BOX OF FROGS

THE FRACTURED FAERY
BOOK ONE

HELEN HARPER

BOOK ONE OF THE FRACTURED FAERY

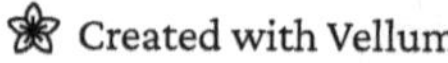

Created with Vellum

FOR JAN AND MICKEY

CHAPTER ONE

The man lying next to me was definitely dead. It wasn't the glassy white caul on his eyes or even his unnatural stillness that gave it away. It was the fact that his head was entirely detached from his body, as if someone had unscrewed it like a burnt-out light bulb and dropped it casually on the ground.

I had the feeling I should probably be screaming. Instead I blinked and rolled away, dew from the perfectly manicured grass beneath me soaking through my thin blouse. Then I got to my feet, the sudden nausea tearing through me suggesting that standing up was a mistake. I grimaced. Even my mouth tasted foul – like wet dog.

Rubbing my hand over my forehead, and avoiding glancing at the body again, I looked around. Where the hell was I? The chill night air offered no clues but, over to my left, there was something tall and thin standing upright. A sign, perhaps.

I staggered over. My chest hurt as if I'd cracked a rib or two. I made it all the same, my legs shaking with astonishing violence. I was forced to clutch onto the metal pole as soon as I reached it in order to remain upright. The small triangle of material attached to the top of the pole hung limply. I squinted at it before my gaze drifted downwards and I dimly registered the hole. A golf course, then. How had I ended up here?

I tried to think. The last thing I remembered was... My stomach dropped. Nothing. *Nada.* Zilcheroony. I strained every brain cell I had but there was just a deep, dark chasm of nothingness. Then another horrifying thought occurred to me and, with desperate fingers, I searched my pockets. No purse. No identification.

I slapped myself around the cheeks in a futile bid to wake myself up. My fingers came away wet, sticky and dark with blood. I felt the sting of pain.

Suddenly my location and how I'd arrived here, not to mention what had happened to the corpse lying less than thirty feet away, drifted into insignificance. My cracked lips formed the words, a croaked whisper breaking the silence. 'Who am I?'

As if in response, the wind strengthened and lifted my hair. I grabbed a curl and examined it: mousy brown. If I had a mirror maybe my reflection would jolt some memory but I was unlikely to find one out here. Wherever *here* was. Whoever *I* was.

With my heart in my mouth, I stumbled back to the corpse. If I didn't possess any ID, maybe he did. I fell to my knees by his chest and started fumbling with his clothes, trying to ignore the faint green tinge to his now-clammy skin. Surely he hadn't been dead for so long that he was already beginning to rot? Perhaps it was simply the dark night that was imbuing his body with the strange hue. I clamped down my nausea.

Whoever he was, he was dressed for darkness, all in black like some kind of Hollywood villain. Black anorak, black shirt, black trousers. Even the buckle on his belt was matte black. I might not have known my own name but I knew that my John Doe had cash. Every item of his clothing was heavy and expensive.

I reached into his anorak pocket and drew out a single object – a solid metal sphere with a clip attached. Some sort of key fob, I guessed, although there were no keys attached to it. Disappointed, I kept searching. In his trouser pockets I found a half-empty pack of mint chewing gum. There was nothing else.

I pulled away, the scent of his aftershave combined with the reek of his blood doing nothing for the state of my stomach. Then I hesitated and leaned forward again, pushing him onto his side. My fingers delved into his back pocket. Empty. This time, however, as I drew away once more I spotted the sword lying on the ground. The man's body had been concealing it.

Even with the congealed blood staining its surface, the blade was obviously well looked after. I touched it gingerly with the tip of my finger, hissing when it sliced through my skin. A moment later, the cut began to burn. Grey smoke rose from my flesh, wisping upwards into the air. I yelped, desperately rubbing the wound against the wet grass. The smoke dissipated but my finger still throbbed with pain. Gasbudlikin bastards. The blade was poisoned. A chemical perhaps, or some designer compound. No: acid. It had to be acid.

I looked in horror from the man to the sword and back again. A distant part of my brain told me to run, as if the man or the sword or both of them were about to rise up and attack me, but my feet felt like lead. A voice in my head screamed at me to move but my body simply wouldn't obey.

I licked my lips. My thoughts were almost as sluggish as my limbs. Amnesia, concussion and a dead body – it was a hell of a way to spend a night. I gritted my teeth, willing myself to turn away but, before I could achieve such a heady goal, I paused. Something about the way the anorak lay against the man's spine didn't look right.

Avoiding going anywhere near the damn blade again, I lunged towards him with outstretched hands and flipped up the material. A leather sheath – black again, naturally – lay snug against his back. It had to be designed for the very sword that now rested on the ground between us.

'You brought me out here,' I whispered, raising my uninjured hand to the gash on my cheek . 'You lured me here and you tried to kill me.' A nervous laugh rose to my lips. 'It didn't work, you evil arsebadger. I got you first.' Obviously.

I should call the police. The boys in blue would keep me safe and investigate this crime. I might have killed the man in black but any fool would recognise it was in self-defence; he was twice my size and he'd brought his own damned poisoned sword.

I nodded. Get off this golf course. Find a phone. Call the coppers. If I'd been reported missing by those who loved me, the police would know about it. I could be returned to the bosom of my loving family within hours. I ran my hands over the slight curve of my stomach. Did I have children? Were they crying for me even now?

I spun round and my body finally obeyed my commands. I whooped weakly. No doubt this amnesia business would wear off quickly too. With any luck, my nightmare was already coming to an end.

An old red phone box stood in front of the single-storey clubhouse. It might have been there purely for nostalgic reasons but I was pathetically grateful all the same. When I lifted the cracked plastic receiver and heard a dial tone, I almost sobbed. I punched in 999, barely pausing to wonder how I could remember that number but not my own name. I was connected almost immediately.

'Hello. Emergency service operator. Which service do you require?'

Her voice was calm and reassuring but my mind went completely blank. 'Uh...'

'Ambulance, fire or police?'

My attacker was dead. There was no paramedic, doctor or surgeon in the world that could bring him back to life. 'Police,' I whispered. 'I need the police.'

'I'm connecting you to the police now.' There was a click. My fingers tightened round the receiver and I tried to remember to breathe.

'Police. What's your location?'

'I'm at...' Gasbudlikins. What was the name of this golf course? I twisted away and craned my neck towards the club-house entrance in the hope of spotting a sign. Less than a second later, there was an explosive crack. Glass and plastic shattered. I screamed and turned back. The phone had been obliterated. As I struggled to compute what was going on another crack followed, together with more breaking glass.

I gaped at the destruction, my dull brain taking a moment to catch up. There was no doubt, however: some bastard was shooting at me.

Without pausing to think further, I slammed out of the phone box and ran for cover, heading for the side of the club-house. The glass on the left side of the phone box had broken so my assailant – or assailants – was shooting from that direction. Another shot was fired, just catching my shoulder. Pain flared through me but I didn't stop until I reached the relative safety of the building's far side. It had to be pure adrenaline driving me forward. Nothing else made any sense.

Panting hard, I flattened myself against the pebble-dashed wall. What to do next? I certainly couldn't stay here and hope that the shooter would go away with an ambivalent shrug at my continued existence. I had to find a way to escape while still breathing, otherwise I might as well give up now. I decided I wasn't the giving-up type.

The most sensible course of action was to circle behind my attacker and vamoose in the opposite direction. Unfortunately there was gravel underneath my booted feet; any swivel of my heel or inappropriate step would immediately reveal my location.

Slow and steady, I told myself. And very, very silent.

Rising onto the balls of my feet, I started to tiptoe down the side of the clubhouse so I could skirt round the back and emerge on the other side. I impressed myself with my quiet movements. It was remarkably easy to stay light on my feet; an almost preternatural calm had overtaken me. I had one goal in mind: to survive.

By clinging to the shadows and keeping my movements slow and deliberate, I made it all the way to the opposite side of the clubhouse without having any more pot shots aimed at my head. As I crept closer, I saw two figures silhouetted in the car park, edging along, searching for me. Both were male – and both were massive. They signalled to each other as they sidled along. They were using a single torch to scan the darker corners.

'She's in the wind,' the nearest one said in an oddly accented voice. 'I told you we should have coated the bullets.'

'There wasn't time.'

'You don't bring down the Madhatter unless you prepare. We're not prepared. I got her, I know I got her. If we'd coated the bullets—'

'Shut up. A direct bullet to the heart or head will end her life whether it's coated or not.'

His partner took no notice. 'We're dead men. If we don't kill her and shut her up, then Rubus will kill us himself.'

There was a skittering sound somewhere up ahead and

both men turned immediately. I strained my eyes through the darkness to catch a glimpse of their features but their faces were angled away from me as they investigated the sound. This was my chance.

I stepped out from the safety of the shadows and pelted for the gloomy copse of trees to my right, taking care to maintain my silent footfall. The tiny wood grew closer and closer and exultation coursed through my veins. Then a third man stepped out right in front of me, barricading my path.

While I stared up at his cauliflower ears and wrinkled visage, his mouth twisted in a semblance of an evil grin. 'Gotcha.'

My left arm whipped up, slamming into the underside of his chin and knocking his head backwards. As he went reeling, I threw myself to the ground and kicked his legs out from underneath him.

The curses from the two other bastards told me they'd registered what was going on. When another bullet zipped over my head and slammed into the ground next to me, I knew instinctively that I wasn't going to get lucky a fourth time. Taking control of the situation, I heaved myself up and bounded over to the groaning third man, ducking for cover behind him.

'We're gonna get you now, bitch,' the talkative one yelled.

I paused. There was an odd tremor to his voice; on the surface, he was all confidence but I could swear he was masking some deeper emotion. I mentally shrugged then grabbed the man in front of me and hauled him upright with surprising ease so that his massive body was in front of mine. He had to be at least seven feet tall and his girth was as impressive as his height. It was just as well; his wide frame provided excellent cover. The other two wouldn't shoot me if there was a chance they'd hit their buddy – especially given that they'd already proven they weren't crack shots.

I was wrong on both counts. Before I could open my mouth to yell at the pair to put down their guns, there was a loud bang and a bullet slammed into the chest of the man I was holding, throwing him – and me – backwards. He collapsed on top of me and I had to writhe and wriggle to get out from under him.

I rolled, reaching the relative safety of the trees. They wouldn't fell an oak as easily as they'd felled their partner. I scrambled up, using the nearest tree as cover before I peeked back round.

The two men were advancing, their guns raised. As they got closer, I saw that their features were not dissimilar to those of their dead colleague. Maybe they were related. Shooting your own kin just because he was in the way brought a whole new meaning to the concept of sibling rivalry.

I flicked my glance from one to the other, noting the heavyset eyebrows, deep wrinkles and bald heads. 'Hey,' I called. 'Why don't we talk? I'm sure we could come to some amicable arrangement that ends in all of us walking away from this.'

There was a muted, nasal snort. 'Lady's been injecting her own dust.'

Huh? 'What was that?'

My answer this time was another shot smashing into the tree. Splinters of bark flew off in all directions. I risked another look. The pair had split up, electing to come at me from both sides. Smart move. I was going to die without even knowing my name. That sounded like the title to a bad country-and-western song.

Hands up in the air, I stepped out and both men stopped moving towards me. Starting to measure my life in seconds, I cleared my throat. 'Look,' I said. 'There has to be a way out of this. There has to be something you want. Money? I can get you money.' Maybe. How the hell did I know what was in my bank account? 'Or would you like something else? Everyone wants something.' I pointed at myself. 'I'm no one. Why would you possibly want to see me dead?'

The two men exchanged long looks. Even though neither of them breathed a word, I knew the instant they'd made up their minds and my heart sank. They glanced back at me while I instinctively moved my hands in front of my chest. They raised their guns a fraction more. Then they fired.

No.

Time seemed to slow. I thrust my hands out even further as if to ward off the bullets. I could see their approach, two gleaming nubs of steel coming right towards me – it was like I was watching a film at quarter speed. Their trajectory was obvious.

Blood roaring in my ears, I stepped to the left and avoided them completely. While the bullets continued, whining through the night air before hitting the same tree I'd been hiding behind, I zipped towards the first man. I kicked upwards, knocking the gun out of his hands and scooping it up. I briefly considered shooting him but instead I simply smashed the butt of the gun onto the top of his head. He crumpled. The poor bastard didn't even have time to look astonished.

The other man, the chatty one, was faster. I ran towards him and wrestled the gun from his grip just as the two bullets finally hit the tree and time returned to normal. It didn't matter; I already had the upper hand and both of us knew it. I thrust my elbow into his stomach with all the force I could muster. He collapsed to his knees.

'Don't,' he whispered. There was a faint trickling sound and the unmistakable stench of urine filled the air. I glanced down at the growing wet patch at his groin. Then I brought my hands down on top of his head.

I flicked my eyes from man to man to man. Somehow – I

didn't know how – I had slowed down time. I had taken out three men, each of whom had to be at least twice my size, not to mention being armed. Four men, if you counted the guy out by hole seventeen. They'd been trying to kill me for no apparent reason whatsoever and were dressed in dark clothes, like every stereotypical villain who ever existed. At least one of them had been afraid of me.

One obvious conclusion stared me smack-bang in the face. Any dum-dum could work it out. I grinned and stretched out my arms, feeling the first drops of rain fall onto my upturned face. Well, well, well. I wasn't just a petite woman with bad dress sense and incredibly dodgy luck. No. I was also a superhero with super powers. I even had a superhero name, derivative as it might be. I was the Madhatter – and the forces of evil were after me.

CHAPTER TWO

It was all very well being a superhero but I couldn't do anything about the rain. I did try, gesturing at the sky and waving my hands around in the same manner as when I'd slowed down time earlier so I could literally dodge bullets. I also used the most imperious tone I could manage to order the sky to cease its drippy torment, but that was about as useful as King Canute attempting to hold back the tide.

That thought made me scowl. I could remember a long-dead English king from some history lesson but I still couldn't remember who I was? Ridiculous. All the same, given what little I had learned about myself, calling the police no longer seemed prudent.

'Thank you,' I said primly to the nearest man. 'Without your timely intervention, we'd currently be surrounded by the country's finest. Not involving them is much more sensible. I won't be so rash in the future.'

He lifted his head and blinked at me with the confusion of the concussed. Still, when I raised an eyebrow in his direction, he was a good little boy and let his head clunk back down again. That was better.

What I really needed, besides an umbrella, was cash. With no specific destination in mind and nothing on me beyond one corpse's key fob and some chewing gum, I wouldn't get very far. I needed some silver so I could cross a few palms.

'Compensation,' I said aloud. I crouched beside the first man and started rummaging through his pockets. 'It's only fair, after all. You did attack me entirely without provocation.' I retrieved a wallet, bulging with crisp new bank notes, and helped myself to them. 'I'm being generous,' I told him. 'I'm leaving you ten quid to get yourself a taxi or a pint of milk for when you get home.' There weren't any credit or bank cards but swiping anything like that was asking for trouble.

I nodded, satisfied. Then I unbuckled his heavy, expensive-looking Rolex and slipped it into my pocket.

The second man was equally prepared with the same wad of new notes. As I drew them out, I frowned. It looked like the same amount I'd taken from McNasty Numero Uno. Pursing my lips, I ambled over to the third man, who'd been shot by his mates. Oddly, his chest was still rising and falling. I could have sworn the bullet had hit him dead on in the heart. Not a corpse after all, then.

'You're superheroes too,' I murmured. Then I corrected myself. 'Make that supervillains. I wonder what manner of beastie can sustain a direct gunshot wound to the heart and still be alive?'

I reached down for his wallet, realising at the same time that my shoulder wound no longer smarted, although my finger was still throbbing from the sword slice I'd given myself. No doubt that was what they'd meant by coating the bullets. If they had managed to do that, I didn't think I'd still be breathing. It was helpful to discover that I had my own personal kryptonite. It made sense, I thought reasonably; no superhero was invincible.

Shaking off my turbulent thoughts, I counted the third lot of money. Same. A shiver rippled across my damp skin. The attack wasn't personal, then: these guys had been hired to kill me. The thought was not cheering. All it meant was that next time they'd send someone stronger. Yippee.

By the time I was done, my pockets were straining at the seams. If I was careful, there was enough money to tide me over for some time. All I had to do now was to get as far away from here as possible.

Parked out the front was a large Jeep, which no doubt belonged to my attackers. Figuring that it wouldn't hurt to delay them further by taking it, I hopped inside, pleased to see that the keys in the ignition. Whoever the men were, they were certainly mucky pups; greasy burger wrappers and crisp packets littered the floor and there was a stale odour.

I searched the glove compartment, looking for clues like a good detective. The only thing I found, however, was a flyer for a swish-looking bar called the Metropolitan. The address at the bottom indicated it was in Manchester. That was good. We had to be near the city – and a city large enough and anonymous enough for me to lose myself in.

It was tempting to veer off into the countryside and hide for the rest of my days in a quaint little village but who ever heard of a superhero who lived on farmland? Even Clark Kent had abandoned ruralsville as soon as he'd had the chance. I ground my teeth. Gasbudlikins. It really annoyed me that I could remember that.

As I drove, I tried to work out what else I could remember. Anything to do with myself or my own history had me drawing a big, fat blank, yet I could remember how to drive. Obviously. When I pulled onto the motorway heading into the city, I could also remember a shortcut that avoided the speed cameras. So maybe I was from Manchester? Not that I seemed to possess a

Mancunian accent. Perhaps I'd been privately educated. My brain ached with the effort of trying to jolt my memory and, in the end, I gave up. Tomorrow was another day, after all.

I abandoned the Jeep in a silent side street that was emblazoned with no-parking warnings but appeared to be bereft of security cameras. Then I walked, winding my way through narrow streets until I'd allowed enough distance between myself and the vehicle to be safe.

Before too long, I came across the welcome lights of a Travotel and presented myself under the highly imaginative name of Joan Smith to a weary-looking desk clerk, who helpfully gave me the keys to a small ground floor room without asking for ID. I mentally patted myself on the back for my forethought at getting this room – I needed to be able to exit from the window if any more wrinkled, bald goons came after me.

Then I collapsed onto the bed fully clothed and fell into a blissful sleep.

It was odd that, when I woke up on the bed some hours later, I was considerably more disorientated than I had been when I found myself concussed on a golf course next to a dismembered corpse. I could only assume that I'd been suffering from shock at the time, which was why I'd managed to treat last night with such calm. Now, the fog of confusion that lit through me when I opened my eyes to the blank Travotel ceiling set my heart hammering against my ribcage.

Taking short, shallow breaths, I gave my cheeks a few slaps. The clock on the bedside table indicated it was already gone noon. Perhaps I just wasn't a morning person. I reached for the remote and turned on the television, irritably skipping past the hotel's welcome channel to find the news. North Korea was threatening military action against the south; there were delays on the M5 because of an overturned lorry; VAT was set to increase. There was nothing about a grisly death on a golf course. Even the local news made no mention of it. That was ... interesting. Equally, there were no reports of any missing women. Maybe no one had noticed I'd gone.

I lifted up my blouse and examined my ribs. As painful as they'd felt last night, there was no longer any signs that I'd been so much as slightly bruised. I prodded the skin but there was no flare of agony. My finger where I'd sliced myself on the headless corpse's damn sword was a different matter; it still throbbed and the small wound was looking distinctly green. I supposed it was entirely possibly to get gangrene in your finger. Why wouldn't it be?

Pursing my lips, I headed into the small, windowless bathroom, flicking on the light and catching sight of my reflection for the first time. Green eyes, the afore-noted boring brown hair and, if I did say so myself, a cute upturned button nose with a sprinkling of freckles. I assessed myself as a decent eight out of ten on the attractiveness-ometer, in my late twenties, with clear, healthy-looking skin. I opened my mouth and examined my teeth. Satisfyingly straight, white and even. There was a glint of something towards the back of my mouth. Craning my neck into a most undignified position, I decided it was a gold filling. Well, I shrugged, it could be worse. At least I didn't have braces.

I turned on the tap and let the cold water run over my small wound. It still hurt. I'd have to search for a pharmacy and get hold of some antiseptic when I made it out of here.

Abandoning my finger for the time being, I smiled at myself. 'I am the Madhatter.' I coughed and deepened my voice. 'I am the Madhatter and you have met your match, for I have powers you can only dream of.'

It occurred to me, not for the first time, that perhaps I didn't just have amnesia. If my superhero nomenclature really was the Madhatter then it was possible I was completely insane as well as terminally forgetful. Had I imagined my crazy feat with those bullets? I bit my lip. There was only one way to find out.

I unwrapped the miniscule complimentary soap and gave my face and armpits a quick wash before straightening my clothes and heading out. I passed several other hotel guests along the way and, although I stared hard at each one in case I happened to know them – or vice-versa – all I gained in return were a few scowls and confused looks.

As I tripped through the small lobby, which smelled unpleasantly of bleach, I paused to grab a local newspaper. September 22nd, 2018. There was nothing about the date that jarred. Given all I had to go on were my instincts, I filed it away in my mind then flipped quickly through the pages in case there was a missing person's advert placed by my distraught family, or an article with my face in it. Again I was disappointed. I grimaced and tossed the newspaper aside.

Cool air hit my face as soon as I left the hotel building and I couldn't stop myself from shivering. I was going to have to use some of my newfound wealth to buy some clothes. I stepped off the pavement to cross the road – then halted abruptly as a familiar smell tickled my nostrils.

Turning my head, I spotted an older woman leaning against a wall and inhaling deeply on a cigarette. As she blew out smoke it drifted in my direction, causing both my fingers and my insides to twitch. Huh. I raised up my own hands, sniffed my fingers and examined them for the tell-tale yellow of a smoker. Oh. I felt oddly disappointed in myself. Then again, it had to be stressful work being a superhero. I bit down the temptation to ask the woman for a cigarette and turned away. I had other things to do.

The main shopping streets were busy with the late lunch crowds. I weaved my way in and out of them. What I was looking for was unlikely to be here; I needed somewhere far murkier than The White Company or Jo Malone. Spinning away, I marched down a side alley. Hunched in a doorway was a homeless guy with a sad-looking cap containing a few coins sitting in front of him.

I crouched down next to him. 'Hey,' I said softly. 'How's it going?'

'Fucking fantastic. How does it look like it's going?'

No wonder he wasn't having much luck with the coinage. All the same, I offered him a sympathetic smile. 'I'm new to town,' I told him.

'Bully for you. Tourist Information Office is in the other direction.'

I dug into my pocket and pulled out one of McNasty's fifty-pound notes. The homeless guy's eyes flickered but he didn't reach for it. 'I bet you know this area well,' I said. 'Better than Tourist Information does.'

There was the faintest sneer to his response. 'If you're looking for something to snort, I'm not your man.'

'I don't want drugs. I just want to know what areas I should avoid. I get ... nervous in new places.'

He gave me such a sceptical look that you'd think I'd told him he'd just won the lottery. 'You think I don't know who you are?'

I froze. 'Who?' I demanded. 'Who am I?' When he didn't answer immediately, I whipped up, hauling him with me. 'Tell me!'

'Your lot don't scare me,' he mumbled. 'Threaten me all you like. Cut off my toes. Won't make any difference.'

'What is my name?' I hissed, getting right in his face.

'I dunno. How the fuck should I know?'

'You said you knew who I was!'

'I know you're one of them. I don't know your bloody name.'

I gritted my teeth. 'One of who?'

'You know. *Them.*'

Superheroes. He knew I was a superhero and he knew there were others. I released my grip on his collar. 'How?' I breathed. 'How do you know what I am?'

He raised a grubby shoulder. 'Just do. I see things, don't I? You'd be surprised what I see.'

My pulse rate had picked up. Trying to breathe normally, I opened my mouth to ask him more when he snatched the fifty-pound note from my hand and spun round, kicking his cap with the paltry pile of coins to one side and pelting down the street away from me. From a brief moment I gazed after him like a flabby, half-baked sponge then I took off after him. No way was I letting him go until I knew everything he knew.

He might have had a head start but I was fast. Damned fast. Olympian-sprinter level fast, in fact. I might have been a smoker but the effort I had to put into running after him barely affected me. I leapt neatly over three rubbish bags, using the wall on my left to gain further traction and, within seconds, I was at his back. I reached out to grab him but, before my fingers even brushed against his clothes, he let out a yell. Arms outstretched, he went flying down to the ground.

I came to a skidding halt and narrowly avoided tripping over his prone body. Glancing backwards, I realised what had happened. There was a pothole in the middle of the road, about a metre or so back and his foot must have caught in it. Shame that the hole had beaten me to it; I'd been rather impressed at how quickly I'd caught up to him.

I crouched down and prodded him with a finger. He didn't move; in fact, he didn't even groan or moan or sigh in vexation. Frowning, I turned him over. Gasbudlikins. He was out cold.

Not only that, but there was a nasty gash on the side of his head where he must have struck the edge of the pavement as he went down. The copious amounts of blood streaming from the wound probably weren't a good thing.

Cursing to myself, I doubled back to accost the nearest passerby for their mobile phone so I could call an ambulance. With that accomplished, I went back to wait with him until the paramedics arrived, pouting the entire time. This simply wasn't fair.

CHAPTER THREE

I tried my level best to accompany the homeless guy to hospital but the paramedics were having none of it. They shooed me away before taking off with lights blazing and sirens blaring. I glared after the ambulance, as if dirty looks might encourage it to return, before I eventually stomped off to see if Mr Clumsy had any friends who might also know about 'my lot'. Unfortunately, even though I came across several more homeless men and women, none of them seemed to possess his vital knowledge. On the plus side, they were a darned sight friendlier than he had been, pointing out which streets I would do well to avoid as a solitary, weak female.

I offered my thanks in the form of the Queen's head and then made a beeline directly for the supposed danger zones. It was still only afternoon but I was hoping that I could make myself look like a target tempting enough for someone to attack. That way, even if I accomplished nothing else, I'd have an opportunity to see what else I was capable of. It wasn't a great plan – but it was a plan.

The supposedly dangerous streets weren't quite as seedy as I'd hoped for. Sure, there were some boarded-up windows and the odd dodgy-looking character wandering past with a shifty glint in their eye, but I walked up and down for the better part of an hour and not a single soul tried to mug me. I didn't even get a creepy catcall from the builders who were bricklaying round an old, decrepit cemetery. The more time passed, the more frustrated I became. Clearly patience wasn't my strong suit.

An elderly man, hunched over a gnarled walking stick, paused at the traffic lights not too far from me. I raced over, more than ready to offer my services to help him get across. After all, being heroic didn't just mean grand, life-saving gestures. He didn't so much as glance as at me when I reached him.

He started ambling across the road in a lopsided shuffle. 'Here,' I said, darting round to his side and offering my arm. 'I'll help.'

He raised his head with ponderous slowness and gave me a slitted glare. 'Piss off.'

Somewhat taken aback, I blinked at him. 'There's no shame in accepting help when you need it.'

'Well,' he snapped, 'I don't need help. There's no shame in ignoring plonkers like you, either.'

Deflated, I stepped away. He continued his shuffle, eventually reaching the other side of the road. He half-turned, realised I was still watching him and raised his middle finger in my direction. I huffed. Cantankerous old arsebadger.

Abandoning him to his fate, I headed to my right. There was a sex shop down this road and enough litter to create a small bonfire. While I waited for someone who wanted my help to appear, I started scooping up the crisp packets and discarded bottles, throwing them into an empty plastic bag I'd spotted curled round a lamppost.

The bag was almost full when I heard a small, plaintive

meow. I brightened immediately and scanned up and down the street. I was just as willing to come to the aid of animals as humans.

The cat was on top of a roof nearby and peering down at me. It meowed some more, baleful yellow eyes fixed on me. Its fur was sleek and looked clean; all the same, it was obviously stuck and needed rescuing. I regarded it thoughtfully for a moment, trying to work out the best approach. Maybe one of my super powers was flight. I grinned. That would be fun.

Punching the air with one hand, I jumped upwards, willing myself to soar towards the cat. All that happened was that I fell down and jarred my knee. I braced my hand against the cold pavement to stop myself falling flat on my face and felt a shot of pain through my finger again. Ouchy.

Brushing myself off, I stood up. The cat gazed down at me and meowed once more. 'Don't worry, kitty,' I called. 'I might not be able to fly but I'm not defeated. I will rescue you, I promise.'

I backed up a foot. Handily, there was a red postbox right in front of the house. I clambered on top of it, swaying dangerously before I caught my balance. It was about two metres' leap from here to the edge of the roof. That was do-able, I decided, because even if I didn't have the power of flight I was still the mighty Madhatter.

Sucking air into my lungs, I braced myself for the jump. One. Two. Three. I threw myself forward, arms outstretched, but even with my best effort I only just managed to grab hold of the edge of the roof with one hand. I hung there for a moment, dangling uselessly. Then with a burst of strength and energy, I flung my other hand upwards and grabbed on so I could pull myself up. At least, that was the theory anyway; no matter how hard I tried, I didn't have the strength to yank myself up. Well, that sucked.

'Whatcha doing?'

I almost lost my grip entirely when I heard the voice. From somewhere underneath me and to my right, a small towheaded child was looking up at me with a fixed, curious expression.

'Cat rescue,' I muttered, trying to swing my left leg upwards in a pathetic bid to hook it over the edge of the roof.

'What cat?'

'The...' I began, before I was interrupted.

'D'ya mean this cat?'

I looked at the ground again and realised that the damned feline had already jumped down of its own accord. It sat next to the boy, blithely unconcerned, with the same vaguely curious expression on its face as he had.

'Gasbudlikins!' I exploded, dropping down to the pavement and spinning round. The cat meowed one final time and took off, sauntering down the road away from both of us.

'Do you need help?' I asked desperately. 'Saving from some bullies? Help with your homework? Anything?'

The boy frowned, his brow creasing. 'Actually,' he said, while I started to smile hopefully, 'nah. Fanks, though.' He tripped away after the cat without a backward glance.

My shoulders sank. So much for being a damned superhero. Nobody seemed to want my help. All I'd learned about myself was that I couldn't fly and that my biceps were weedier than an average IT technician's. And my darn finger was even more sore than before. What a waste of sodding time.

I shook myself off and set off in the direction of the Travotel. I'd just have to try again later when it was dark. Besides, I needed to get some supplies.

Making a brief detour, I located a small Boots in the main shopping precinct and scooped up some antiseptic cream and plasters. The other shoppers gave me a wide berth and, when I caught sight of myself in a nearby mirror, I realised why. My cheeks were bright red and there were smudges of dirt all over my face, hands and clothes, mingled with the grass stains from the night before which I hadn't noticed previously. I also reeked. Grimacing, I grabbed some deodorant. No wonder even the cat didn't want my help.

When I stepped out of the shop, it started to rain and big fat droplets of cold yuck landed on my head. Someone opened their umbrella right next to me, almost taking out my eye. I was turning to spit out an expletive when my attention was caught by something else entirely. Or rather *someone* else.

Directly opposite, and probably less than twenty metres away, stood a woman of Amazonian stature. She was completely ignoring the rain and glaring at me with a mixture of shock and fear. She sashayed her hips once, as if in delight, then started to reach inside her coat pocket. I didn't wait to see what manner of weapon she was pulling out. I simply ran.

Fool, I mentally berated myself. Regardless of who I was – or indeed what I was – I knew full well that the bad guys were after me. Wandering around in the middle of day was just asking to be taken down. In fact, if it hadn't been for the rain, I'd probably already be dead.

I pelted round the nearest corner and darted into a shop, making sure to close the jangling door behind me. Chest tight with nervous tension, I whirled round and waited to see if the woman was following me.

'Welcome, dear!'

I ignored the trilling voice of the shop assistant, keeping my eyes peeled on the street outside.

'Terrible weather we're having, isn't it?'

I crossed my arms and continued to stare. There was no sign of the woman and for a moment I debated whether to go back and find her. Perhaps if I confronted her, I'd learn more about who I was. Without the element of surprise on her side, I'd be more likely to gain the upper hand. After all, I'd beaten back all those goons last night.

In the end, however, the persistent shop assistant behind me made the decision for me. 'We have some lovely new clothes in. I just hung them up. There are some warm coats.' She paused. 'You look like you need a coat.'

I supposed I did look like I was in need of proper clothing. Satisfied that my would-be attacker wasn't on my heels, I slowly turned, realising that I was inside a charity shop.

'Hi,' I said, somewhat belatedly. 'Yes, I do need something decent to wear.'

She beamed in delight. 'How about a nice anorak? Or we have these jumpers?'

I started to nod then my eye fell on something else entirely. 'Actually,' I said, 'I'm in the market for something completely different.'

When I finally got back to the safety of the hotel, after doubling back several times to ensure I wasn't being followed, I was soaking wet and shivering. I laid out my new clothes and jumped in the shower. I hadn't appreciated quite how dirty I was but, judging by the colour of the water swirling down the drain, I needed a damn good scrub.

As soon as I was warm and dry again, I tried on the first of my new outfits. The shop assistant had been nonplussed at some of my choices – but she didn't know what I did.

First of all, there was a dark leotard. It fitted snugly and was surprisingly comfortable. To avoid any unpleasant suggestion of camel toe, I pulled a pair of shorts on top. Then I grabbed my *pièce de résistance*. This was what had really caught my eye in the shop: a bright, electric-blue cape. Goodness only knew what it had originally been used for but it didn't matter now. Every superhero needs a cape and now I had one of my own. I'd even managed to snag a mask to cover my eyes and nose. It had some ridiculous flowers on one side, which I yanked off, but I left on the sequins. The Madhatter deserved some sequins, I decided.

As expected, the overall effect was completely ridiculous. However, my reasons for playing fancy dress were twofold. First of all, I needed a disguise to guard against those who were after me; secondly, I wanted the world to know that I wasn't just a crazed person roaming the streets – I really did want to help out. Every other darned superhero in the world had a costume. Surely I deserved one too?

I twirled round several times, practising with the cape to avoid suffocating myself instead of expertly swirling the silky material as I wanted to do. After twenty minutes or so, I reckoned I had it. My first venture into the real world today might have been a total disaster but I was ready for my second one.

I applied cream to my poor finger, slapped on a plaster and waited for night to fall.

CHAPTER FOUR

Obviously, I didn't want to stride out of the Travotel wearing my superhero disguise for all and sundry to see. In fact, by the time it was actually dark, I was starting to regret my plans to dress up.

There was still nothing on the news about any unfortunate events at a local golf course, and I still remembered nothing about myself. I'd spent an hour or two making use of the hotel's business centre but, with virtually no clues to go on, my internet searches weren't very helpful. Unsurprisingly, typing 'who am I?' into the search bar didn't get me very far, regardless of which search engine I used.

If some real clues didn't present themselves soon, I would have to involve the police. In that scenario, it was probably better that they didn't discover I'd been running around the city streets and trying to save people in order to test out my supposed super powers. Neither I didn't think my real self, whoever she was, would appreciate my costume. I could only presume that my amnesia was making me bold. If *I* didn't know myself, I certainly didn't know anyone who would be embarrassed by my get-up.

I told myself that I was being sensible. I doubted the authorities would look kindly on a hero vigilante and, with any luck, my disguise would hide my identity from CCTV cameras as well as potential evil-doers. Anyway, it was important to go with your gut instinct. All the same, it was fortunate that I'd had the foresight to purchase a long raincoat that more than covered my outfit. I dropped some cash and the strange spherical object I'd nabbed from the headless corpse into one of the deep pockets then did up the buttons.

I didn't put on the mask until I was well away from the hotel. Once it was snug and secure on my face, I stashed the raincoat under an old car that didn't look as if it had been driven since the seventies. Doubtless the coat would be safe there until my return in a few hours' time; if nothing else, it was both dry and out of sight.

Once that was done and I was striding along the street once more, I felt as if I'd found myself in the middle of some bizarre Marvel-inspired farce. I whispered under my breath that confidence and aplomb would carry me further than my blue cape and straightened my shoulders.

My first stop was the side street where I'd spoken to the homeless guy. Alas, there was still no sign of him. Given how nasty his head wound had looked that wasn't surprising, but I was still disappointed. So far he was my only viable lead – and I suspected that even he didn't have much to offer.

Once I'd established that he wasn't anywhere nearby, I veered off to the seedy area where I'd tried to play hero earlier. I did, however, avoid the cat's street. I might seem to possess a high embarrassment threshold but there was only so much humiliation I was willing to put myself through.

I pitter-pattered my way along the pavement, keeping a close eye out for anything untoward. It had finally stopped raining and the clouds were clearing. That was good. I couldn't remember a full twenty-four hours of my life but so far most of it had included rain; anything that didn't involve getting wet could only be deemed positive. I hadn't tested it yet but I was fairly certain my cape wasn't waterproof.

A small group of people appeared from the gloom on the other side of the street. They were laughing, merry with alcohol although not yet so sozzled that they couldn't walk in a straight line. One of the men lifted his head and spotted me, grinning when he took in my costume. 'Hey!' he yelled. 'Where's the fancy-dress party?'

'I'm not going to a party!' I called back. 'I'm a superhero! I'm looking for someone to rescue.'

All of them laughed and the man who'd hailed me clutched his chest melodramatically. 'Rescue me! I'm being kidnapped and taken to yet another pub where these bastards will force me to drink more beer.' His voice rose. 'Help! It's not even a good pub. It's that poncey Metropolitan place.'

I paused. Well, hang onto your superhero tights. Providence was finally smiling on me. I shook out my hair and sprang across the street. 'I must save you from a fate worse than death,' I boomed.

'Please, please, Miss Superhero Lady.'

'I am the Madhatter,' I intoned.

'Please, Miss Madhatter. Please help me.' The man, who close up was rather good-looking with strawberry-blond hair tied back in a daft man bun and sparkly blue eyes, fell to his knees, clasping his hands together and raising them towards me. He wasn't exactly the sort of person I'd been looking for but this was far too good an opportunity to pass up. It certainly beat walking around the cold streets of Manchester hoping that someone would get attacked simply so I could try and save them.

I tapped my mouth as if deep in thought. 'I can't save you

from the pub,' I told him. 'But I can accompany you as your bodyguard to prevent anything untoward from happening.'

The man's eyes danced. 'I've always wanted a bodyguard,' he grinned. He looked me up and down, clearly enjoying what he saw. 'Especially a superhero bodyguard. I can only pay you in beer though.'

Did I like beer? I smacked my lips and beamed back. 'Done.'

He stuck out his hand. 'Dave.' He waited. There was no doubt as to what he expected in return.

Uh... 'I can't tell you my real name,' I said conspiratorially. 'It would compromise my secret identity.'

Dave was momentarily deflated. 'Don't worry, boyo,' one of his mates said. 'Your last girlfriend was mad too.'

Dave leaned towards me with a rueful expression. 'He's right. She kinda was.' Then, as if he'd overstepped the mark, he tried to backtrack. 'In a fun way. She wasn't bad. She just, er...'

I touched his arm. 'Let's just get that beer, shall we?'

I was rewarded with another disarming grin. 'Let's.'

His friend leaned in. 'He's been desperate to get to the Metropolitan Bar all night,' he confided.

I smiled. Him and me both.

~

As it turned out, the Metropolitan Bar wasn't far away; in fact, I'd probably run past it during my escape bid from the Amazon woman. Despite Dave's chatter and questions, each of which I neatly deflected, I felt a tight coil of fear inside me as we went in. I was half-expecting to be jumped on by several evil goons. Instead, not a single person glanced in my direction.

Scanning the crowd, I searched for any sign of bald villains or potentially nasty killers but the punters appeared innocuous.

Unless the woman in the far corner was planning to stab me to death with one of her dangly earrings, or the short guy nursing a pint was hiding a machine gun inside his ancient Oasis T-shirt, I reckoned I was probably okay.

Dave and I strolled up to the bar, his friends apparently deciding that it would be wise to give us space. He glanced down at me. 'Have you been here before?' he asked.

I shook my head. 'Nope,' I said cheerfully. 'First time.'

The woman behind the bar, with a neat blonde ponytail and a cheerful smile, ambled over. She took in my mask and costume and seemed unconcerned that I looked like an idiot. Then her eyes met mine and she squinted. 'Oh. It's you.' Her friendly smile vanished and she glanced behind her as if seeking help. 'Long time no see.' She certainly didn't sound very happy. But—

She was addressing me. And she knew me.

I stared at her, my expression as blank as my memory, while Dave nudged me in the ribs. 'First time here?' he murmured.

I paid him no attention. 'You know me,' I breathed, finding my voice and focusing my attention on the woman. 'You know who I am.'

Her expression flickered. 'No. No, I don't.' She turned her attention to Dave. 'What would you like to drink?'

I reached forward and grabbed her arm. She stiffened immediately. 'Yes, you do. How do you know me?'

She yanked her arm away from me and turned to the barman. 'I'm taking my break,' she said. 'Can you serve these two, please, Phil?'

He grunted and she all but sprinted away and through a solid-looking door marked 'Staff Only'. By my side, I felt Dave shoot me a wary look. I forced a smile in his direction and shrugged. 'Secret identity,' I reminded him, as if my exchange with the woman had been nothing but banter. 'No one's supposed to know who I am.'

We got our drinks and, ignoring the prickle of discomfort across the back of my neck, Dave and I sat at the same table as his friends. I made sure that I had a clear vantage point to the door; if that woman reappeared, I wanted to know about it.

'So,' Dave said, taking several swift gulps of his beer as if alcohol could rescue him from the crazy woman he'd somehow entangled himself with, 'tell me more about yourself.' He shifted away from me slightly; clearly I was making him nervous. His eyes kept flickering around the room, as if he were searching for rescue. 'Not your name. Tell me something else.'

He'd already served his purpose but all the same I felt a bit sorry for him. I took a small sip of my drink and savoured the taste, letting the bubbles tickle my tongue. 'I like beer.' I burped loudly for extra effect before grabbing the edge of my cape and using the corner of it to wipe my mouth. With that done, I scratched my crotch rather vigorously.

Dave's cheeks coloured, embarrassed for me. 'Good. That's...' he hesitated '...good.' Then, apparently deciding that ignoring me would be the safest course because I wasn't the sort of lady he'd thought I was, he turned to his friends and immediately engaged them in a supposedly riotous conversation about a game of football.

I smiled. Now, when I disappeared to find my errant barmaid so I could interrogate her, he would be unlikely to care. In fact, he'd probably be relieved.

I leaned away from him and his mates. The discomfort I'd felt earlier was increasing. If I hadn't known better, I'd have thought that someone was watching me. No one in the bar area was glancing in my direction but there was a CCTV camera in a far corner and I was right in its line of sight.

I stood up and ambled over to the bandit machine on the

other side of the room. I half-turned and started to fumble in the pocket of my shorts as if I were looking for some change to gamble away. The camera followed me, its tiny lens swivelling in my direction. Bingo. I'd definitely made the right decision in coming here.

I might have run away from the Amazon in the street but I'd been caught unawares and I'd panicked. That wasn't going to happen again. This time I was here on purpose and I was prepared to do whatever I could to take charge of the situation.

What had happened with the bullets the previous night hadn't been my imagination; I was sure of that. It might have been the adrenaline that awoke whatever powers lay inside me; all I had to do was to recapture that feeling and utilise the same skill now.

I raised my arms slowly, vaguely aware of Dave eyeing me as I did so. Then I whispered under my breath, 'Come on.'

There was a brief tightening in my stomach, followed by a muted whooshing sound. The people around the edges of the bar blurred slightly and the high-pitched chatter around me dulled. I gazed round in astonishment. I'd done it – I'd slowed down time again.

I didn't know how long it would last, however. Shaking myself, I closed my gaping mouth and vamoosed through the staff door. With any luck, all the CCTV would pick up would be a blur of electric blue. As the door closed behind me, I allowed myself a Wonder Woman spin. Take that, arsebadgers!

The bar might have been all sleek lines and burnished mahogany tables but the staff quarters beyond were somewhat shabbier. There were numerous health and safety posters lining the walls in the small staffroom, a few rickety chairs and a tea-stained table with an electric kettle and an array of mugs. There was no sign of the woman who'd recognised me.

Figuring that she probably wasn't carousing with the chef

or the kitchen porter, I skipped past the door marked 'Kitchen' and headed instead for the two doors near the end of the corridor. One led into a suspiciously empty office that had a bank of television screens that were obviously fed by the CCTV cameras, including the one that had been tracking me. The other led outside.

I popped my head out and there, leaning against the wall and blowing out a cloud of slowly dissipating cigarette smoke, was my target.

As soon as I stepped outside to join her, the air around me seemed to crackle as if the air molecules were tightening. A heartbeat later, the smoke that the woman had been exhaling abruptly picked up speed. Time had returned to its normal pace. That was uber groovy. Maybe I wasn't a superhero. Maybe I was a Time Lord. Or Lady.

The woman turned towards me. The moment she caught sight of me, her nostrils flared and she sprang away from the wall, backing away. There was nowhere for her to go; behind her was a seven-foot wall and in front of her was, well, me.

I figured I'd be more likely to get information from her if I didn't leap into threatening mode. Trying to keep emotions calm and the atmosphere peaceful, I held up my hands with my palms facing her. 'I just want to talk,' I said, in what I thought was a soothing tone.

Her cigarette dropped to the ground, hissing as it hit a puddle. She jumped away from me until she was pressed against the wall. 'Stay away from me. I've not done anything. I don't know anything!'

I swept my gaze across her. I didn't get the same sense of menace as I'd had from the other woman earlier today; all I was getting was fear. 'You're frightened,' I said. 'Why?'

'I ... I...' Her jaw worked uselessly while her eyes darted from side to side.

'I promise I won't hurt you. I won't do anything.' I changed tack. If she was afraid, that was her look out. I had questions I desperately needed answering. Trying not to reveal that I couldn't remember my own darned name, I fudged slightly. 'I need to know when I was last in here.' My voice rose. 'When was I last in this pub?'

She swallowed. 'Maybe six weeks ago.' Her expression clouded with confusion. 'Don't you—'

'And who was I with?' I interrupted. I was the one asking the questions here.

'You...'

'I'll take it from here, Jodie,' said a smooth male voice from behind me.

Her relief was palpable. She scooted away from the wall and past me, while I turned with a scowl and moved to stop her. The man stepped out from the shadows and gently pushed me away so she could escape back into the pub.

The anger I should have felt was superseded by a strange, squirmy sensation in the pit of my tummy. He hadn't been in the pub earlier – I'd have noticed him if he had been. He was the sort of man who commanded attention. The very air around him crackled and I sensed uncoiled power and danger emanating from him.

His frame was large but there wasn't an ounce of fat on him. His hair was dark, almost black, with the faintest hint of a curl, and he had a shadow of stubble around his jaw. Eyes as green as my own glittered at me, not with malice or humour but with barely controlled fury.

'You shouldn't be here,' he growled. 'You shouldn't be strong-arming my staff. And you certainly shouldn't be manipulating time for your own ends. You know it's forbidden.'

I licked my lips. His eyes tracked the movement. 'Look,' I said. 'I don't know who you are...'

He took a step towards me. All of a sudden I caught a whiff of his musky, male scent. His fists clenched and unclenched. 'What game are you playing this time?' He flung out an arm, motioning at my body. 'And what in Fey are wearing? You didn't really think we wouldn't realise who you are with that mask on, did you? Or are you trying to be cute? Because there's nothing about you that's ever going to be cute or endearing.' His voice dripped with disdain. 'Just how stupid do you think I am?'

He really wasn't very nice at all but he clearly knew me, just as the barmaid had. No doubt I was dealing with yet another bad guy here and he was obviously aware of my super powers as well as my identity.

Desperate to discover more about myself, I blocked out the insults; I wasn't sure I had any choice. 'The outfit is a long story,' I muttered. 'But I'm not playing any games.' At his sceptical scoff, I widened my eyes. 'I mean it. I...' Gasbudlikins. I couldn't think of any way to get the information I needed without telling the truth. 'I can't remember anything.'

His lip curled. 'What the hell is that supposed to mean?'

I kept my tone as pleasant as possible but this arsebadger's attitude was starting to irritate me. 'Exactly that. I woke up last night on a golf course and—'

'Your finger,' he said suddenly, sniffing the air while his gaze dropped. 'You've been poisoned.' He let out a short laugh. 'That's why you're here.'

I frowned down at the small plaster wrapped round my index finger. Poisoned? How could he tell?

My expression must have given me away because Dark and Despicable snorted. 'Do you think I'm stupid, Madrona? You reek of rowan.' He smirked. 'You should get that seen to. I'm sure Rubus will be able to help you. I'm not wasting my supply of nux on the likes of you.' He leaned his head closer to mine and my pulse rose. 'Now scat. Don't come here again. You're lucky you're walking away and I'm not laying you out. The truce benefits you more than it benefits me. Leave that poor human guy alone, as well. He doesn't need you tainting him.' His eyes glittered with warning. 'Otherwise I won't be so lenient next time.' He moved away abruptly.

Realising he was leaving, I lurched forward. 'Wait!'

I was too late. The door slammed shut, leaving me alone on the street and gaping. I shook my head slowly and tried to think through what he'd said. I was Madrona, then. What the hell kind of name was that? Who was Rubus? What was nux? And, more to the point, why on earth did that rude man with a serious attitude problem seem to hate me so much? Lay me out? How dare he!

I ground my teeth, stepped back to the door and tried to open it. It was stuck fast, however, and no matter how hard I tried it wouldn't budge. Big deal. This wasn't the only entrance. I marched to the front door. It was wide open and, with my shoulders squared, I walked through it. Or rather, I tried to walk through it but I didn't get my foot past the threshold. The door might have looked open and the pub might have appeared welcoming but I couldn't seem to get myself inside. And there was no earthly reason why.

'Excuse me.'

I turned my head. A couple stood right behind me. The man, eyeing me curiously, gestured at the door. 'Are you going in?'

Uh... I raised my hand in vague defeat. 'After you.'

He shrugged and walked past me with his girlfriend in tow. The pair of them strolled inside, disappearing within seconds. I stared and then started after them. Once again an invisible barrier kept me out.

I looked up and realised there was yet another CCTV camera

angled towards me. I glared up at it, giving it the finger. 'Fuck you,' I mouthed. Then I turned on my heel and strode away. That man with the sexy stubble, glittery green eyes and high desirability factor was clearly nothing more than a nasty piece of work.

CHAPTER FIVE

Wending my way back through the cold, dark streets, I decided to look on the bright side. I might not yet be doing a great deal to fulfil my superhero potential but Dark and Despicable – DD for short – had given me plenty of information.

My name was Madrona. It was a stupid name, and one had to wonder what on earth my parents had been thinking of, but it gave me a clue as to why the golf-course goons had called me the Madhatter. It wasn't that I was crazy or that I had a peculiar fondness for large hats, it was because the first three letters of my real name matched my heroic pseudonym. I appreciated the symmetry. Clearly, I was a being of higher intelligence as well as super powers. I'd suspected as much.

DD was obviously fully aware of my time-bending super powers. In fact, he apparently had some powers of his own, daring to block me from re-entering his pub. Despite his unpleasantness, he was someone I needed to visit again in the near future.

So, although my night hadn't been quite the success I'd hoped for when I'd ventured out, I could hardly dismiss it as a total failure.

I skipped over a few puddles. The worrying thing was my finger. If anything, it hurt even more – although that might have been a psychosomatic result of DD's reference to poison. Regardless, the antiseptic cream I'd slathered over the wound wasn't doing any good. I had to find some of this nux stuff, whatever it was.

With that thought in mind, I abandoned my plan to buy a greasy kebab to munch while I trudged back to the Travotel and veered off towards the bright white lights of a twenty-four-hour pharmacy. Perhaps nux was a generic name and whoever was inside could help me locate it. With any luck, I wouldn't need a prescription to buy the stuff.

After the gloom of the streets outside, the searing white walls and overhead strip lights were almost painful to my eyes. The only person in the shop was the pharmaceutical assistant. Rather than pointlessly perusing the shelves, I walked straight up to him and laid my palms flat on the counter. I meant business.

'Good evening,' the man said. 'Cool costume. How can I help you?'

'Technically,' I told him, 'it should be how *may* I help you.' The words were out of my mouth before I had the chance to think about them. As soon as I realised what I'd said, I winced. Gasbudlikins: I was some sort of grammar freak. Well, that was a horrid revelation; people who got irritated by split infinitives and verb usage did not strike me as the sort of people who had many friends. Maybe that was why everyone seemed to hate me, rather than the fact that I was the sole superhero in a sea of nasty villains.

'Sorry,' I hastily apologised. 'I've just come from my late-night English class and my brain is still in teacher mode.' I offered the man a rueful smile. 'Old habits die hard.' It may have been a white lie, at least as far as I was concerned, but I impressed myself with how glibly it tripped off my tongue.

'I had a teacher like you once,' the man said, not unpleasantly. 'He taught maths though, not English. I always suspected he was a frustrated writer. Not a bad bloke. He didn't dress up like you; he was a bit of a tweed man really. Still, he helped me once when I was getting bullied.'

I stared at him. I didn't want his life story but that was what I got for playing nice and apologising. Then I winced again – what was wrong with me? I shook myself and tried again. I was a nice person. I was a good person. 'How ... lovely for you,' I said faintly. Unfortunately, my words came across as pathetically insincere, even to my own ears. Small talk was not my forte, I decided; I should stick to business as I'd originally planned. 'Anyway,' I said with forced cheer, 'I am looking for nux.' I curved my mouth into a semblance of a smile. 'Do you have any?'

The man blinked. 'Say what?'

Maybe he was hard of hearing. 'Nux,' I said. 'N. U. X.' I spread my arms out with a flourish. 'Nux.'

'Er, is that a generic name?'

I scratched my head. 'I'm not sure,' I admitted. 'It's for ... a friend.'

The man looked sceptical. 'And did your *friend* say what it was for?'

'That's personal,' I said stiffly.

His customer-service smile did not waver. He was obviously used to dealing with awkward people like me, especially at this time of night. 'If you could give me an idea why your friend needs this nux, I'll have a better chance of locating it or finding a suitable alternative.'

What was I going to tell him? That it was for a festering wound caused by a tiny nick from a magical sword that happened to be coated with poison? 'Why don't you just look it up on your computer?' I suggested.

His expression told me everything I needed to know. All the same, he stepped over to the open terminal on the counter and began to tap the keys. As he did so, the door behind me jangled as another customer entered.

'I can't find anything,' the assistant said. 'Unless you mean Nix.'

'No,' I answered. 'It's definitely nux that I'm looking for.'

'Are you sure? Because if it's for the common cold, then Nix is definitely what you're after. You must have seen the advert on television.' He began to hum. '*Nix that cold and you will be feeling bold...*' At the look on my face, his voice trailed off.

'I don't watch much television,' I mumbled.

'You don't watch much television?' came a cultured female voice from behind me. 'What? Not even that glorious soap opera *St Thomas Close*?'

My brow furrowed and I turned towards the blonde woman who'd spoken. I didn't have a clue what she was on about but the pharmaceutical assistant looked awestruck, his jaw dropping as he gazed at her in awe. 'You're... You're ... Stacey!' His cheeks went bright red in a most fascinating fashion.

She flashed him a brilliant red-lipsticked smile. 'That's my character's name,' she said. 'My real name is Julie.'

'Of course! Of course! I knew that,' he babbled. Completely ignoring me, he scrabbled around for a pen and a piece of paper. 'Can I have your autograph?' Then his face lit up as an even better thought struck him. He delved into the pocket of his white coat and drew out a smart phone. 'In fact, how about a selfie?'

Stacey or Julie or whoever she was smiled politely. 'Certainly,' she said. She was twisting round to get into position for what I supposed was her best angle when, out of nowhere, a hulking man wearing a dark suit appeared. I gaped at him. He must have been lurking around the condoms.

'No photos,' he growled.

Julie gave a small titter, which was entirely at odds with her well-heeled, older-woman appearance. 'Mark, darling,' she chided. 'This man is perfectly safe.'

A small muscle ticked in Mark's jaw. 'You don't know that,' he said. 'And you don't know what he will do with the photo afterwards.'

Julie rolled her eyes. 'He's hardly asking me to get my kit off. Look at him! He's about as threatening as a dormouse.'

Mark, who I assumed was her bodyguard rather than an over-protective toy boy, folded his arms and glared. Julie sighed. 'Sorry,' she said. 'I can't be too careful.'

Interesting. I inspected her more closely. Even for someone who was sensitive about her age, she was wearing a lot of make-up. I noted the barely visible dark circles under her eyes. My gaze drifted back to Bodyguard Mark. He was frowning at me as if I were about to pounce on her. Then he moved forward, insinuating himself between his precious Julie and me.

'I can assure you,' I said. 'You don't have to worry about me. I don't even know who she is.'

Bodyguard Mark ignored me and addressed the pharmacy assistant. 'Here,' he said gruffly, passing over a prescription and angling his body away so that I couldn't peer over his shoulder to read it. He needn't have bothered.

'Valium?' The assistant's eyebrows shot up his forehead. He glanced at Julie who tilted up her chin and dared him to continue.

Bodyguard Mark reached across and put a warning hand on his arm. 'Patient confidentiality,' he snapped.

I hadn't thought it was possible for the assistant's cheeks to get any redder but they did. He coughed loudly and turned away. 'I'll just be a minute.'

Unable to resist, I smiled and called out, 'Can I borrow your phone?' I glanced at Bodyguard Mark. 'Do you have the number for the *Daily Journal*?'

He took a threatening step towards me but Julie laughed. 'She's yanking your chain,' she said. 'Believe me, I've been in this business long enough to know about my fans' real motivation.'

I thought about reminding her that I had no clue who she was and so I definitely wasn't a fan but I'd probably pushed my luck enough for one night. In any case, the assistant had already counted out the Valium pills and was passing them over. 'Here you go,' he said, holding them out to Julie.

Bodyguard Mark reached out and palmed the bottle, before rolling it around in his large hands. Then, as we all watched, he unscrewed the lid and examined the contents. He might have the build of Arnold Schwarzenegger but he was all brawn and no brains.

'Seriously?' I asked. 'What are you expecting to find? Have you been properly trained? If you really want to check those pills, you should be doing it in privacy not out here in the open where anyone can see you. You're broadcasting her weak spots for all the world to see. Why did you even bring her here? If you're protecting her, you should have left her in a safe place and come to get the prescription yourself.' I glanced at Julie. 'I don't know what you're paying this guy but, whatever it is, it is far, far too much.'

'How do you know all this?' she asked. 'Are you in the protection business too?'

I hesitated. Maybe I was. Maybe that was how I put my superhero skills into action and how I knew that the faint ripples in the fabric of his suit meant Bodyguard Mark had a shoulder holster with a gun neatly tucked away inside it. I also knew that an old injury was causing him chronic lower-back pain that he was doing a decent job of concealing. 'You could say that,' I said eventually.

'Why the fancy dress? Are you in amateur dramatics?'

Amateur melodramatics only. 'No. I just...' I raised a shoulder. What the hell. 'I wanted to dress up because I'm a superhero. Jeans and a T-shirt just don't seem to match my personality in the same way that an electric-blue cape and a leotard do.'

Julie grinned. 'You go, girl.'

She might have been charmed but Bodyguard Mark seemed to be under the impression that I was trying to poach his client. He gave me a narrow-eyed evil look, which might have stopped me in my tracks if I hadn't just had an encounter with the embodiment of evil himself, and began to hustle Julie out of the shop. She managed a light-hearted cheerio before the door jangled shut after them.

'I didn't even get a selfie or an autograph,' the pharmacy assistant said mournfully. 'No one will believe me when I tell them she was here.'

'Well, I didn't get to keep my place in the queue,' I snapped. 'What about my nux?'

'I still have no idea what you're talking about.' He shrugged. 'I've never heard of it before and there are no details of it in our system. I suggest you try the Batcave instead.'

I put my hands on my hips and shook out my cape. 'You making fun of me?'

'Heaven forbid,' he said. He motioned towards the shelves. 'You're welcome to search for yourself if you wish.'

I gave the various items on display a cursory once-over but unfortunately I didn't know what I was looking for any more than he did. Eventually I gave up and stomped out. I'd have to try the internet instead. I could probably order the darn stuff online.

Massaging my poor finger, I continued on my way. The rain had started once again. I was about to pick up my feet and make a run for it before my costume became entirely waterlogged when I spotted the gleaming car on the opposite side of the street. It was at a standstill but its engine was running and the passenger door was wide open. Given that the number plate was JOOLZ, it didn't take a genius to realise who it belonged to.

I cursed. That bodyguard really was next to useless. Even a child would know that taking such an expensive and showy vehicle out with Julie Whoever's name emblazoned on it was a stupid move. I stomped over. It had been kind of fun winding him up in the shop but now I was getting irritated.

I went round the back of the car, ducking my head towards the open door. 'Seriously,' I said, 'you really need to think about...' I stopped. The car was empty. I frowned and checked the driver's seat. Nope. Definitely empty. Bodyguard Mark was stupid – but there was no way he was this stupid.

I craned my neck round. There was no sight of anyone else. There was, however, a dark alleyway up ahead to my right. Ah ha. Twirling once more for effect – although my cape was now too wet to do more than flap uselessly – I sneaked over and peered down it.

There was a prone body lying on the ground a few metres up the alley. I couldn't see the face but I was willing to bet my groovy sequined mask that it was Bodyguard Mark. Further up, shrouded in heavy darkness, two figures were scuffling. There was a muffled, high-pitched shriek. I guessed Julie hadn't hired a bodyguard just for show then; she really did need saving.

'This,' I murmured under my breath, 'can only be a job for the Madhatter.'

Wasting no further time, I raced towards them. Whoever

was attacking Julie was making a meal of it. He towered over her with one gloved hand clamped over her mouth and the other holding her in place. She still managed several sharp kicks against his shin and, even though he was wearing a skanky-looking balaclava, his oomphs of pain made it clear that he was struggling.

'I am the Madhatter!' I yelled, barrelling towards them. 'You will stop now or suffer the consequences!'

The attacker slammed his elbow into Julie's temple and she crumpled. Then, with the casual, practised movements of a pro, he reached into his belt and drew out some kind of Taser.

Easy peasy: I'd just warp time as I had before and beat him to the ground before he could pull the trigger. Concentrating, I reached for the power. I felt a familiar tightening in my stomach but this time nothing seemed to happen. I tried again. Gasbudlikins. Whatever magic I'd drawn on before wasn't working. I came to a skidding halt, just as Julie's attacker smiled and raised the Taser.

Two small darts shot out and connected with my tummy. There was a brief tingle – and nothing else. I frowned. 'That tickles.'

Behind his own mask, the man's eyes widened. He shook the Taser as if willing it to work. 'Fucking...'

I lashed out, punching him in the stomach as hard as I could. Unfortunately, the action seemed to do my hand more damage than it did him. He threw the Taser down and faced me, teeth bared. I shook my hand in the air as if to flick off the pain. 'Ouchy. Are you wearing a steel corset?'

He was apparently unwilling to participate in small talk and flung himself towards me once more, fists swinging. I must have been some sort of hand-to-hand combat expert in a previous life because from a mile off I could see he was aiming for the right side of my head. I neatly dodged him, spun round and grinned. 'You're the human equivalent of a participation award.' My quip would have sounded better if my rain-sodden cape hadn't spun with me and smacked me wetly in the face as I was saying it. Why on earth did superheroes wear shit like this?

I didn't have time to ponder on the dress code of noble protectors for long. The man snarled and wasted no time in advancing and reaching out to grab a hank of my hair. This time I wasn't fast enough and he snagged enough to pull me towards him. It felt like my scalp was being yanked away from my skull and I shrieked. Bloody arsebadger.

I twisted and turned in a bid to free myself. Fortunately for me, Julie took this moment to join the fray, leaping onto his back with her fingers scrabbling towards his eyes. As she jabbed her thumbs towards his eye sockets, he howled and let go of my hair. I took full advantage of my reprieve and darted forward, scooping up the Taser from the ground. As the man whipped round, throwing Julie onto the hard pavement, I leapt forward and pressed the muzzle into the bare skin just visible at his neckline. I pulled the trigger and, hey presto, this time it worked. He jerked and screamed, his body juddering for a few seconds before going completely limp.

Throwing the Taser away, I dusted off my palms and smirked. 'Not such a bright spark now, are you?'

Julie coughed and rolled on to her side. I nipped over and helped her to her feet. She glanced from the man to me and back again. 'That was ... amazing.'

I nodded. 'It was rather.' I knelt down beside the still-prone man. 'Let's see who we're dealing with, shall we?' I reached for his balaclava just as flashing blue lights illuminated the street from near where Julie's car was parked.

She clutched at my arm. 'No police.' Her voice was low and filled with vibrating alarm.

I looked at her curiously. 'You should talk to them,' I advised. 'This guy wasn't trying to kill you. He had a stun gun, not a shotgun. He probably wanted to abduct you.' My tone was matter-of-fact but fear still flared in Julie's eyes. 'They can take him in for questioning and find out if there are others.'

Her panic only increased. 'No. I can't let that happen.' She swallowed. 'I won't be that actor on the front page of every tabloid rag because I have a stalker. I value my privacy. If we go to the police then all that disappears.'

Part of me wanted to point out that if she really thought that much of her privacy perhaps she shouldn't drive around with a flashy car and a personalised number plate. I was rather taken by her use of the word 'we', however. Not to mention that I had my own reasons for avoiding the police; if they connected me to the still unpublicized events at the golf course, I'd have a lot of unpleasant questions to answer. After all, if I'd been going to report what had happened to me, I should have already done so.

I shrugged. 'As you wish. Get that useless bodyguard of yours to his feet and I'll deal with the coppers.'

I sauntered over as a uniformed policeman emerged from the panda car and began to inspect Julie's empty vehicle.

'Hey, officer!' I called out cheerily. 'How are you this fine evening?'

'Stay where you are,' came the unimpressed response.

I stopped in my tracks. 'Is there a problem?'

The policeman, together with another uniformed companion who appeared behind him, walked towards me. 'Whose vehicle is this?'

'Julie's,' I said confidently.

'Julie who?'

Er... 'Julie who plays Stacey in that soap opera.' Gasbudlikins. What was it called again? '*St Tomahawk Close*.'

He peered at me. '*St Thomas Close?*'

I snapped my fingers. 'That's the one!'

There was a shuffling noise and the lady herself hobbled up with a groaning Bodyguard Mark leaning heavily against her. It was a wonder she didn't collapse under the big man's weight. 'Hello!' she cooed. 'Sorry. I know I shouldn't have parked there but it was an emergency. My friend here wasn't feeling well and needed to throw up.'

Both policemen paused and did the sort of double take that I was starting to suspect passed for normal when you were a soap star. 'You're Julie Chivers.'

She attempted a curtsey; unfortunately, with Mark by her side, she ended up merely staggering. The first copper threw himself forward and quickly took Mark from her, hooking the bodyguard's arm round his shoulder. 'Here,' he said. 'Let me help you.'

She giggled. 'Thank you so much. He is soooo heavy. I told him he shouldn't have had so much to drink but...' She shook her head in dismay. 'What can you do?'

As if answering her, Mark groaned and tried to speak. She hushed him. 'Don't try to talk, dear. We're getting you back to the car now with the help of these wonderful police officers.'

The wonderful police officers immediately took her veiled suggestion and half-dragged, half-lifted Mark into the back seat. He fell forward inside with just his feet sticking out. Trying to be helpful, I scooted up and gently pushed them in. Mark curled up into the foetal position and groaned some more. Honestly, 'the bigger they are, the harder they fall' was more of a truism than I'd realised.

'He's a friend of yours?' the policeman asked.

Julie pursed her lips. 'Friend of a friend.' She pointed at me. I wasn't sure I appreciated being dragged into her tale but it was a bit late now to do anything about it. 'We were at a party.'

'Fancy dress?'

She smiled. 'No.'

I cleared my throat. 'I thought it was a superhero-themed party but I...'

'She was wrong.'

I nodded. 'I was wrong. And embarrassed. Horribly embarrassed. Admittedly not as embarrassed as Mark will be in the morning, but still.'

Neither policeman was interested in what I had to say. Clearly they only wanted to hear from Julie. 'Who's driving?'

'I am.' She smiled brilliantly. 'It's my car. I've not had anything to drink, I promise you.'

She was an actor – she lied for a living. I was sure that both policemen would remain suspicious despite her glib words. Instead, however, they grinned at her. 'You're not like Stacey on *St Thomas Close* then.'

Julie laughed. 'No. She is something else.' She clasped her hands together. 'Anyway, we should get this poor man home. Unless there's anything else?'

I was expecting them to ask her for an autograph but unfortunately they suddenly seemed to remember who they were and what job they were supposed to be doing. One of the coppers craned his neck down the small street. 'Is there anyone else down there?'

I held my breath, praying that the balaclava-wearing attacker didn't take this moment to moan or stand up. When I glanced towards him, though, there was no sign of the man; the lump where his body had lain had vanished. I couldn't decide whether that was good or not.

If Julie was as surprised at his disappearance as I was, she didn't let it show. 'Not a soul, luckily enough. Not even a dodgy paparazzo.'

'Fair enough. We'll let you off this time. But you shouldn't leave your car with the engine running like that – someone might steal it.'

'Or worse,' added the other policeman with a grim edge.

Or worse indeed, I thought.

Julie smiled. 'Thank you. We'll take more care in the future.' She glanced at me. 'Coming?'

I couldn't say no. I plastered on a smile of my own and walked round to the front passenger seat. 'Let's go.'

'Thank you again,' Julie trilled. Then she hopped in, closed the door and we quickly drove off.

CHAPTER SIX

The next morning, I lay spread-eagled on the hotel bed and contemplated my next move. Perhaps dressing up in a superhero costume hadn't been the greatest idea in the world and, given that Julie had dropped me off last night, I'd not retrieved my overcoat from where I'd stashed it under the old car. Instead, I'd dripped through the hotel lobby with both mask and cape still on. The costume had served neither to hide me from the police nor conceal my identity, so caring about it by that point had seemed entirely pointless.

I was frustrated that I couldn't remember anything useful about myself and I was desperate to investigate more. And now it wasn't just the small wound on my finger I had to worry about; my entire hand was starting to throb, pain radiating across all my tendons. The smart move would be to find some of this nux stuff and sort my health out once and for all.

DD had mentioned a fellow named Rubus who could help me out. I decided I'd start my search for him. If I could find him, not only might I find the antidote I needed but I might also learn who I really was and exactly what I was capable of. That Taser last night hadn't affected me so, while I knew I wasn't invincible, there was definitely more to my abilities and strengths than I appreciated.

I'd only just rolled off the bed, shrugged on a bathrobe and turned on the small kettle when there was a knock at the door. My body tensed. Theoretically, apart from Julie, no one knew I was here but that didn't mean she hadn't bandied my details about or that I hadn't been tracked.

I darted over to the window and opened it so I could squeeze through in a rush if I needed to, then unplugged the half-boiled kettle. In a pinch, I could throw hot water at an assailant. There was another loud knock and, kettle in hand, I edged over to the door and answered it, leaving on the chain.

'Yes?'

It wasn't housekeeping as I'd hoped. Instead the stern, unlined features of a suited man whose face I didn't recognise looked back at me. He had dark thinning hair and an abnormally large forehead; his skin was completely blemish free. Either he had an excellent dermatologist or he was wearing make up.

'Miss Smith?' he enquired. 'Joan Smith?'

I struggled for a moment to remember if that was the name I'd given when I checked in. 'Uh, that's me. Joan. Joany Baby. Joan Smith. Hello. I'm Joan.' Clearly Joan was also a blathering idiot.

He didn't smile. 'I'm Mike Timmons, the hotel manager. Am I correct in thinking you checked in two nights ago?'

I wasn't the only one who was an idiot. This was a hotel chain with well-established computer systems. Mike Timmons didn't think I checked in two nights ago, he knew. Now even more concerned that this was some sort of set up, despite both his demeanour and clothing screaming hotel manager, I hefted the kettle and tried to smile. 'That's correct, yes.'

'You paid cash.'

'Yes, I paid upfront. Why? Is there a problem?'

'No, no problem. We just don't appear to have any identification for you on record. It's important for health and safety reasons to keep an official log of all our guests. A credit card will suffice.' He smiled, displaying even, white teeth. His green eyes flashed.

Something tugged at me, an errant thought that something wasn't quite right. My instincts had served me fairly well so far and I wasn't about to ignore them now. Besides, it wasn't like I had a credit card to give the man.

'I only just woke up,' I said pleasantly. 'Give me half an hour and I'll pop down to the front desk and sort all this out.'

Timmons didn't blink. 'I'd prefer it if we sorted this out now.'

Okay. Something was definitely up. Yes, he was well within his rights to demand identification but planting himself at my door and refusing to leave until I did as he asked was not the way to gain yourself a five-star review on Trip Advisor.

I lifted up my chin and met his eyes. 'I'll be at the front desk in half an hour,' I repeated. 'I'm not even dressed yet and this is starting to feel like intimidation.'

Timmons didn't back down. Instead, he leaned forward, licked his lips and smiled even more brightly. His smile didn't reach his eyes. 'I'll let you off with the ID part,' he said, lowering his voice to a whisper, 'if you give me some.'

I stared at him. Unbelievable. I'd thought he'd looked rather sleazy but this was beyond the pale. 'No chance. I'm not some prostitute. I'm not going to drop my robe and spread my legs for you. What do you take me for?'

Something akin to disgust flashed in his eyes. 'Ew.' His eyes widened, as if he hadn't meant to say that aloud. He took a step back and bit his lip. 'I'm joking.' He twitched. 'I really am. Don't tell Rubus. I just need ... some stuff. I don't want to offend you but you did come to my hotel. I won't tell anyone you're here if you just give me some.'

His abrupt volte-face from stern jobsworth to a grovelling excuse for a man would have given me pause if his other words hadn't had me unhooking the chain and flinging the door wide open so I could confront him. 'What do you know about Rubus?'

Timmons paled. 'What do you mean?'

'Who is he? What does he have to do with me?'

His eyes darted from side to side. 'Is this a test?'

'What?' I gritted my teeth and stepped forward. Somehow I was having a bizarre conversation with an even more bizarre man that seemed to be nothing more than questions fired at each other, with no one giving any answers. 'Stop beating around the bush,' I snapped. 'Answer me.'

He hissed under his breath, 'I just want some fucking dust. I don't want to antagonise Rubus. Give me some and I'll leave you alone. You can stay here for as long as you want – free of charge – and I won't ask any more questions.'

I folded my arms and tilted my head to one side, examining him from head to toe. Those hulking brutes out by the golf course had mentioned dust as well. Somehow I doubted it had anything to do with cleaning. 'You want some dust,' I said slowly.

Timmons threw up his hands. 'Isn't that what I said? Not much. Just an ounce or two will do.'

As he spoke, I realised that there was definitely something not quite right about the man. It was almost as if he weren't entirely human. Taking a chance, I swallowed and leaned forward. 'What are you?'

He gazed back at me stupidly for a second. 'Huh?'

I was growing tired of all this prevarication. I put the kettle aside, grabbed him by the lapels, hauled him into my room and slammed the door shut. Then I whirled round to face him, using the base of my hand to hit his chest and knock him backwards.

'You can't do this,' he stammered. 'You can't hurt me. The truce—'

'What truce?'

At this, his eyes flared in fear. I sucked a deep breath of air into my lungs. The man obviously thought I was threatening him. Well, if that was what it took to finally get some answers around here, that was what I was going to do.

'You heard me,' I snarled. 'The truce,' whatever it was, 'means nothing to me.' I jabbed him again in the chest. 'You came to me. Don't forget that part.'

The look in Timmons' eyes suggested I'd just committed the ultimate heresy. 'You ... you ... can't do this.'

I wasn't doing anything – yet. 'I can do whatever I want,' I said airily, as if I knew exactly what was going on. 'Now tell me who Rubus is and where I can find him.'

'I only want dust!' he whined. 'Morganus will hear about this. Mark my words, Madrona, you'll regret this. Even if you kill me, you'll get what's coming to you.'

I started. Kill him? I might have been playing the role of tough guy – or gal – but I wasn't sure when death had entered the equation. I opened my mouth just as Timmons did the same. He wasn't trying to chat any longer, though; his pupils became pinpricks and his eyelids narrowed into slits. His cheeks bulged and then, with bared teeth and in a manner akin to a crocodile, he snapped at me.

I sprang back. What the hell? He lunged in my direction and I flung up my hands to shield myself. He didn't touch me, though; instead he barrelled past me, yanking open the room door and escaping into the corridor. I darted after him, only to hear one high-pitched laugh as he disappeared round the corner.

I was about to go after him when another door opened and a couple emerged. 'Morning!' said the woman cheerfully. She took her partner's hand and they ambled away in the same direction as Timmons. I fumbled a half wave and, cursing under my breath, retreated into the room.

Heart pounding against my chest, I wasted no more time. I hastily pulled off the robe and grabbed some clothes. Real clothes. The crappy superhero costume, which hadn't helped me at all, could stay crumpled on the bathroom floor. I wriggled into the jeans I'd bought from the charity shop and hauled a Led Zeppelin T-shirt over my head. Without bothering to untie the laces, I thrust my feet into the pair of canvas shoes I'd also purchased and sprang back to the door.

I'd barely turned the handle when the phone rang. I hesitated. It was Timmons. It had to be. Whatever manner of beastie super villain he was, he had decided it was easier to confront me over the airwaves than in person. I debated for a split second and then turned to answer it.

'Hello!' trilled a female voice that most definitely wasn't Timmons. 'I'm not sure if I have the right room or not. This is Julie Chivers. We met last night?'

My brow furrowed and I almost hung up but something stopped me. 'Yes,' I said slowly. 'This is ...' Joan? Madrona? The Madhatter? 'Me,' I finished lamely.

'Excellent! I'm in the hotel lobby. I was rather hoping I could take you out for breakfast.'

I grimaced. This was hardly the time. I was about to tell her that when a soft rustle outside the door caught my ear. I tiptoed over. This time I didn't open the door, I did the sensible thing and peeked through the spyhole instead. When I saw who was out there I immediately stiffened. Three men. And I recognised them. It was the assassination-hungry arsebadgers from the golf course: McNasty One, Two and Three. No doubt Timmons had called up the cavalry to bring me down.

I'd succeeded against them once because they'd apparently not coated their bullets with rowan but I doubted I could count on such good fortune the second time around. Well, regardless of how many creepy buddies of indeterminate ethnicity Timmons sent my way, I'd escape them all.

'Julie,' I said quickly and quietly into the receiver as I scurried over to the window and hoisted it open. 'Breakfast sounds fab. Did you bring your car? If you start up the engine right now, I'll meet you out front.'

She murmured acquiescence. I hung up and hopped out of the window, taking care to close it behind me. I was halfway across the hotel car park when I heard the sound of splintering wood; they'd not wasted much time in breaking into my room. I grimaced at the thought of abandoning yet another potential clue. Risk versus reward, however – and I had to protect myself first. Superhero though I may be, I wasn't invincible. And I wouldn't find out anything if I ended up dead in a dreary hotel room.

I scooted round to the front of the hotel just as Julie arrived in her car. She wound down the window but I didn't wait; I simply hopped into the front seat next to her.

'Let's go,' I said, glancing in the rear-view mirror. As expected, my old golfing buddies hadn't taken long to establish how I'd escaped from the room. They were already racing across the car park towards us.

'I'm sure we could get breakfast here,' Julie began.

I shook my head. 'Drive.'

The urgency of my tone must have filtered through. She put the car into gear and, wheels squealing, drove out of the car park. I spotted Timmons coming out of the hotel's front doors with a mobile phone clamped to his ear and his goons running up to join him. All four of them glared nastily after us.

I relaxed into the seat. As vexing as it was that the best option was to run away, I couldn't have made a better getaway if I'd had months to plan it.

CHAPTER SEVEN

I was prepared to dump Julie as soon as we were far enough away from the hotel to be safe but my stomach was grumbling and a decent breakfast seemed prudent. Besides, I figured that the least I could do was to sit with her as she'd requested. Maybe the poor woman had no friends and was looking for a good mate to hang out with and beat up the occasional man. It turned out I was half right.

'I want you to be my bodyguard,' she said without preamble, once we'd made our food orders.

I choked on my coffee. 'Excuse me?'

She smiled. 'You've proved yourself far more competent than Mark. Not to mention that you're obviously not the slightest bit star-struck.'

I wasn't star-struck because I still didn't know who she was. I used a napkin to pat away the coffee dribbles on my chin and pretended to take her job offer seriously. 'Hmmm.'

'You'll be amply compensated,' Julie assured me.

I'd already been amply compensated by the golf-course goons; I wasn't short of money. 'I appreciate the thought,' I said. 'But I'm not sure my schedule will allow me to take up a full-time position.'

She tapped her perfectly manicured nails against her cup. 'It's not really full time. It's barely even part time. I'm on set most of the day and the production company have serious security, so I only need you when I'm not working. Three nights a week and maybe the odd weekend or two, tops. Honestly, it's easy money.'

'You don't know anything about me,' I pointed out. Hell, *I* didn't know anything about me. 'I could be a psycho killer.'

'Your name is Joan Smith.' She smiled at my expression. 'The hotel receptionist told me. People take one look at me and generally fall over backwards to give me what I want. That's why I like you. You don't want anything from me. You're different.'

Different was certainly a word for it. 'Look, Julie,' I said. 'The thing is, my name isn't Joan. I think it's Madrona but I can't be completely sure. I've got amnesia. I woke up in the middle of a golf course two nights ago and I can't remember who I am or what's going on.'

Her eyes widened fractionally but she didn't miss a beat. 'Amnesia? Wow! *That's* why you don't know who I am!'

'No,' I said, without thinking. 'I remember pop-culture stuff and how to drive and things like that. I just don't remember *me*.' I shrugged. 'I guess the old me didn't watch your soap opera.'

'Oh.' Somewhat deflated, she leaned back.

'So,' I said, the very definition of earnest optimism, 'I can't work for you because I have to spend my time trying to find out who I am and why people are trying to hurt me.' And what dust is. And why I have super powers. And who Rubus was. And Morganus. And where I could get some nux from. And... Gasbudlikins. It was never-ending.

Julie mulled this over for only the scantest of moments. 'But that's why this job is perfect. Most of your time will be your own. I'll give you somewhere to stay –I've got some excellent guest quarters in my house. You can work for me occasionally but mostly work for yourself. And,' she added with a triumphant flourish, 'I can help you out more than you realise. A few years ago, Stacey, my character, was hit on the head by her son's girlfriend's fiancé and she got amnesia as a result. I know all about the condition.' She rolled her eyes at my expression. 'Don't look at me like that. It might be a soap opera but we still do our research and try to make everything as realistic as possible. I can already tell you that, if your name is Madrona, we're onto a winning start. I've never heard that name before so I'm sure a simple internet search will help us. And have you considered the police? They could put out an appeal. Someone might have reported you missing.'

'I don't want the police involved,' I interjected hastily.

'Is that because you're a superhero?'

I blinked at her. 'Pardon?'

'Last night you said you were a superhero. I imagine that you'd want to stay under the radar if that's true.' She smiled as if amused. This was certainly a far more light-hearted Julie than the one who'd been under attack last night.

'I'm not crazy,' I said stiffly. 'Besides, you can't talk. You didn't want to call the police last night and you have an even better reason to request their help than I do.'

Julie didn't take offence. 'I already explained about that.'

I met her eyes. Keen intelligence gazed back at me. I sighed and pushed my hair out of my eyes. 'I'm not normal.' I wasn't quite sure why I was trying to talk myself out of this almost perfect job.

She laughed. 'Darling, none of us are normal.'

'What I mean is that I wasn't kidding about the superhero

thing. I do have weird powers. I don't know where they came from or what they mean but,' I shrugged, 'I really do think I'm a superhero.'

To her credit, she didn't get up from the table and run away screaming. 'Tell me more.'

'You saw what happened with the Taser,' I said. 'When your bad guy tried to use it on me. *Nothing* happened. I felt a bit of a tickle and that was it.'

'I thought it had just run out of juice or something.'

'No. I was able to use it on him a moment or two later. There was nothing wrong with the gun.' I looked down at the table. 'I can also do things with time. Slow it down so I can gain the upper hand, I mean.'

She arched an eyebrow. 'Really? What else?'

'I don't know. I told you, I've got amnesia. There might be lots of other things that I'm capable of. There might be nothing.'

Julie regarded me thoughtfully. 'I still don't see any reason why you can't come and work for me. If you do have super powers, you're the perfect bodyguard. And I can help you experiment to discover your potential. There might be more untapped magic inside you that you don't know about.'

'You're taking this very calmly,' I told her. 'Don't you think I'm nuts?'

Her answer was frank. 'If it weren't for you, goodness knows where I'd be right now. Chained to a radiator, if I was lucky.' She reached out for my hand. 'Mark was twice your size and came at a premium cost, and look what happened to him. You succeeded where he didn't. It stands to reason that there's far more to you than meets the eyes. Besides,' she grinned disarmingly, 'this sounds like it's going to be a two-way street. We need each other.'

It seemed too good to be true. I'd effectively told her I

thought I was Supergirl and she'd not blinked. Plus, she was offering me the perfect job, at the perfect time. 'Tell me about that man,' I said slowly. 'The one who attacked you. You were obviously expecting something like that because you'd hired Mark to protect you.'

For the first time she looked uneasy. 'A few ... incidents have occurred.'

'Such as?' I pressed.

'Nasty letters. Someone calling my home and breathing down the phone. That kind of thing. I didn't think much of it to begin with – I get a lot of nutty fans. Then things escalated. You saw Mark checking the bottle of pills?' I nodded. 'I was poisoned,' she told me flatly. 'I almost died. Someone spiked a bottle of water that I took to the gym. We checked the CCTV camera but they were too smart to get caught that way. Then there were the body parts.'

I stared at her. 'What?'

Julie shifted in her seat. 'Not human. There was a cat's leg, all bloody and bound up. Then a dog's tail.' Her mouth turned down. 'They were shoved through my letterbox.'

'Someone was sending you a message.'

'Yes.'

Sick. I pushed aside my disgust. 'Do you still have the letters?'

She shook her head. 'No. I threw them out.'

'And the ... animal bits?'

She made a face. 'No.'

I wrinkled my nose. It didn't give me much to go on. 'Do you have reason to suspect anyone in particular?'

Julie raised her hands helplessly. 'No. I have a list of people who've crossed the line. Fans, people like that. My agent drew it up for me. Mark has a copy. We've been through it but I don't think there's anyone on it who fits this profile.' There was something about the way her eyes shifted that suggested she wasn't telling the whole truth. Rather than put me off, I was more intrigued.

I tapped my mouth. This did indeed seem like a job for someone who believed they were a superhero – and it certainly beat tramping the streets searching for random people in need of help. 'Okay,' I began. 'I'll help...'

Her face broke into a wreath of smiles. 'Thank you! Thank you so much!' She reached into her pocket and drew out a key. 'This is for my house.' She passed it to me, grabbed a napkin and scribbled down the address. 'I've got to be on set in an hour and I won't be home till after eight, but you can go and make yourself comfortable. It'll also give you some time to do your own investigations into yourself.' She bounced up and planted a kiss on my cheek. 'This is going to be great, Madrona. You won't regret it.'

Before I could say another word, she scooped up her bag and launched herself out of the café as if she were afraid that I'd change my mind. The door had just clanged shut behind her when the waiter appeared with two plates in his hands. He glanced at Julie's empty seat.

'Ms Chivers has gone?' He was visibly disappointed.

The salty aroma of bacon hit my nostrils. 'Yep. Just as well too.' I grinned at the plates as if they were long-lost friends. 'I'm starving.'

~

Although I wanted to get to Julie's house before she returned from work so I could investigate her home security, I had more than enough time to focus on my own problems first. I drew up a mental list, prioritising each item. As soon as I'd finished eating, I made a beeline for the city library, using the directions of various passers-by in order to get there. There were no signs of Timmons and his crew nor of tall Amazonian women nor, disappointingly, of green-eyed Dark and Despicable. That was a good thing, I tried to tell myself. I almost believed it.

The library building was satisfyingly old and impressive. Fashioned out of granite, it was a large, imposing, circular structure with towering grey stone columns at the front and smaller versions encircling the third-floor façade. It didn't look in any way familiar to my poor damaged mind but I was still impressed. I loped up the stairs at the front and entered.

A sign dangling from the ceiling directed me to the line of computers. Sitting down at the only empty monitor, I tapped on the keys. A login screen appeared. With neither a username nor a password, I glared at it for a long moment, as if I could will it to permit me access through sight alone. When that didn't work, I sighed audibly and stalked to the front desk.

The bespectacled clerk, whose attention was wholly on the screen in front of him and whose name tag proclaimed him as Ernest, completely ignored me. I coughed loudly. Without glancing up, he held up his index finger indicating that I should wait.

'I want access to the computers,' I said in an overly loud voice. Several people turned their heads to look at the person who was daring to interrupt the librarian from his game of Solitaire.

'Just a moment.' Ernest still didn't look up.

I drummed my fingers on the reception desk and regretted it almost instantly when pain flared up through my arm from my finger. I yanked my arm back and cradled it against my body. Bloody hell, it hurt. 'Ernest,' I said. 'If I were going to pick a name for a librarian, it would be Ernest. Are you called Ernie for short? Do you have a friend called Bert? Are you earnest, Ernest? You look earnest. I...'

He looked at me. Excellent. I smiled at him beatifically; that was better.

As if the weight of the world were on his shoulders rather than that of a few books, he sighed. 'What can I do for you?'

'I would like to access the computers.' I paused. 'Please.' See? I could be nice.

'Are you a member of this library?'

Probably not. 'Nope.'

'I'll need your name and address and two forms of identification. You'll need to fill in this form,' he said, pulling out a lengthy sheet of paper attached to a clipboard from a drawer. 'And then you can book a computer.'

I stared at him. 'I don't want to move in, Mr Wiffle-Waffle. I just want to use a computer.'

'Mr what?'

'Ernest. Mr Ernest.' I smiled again. It didn't appear to appease him.

Using the tip of his index finger, he slid the bridge of his glasses up his nose. 'We can offer you a temporary membership for today but you'll still need to fill in the form. And show me ID.'

'I don't have any.'

Ernest didn't appear in the least surprised. 'Then I'm afraid there's nothing I can do.'

'I...'

A grey-haired woman arrived and peered at me. 'I'll deal with this customer, Ernie,' she said. 'You go take your break.'

'It's your funeral,' he said darkly. He didn't waste any time in stomping off.

You wouldn't think it would be this hard simply to gain internet access. I tried again, glancing at the woman's name badge. Paeonia: unpronounceable as well as daft. 'Hello. I would like to use one of the computers. I don't have ID but I promise I'm a good person.'

Paeonia's green eyes shifted from side to side, as if she were checking for eavesdroppers. Then she dropped her voice to a whisper. 'You got any dust?'

I almost shrieked. 'What the freak is dust?'

'Keep your voice down! You only had to say no. Honestly.' She rolled her eyes to the heavens.

I gritted my teeth. The conversation might have taken a wholly unexpected turn but that wasn't necessarily a bad thing. I wasn't getting anywhere fast by being honest so I had to switch tactics – and as smoothly as possible to avoid raising suspicion. 'Okay,' I said, waggling my eyebrows in a conspiratorial fashion. 'I was just checking. You can't be too careful.' I leaned forward. 'I can't get you any dust until I know for certain that you know what it is and what to do with it. It's ... important stuff after all. I need to know you're worthy.'

She bobbed her head as if she completely agreed with me. 'Oh, I'm worthy. I've taken it many times before. I love pixie dust,' she said reverently. 'I don't know what's in it, of course. It's a secret formula. But it makes all of this,' she waved an arm around, 'just a little bit easier to manage.'

'Hmmm.' I nodded sagely in return. 'You say you've taken it *many* times before?'

'Oh yes.'

I gripped the desk with both hands. 'What does it look like then?'

Her brow creased. 'Grey. Sparkly. Like ... dust.'

Duh. I should have guessed. 'Why are you asking me about it?'

Her eyes darted from side to side once more. 'Because you're Madrona.'

Huh. I was obviously quite a prolific superhero if so many

people knew my name. Dust sounded like it was some kind of medicine – or drug. Whatever it was, it was clearly doing some good. By this woman's own admission, it made everything better. I pursed my lips. Was I a doctor?

'Have we met?' I enquired.

'Oh no. I saw you once in the street with Rubus but we've never officially been introduced. Everyone knows who you are, though.'

I nibbled on my bottom lip. 'Well, I still need to confirm that you're trustworthy and that you know what you're getting yourself into. So tell me everything you know about Rubus.'

Another library customer appeared at my side. 'Hello! Can you tell me where the historical fiction section is?'

I turned. 'It's very rude to interrupt.'

'It's over there,' Paeonia said, pointing. She glanced back at me once the customer had gone. 'You're testing me. I'm not an idiot. I won't say a word about Rubus.' She drew a line across her lips. 'Don't worry about that.'

Gasbudlikins.

A man in a wheelchair trundled up. 'Good afternoon. Do you have the key for the disabled toilet?'

I rolled my eyes. This time, the woman moved a bit faster before I could snap at this new irritant. She quickly handed over a large key and he wheeled away.

I had about a million questions. She might not be willing to talk about Rubus but I reckoned I could glean plenty more information from her. 'Okay,' I said. 'You seem like you're ... good enough for some dust. I'll bring some in tomorrow.' But of course, once I received the answers I was looking for she wouldn't even see me for dust. Boom boom.

'You don't have any on you now?' Her shoulders drooped. 'Are you sure?'

'I could maybe try to get hold of some,' I demurred. 'If you tell me where I can get some nux.'

She drew in a sharp breath. 'Nux? But...' Her face paled dramatically as her eyes flickered to yet another bloody customer behind me.

I sighed loudly and stepped back so she could deal with whoever it was. Then I froze. Dark and Despicable glared at me with frosty rage then grabbed my arm. 'This conversation is over.'

'Wait, I—'

'I mean it, Madrona. You're coming with me.' He lifted his green-eyed gaze to Paeonia. 'You should watch yourself,' he added coolly.

She looked utterly terrified. 'I'm sorry. I mean it! I'm really sorry! It wasn't me, though. It's all her fault.' She pointed a long bony finger at me.

Irritated, I tried to wrench myself out of DD's grasp. I wasn't beyond making a scene if I needed to.

'Don't try anything,' he murmured in my ear, his voice like tempered steel sheathed with pure silk. 'Not unless you want more rowan flooding your system, Maddy.'

I felt something jabbing the side of my ribs. Rowan. That was the stuff that I'd been poisoned with. The arsebadger was threatening me! Unwilling to risk it, I gritted my teeth and forced my body to relax. A moment later, and with an iron grip, DD led me straight out of the library at high speed.

CHAPTER EIGHT

When we reached the steps outside, I felt DD's weight shift and the sharp object pressing into my side disappeared. I whirled away from him. 'What exactly do you think you're doing?' I demanded.

He casually slipped his hands into his pockets before I could see exactly what manner of rowan weapon he was carrying and regarded me disdainfully. 'I might ask the same of you.'

'You threatened me!' I spat. 'In a library of all places!'

'You're soliciting custom, Madrona. Spreading your tentacles across the city – as if you didn't have your talons in everything already.'

I glared. 'Well, it's either tentacles or talons. I don't think it's physically possible to have both.'

He didn't blink. 'So you're admitting it. You were selling your disgusting dust out in the open. In broad daylight.'

'Hardly,' I scoffed. 'I just wanted to use a damn computer to do some research. That woman approached me, not the other way around. Besides, what's it to you?'

DD's nostrils flared slightly. 'You dare ask that of me?'

For goodness' sake. It was like having a conversation with a brick wall. I stepped towards him to indicate that I wasn't in the slightest bit afraid of him. 'Why is this dust stuff so abhorrent to you?'

He gazed at me in abject disbelief. 'You have got to be kidding me.' He tutted loudly, turned on his heel and strode away, calling over his shoulder, 'Don't let me catch you selling again.'

Nuh-uh. I wasn't going to let him get off that easily. Not this time. Forgetting that he'd only just threatened me, I sprang after him and grabbed his arm.

He turned back, sneering as he gazed at my hand clutching his elbow. 'Let go of me.'

'Why? It's alright for you to manhandle me but when the shoe is on the other foot, I'm some sort of evil being? I told you,' I hissed, 'I've got amnesia. All I'm trying to do is find out who I really am. Not to mention who *you* are.'

'And I told you,' he snapped back, 'that I'm not falling for your games. Not this time.' He continued staring at my hand. 'Why in Fey haven't you sorted that wound out yet?'

I let go of him. 'Have you not been listening? I. Have. Amnesia. I don't know who I am. I don't know who you are. I don't know what's wrong with my finger except that it hurts like hell and you told me I'd been poisoned by rowan and I should get some nux to heal it. Except I don't know what nux is. I tried a pharmacist and he just thought I was nuts.'

For a moment he looked at me with fathomless eyes. 'Rubus,' he began.

'I don't know who Rubus is!' I shrieked. 'Bloody hell, DD, why can't you just put aside your own issues and listen to me?'

Something odd sparked in his expression. 'DD?'

'Well, I don't know your real name, do I? I can't remember it.'

He moved up to me until we were barely inches apart. He

really did smell very good. I inhaled deeply while he merely frowned. 'What does DD stand for?'

His scent was making me feel light-headed. 'Dark and Despicable, of course.'

He laughed aloud 'Right.'

'You've got to admit that it fits.' I shrugged.

The corner of his mouth crooked up as if he were amused. 'Come on, Maddy. Stop this idiocy and just say my name. You used to scream it to the heavens when I made you come. You used to whisper it in that husky, aroused voice of yours when I kissed you on that special spot on your neck.'

My jaw slowly dropped. 'You and me? We ... did the dirty? Made the beast with two backs? Loaded the clown into the cannon?' I scanned him up and down. Well, go me. Although it was hardly surprising that I'd dumped him in the end, given what an arsebadger he was.

He curved his head down. 'Up until,' he murmured huskily, while I held my breath, my fingers longing to reach up and gently rub against the stubble at his jawline, 'you betrayed me.'

I exhaled loudly and stared at him. When he pulled back again his eyes were cold and distant.

'I...' I swallowed. 'What did I do?'

A muscle ticked in his cheek and he gazed at me, apparently unwilling to say. I stared him out. He was the one with all the answers – not me.

'Fine,' he said eventually, after the drawn-out silence apparently became too much. 'You say you've got amnesia and you don't remember who you are? Well, then I'll show you.' He turned away once more and began walking across the pedestrianised square. When I didn't follow him immediately, he looked back at me. 'Come on then.'

'Are you going to hurt me?' I asked, raising my voice.

'As if I could,' he muttered. He raised his eyebrows. 'Last chance, Madrona. Come or don't come. It's your choice.'

Like I really *had* a choice. I watched him stride away for a moment or two and then raced to catch up with him. 'Before we go,' I said, 'just tell me one thing. What is your real name?'

He blew air out through his pursed lips in exasperation. 'Morganus,' he said. 'But call me Morgan.'

~

Morgan marched along the street at breakneck speed. I was sure he was waiting for me to complain so I made a point of keeping up with him. At least the question of both his name – and the identity of the mysterious Morganus – had been solved.

I had a horrible uneasy sensation deep in the pit of my stomach that suggested I might not like the answers to my other queries. Maybe I wasn't the wonderful superhero I thought I was. Maybe I was nothing more than a cuckolding dust dealer. I couldn't quit now, though; I had to know the truth. Besides, who was to say that Morgan's truth was the same as my truth? I didn't feel like the bad person he clearly believed I was. Sure, I had a mean streak but I wasn't the damn Sugar Plum Fairy. I couldn't be nice all the time.

I was so caught up in the turmoil of my own thoughts that I didn't notice when he stopped. Almost inevitably, because I was a step or two behind him despite my best efforts to keep pace, I collided with his body. He let out a muttered expletive and all but leapt away from me.

'Is it contagious?' I asked, genuinely curious.

His eyes narrowed at me. 'Is what contagious?'

'You know.' I held up my finger. 'This rowan poison business.'

'Don't be silly.'

'Then why did you jump away from me like that?' I enquired. 'In fact, when you grabbed hold of me in the library you were determined to let go as soon as you possibly could.' I sniffed at my clothes. I smelled reasonably clean.

All he did was answer my question with another question. 'As far as I can tell,' he said, 'the only thing you seem to have forgotten is how to filter your thoughts. Do you say every single thing that crosses your mind?'

I considered. No, not everything – but perhaps more than was comfortable. 'Would it be better if I didn't say what I was thinking? If I hid my thoughts and my agenda and pretended to be something I'm not?'

Morgan's lip curled. 'I honestly cannot believe that you of all people are asking me that.' He shook his head in disbelief.

I shrugged. Whatever. The man was clearly determined to avoid giving me a straight answer to anything, despite his reluctant promise to the contrary. 'Never mind,' I sighed. 'Why have we stopped here?' I looked around.

Morgan watched me carefully. 'You really don't know?'

I glowered. 'I've got...'

'Amnesia. Yes. So you keep saying.' He ran a hand through his jet-black hair. 'Just wait a minute and all will be revealed.'

I frowned and looked around. We were in a small, nondescript street not too far from the city centre. There was a Polish supermarket on the other side of the road and a tasty-looking kebab shop right behind us. Up in front by the corner stood a pretty church, complete with steeple and rusting weather vane. There were a few people dotted here and there but they all looked as if they were going their own separate ways to their own separate destinations. None of them paid either Morgan or me the slightest bit of attention.

I began to hum tunelessly, keeping myself occupied. Morgan stiffened and shot me a quick look. I didn't bother to glance in his direction; instead I tapped my foot in time to my tune and leaned casually against the wall. He tutted and checked his watch. He gave a brief nod of satisfaction and, a few seconds later, the door to the church opened and people began to pile out.

I gazed at them all, confused. Although they came in all shapes and sizes, with different styles of clothing and a range of ages, there was something in all of their faces, some twist of pain, which was remarkably similar. I frowned. 'Were they praying?' I asked.

Morgan shot me a look from under his eyelashes. 'AA.'

As I tried to make sense of this, a tall man with stooped shoulders shuffled out. He cupped his hands to light a cigarette and I felt a tug of nicotine longing. Then he glanced to his right and spotted us – or should I say he spotted Morgan. His expression lightened then he spotted me and he seemed to cower.

A few of the others clapped him on the back as they departed but he only had eyes for us.

Once most of the others had dispersed, Morgan called over to him. 'It's alright, Vandrake. She's on a close rein.'

I stiffened. I didn't feel I was in a position to say anything but, all the same, I managed a quick snipe at Morgan. 'A tight rein? Does that mean you still want to ride me?'

It was Morgan's turn to stiffen. Just his shoulders, not any other part of him. He kept the friendly smile directed at Vandrake; he was far more of an expert at dissembling than I was. And what was it about people with strange names?

'Either we're doing this, Madrona, or we're not. It's entirely your call,' he murmured under his breath.

I raised my shoulders in an irritated shrug. Fine. Whatever.

Vandrake walked over, reluctance dogging every step. When he reached us, he made sure to side step so that Morgan's large frame was blocking me.

'What is she doing here, Morgan?' He took a long, shaky drag on his cigarette.

'Don't worry about her. I won't let her touch you. In fact, she won't even talk to you. I promise.'

I opened my mouth to interrupt and tell him in no uncertain terms that he couldn't prevent me from speaking but when Morgan's head turned towards me and I saw the dangerous glint in his eyes, I changed my mind.

'How did the meeting go?' Morgan asked softly.

Obviously still disturbed by my presence, Vandrake wrinkled his nose and obfuscated. 'S'okay. I'm not giving away any truths, if that's what you're worried about.'

'The thought never even crossed my mind,' Morgan said.

I wasn't sure that Vandrake even heard him. 'I've told them it's cocaine. I thought about saying heroin but then I'd probably be expected to be on methadone for the withdrawal and I'm not sure I could pull off those conversations.' He flicked ash onto the pavement. His hands were still trembling.

'It's alright,' Morgan reiterated. 'I know you wouldn't give us away or allude to anything out of the ordinary.' He reached out and squeezed Vandrake's shoulder. 'You're doing really well. I'm not here to jeopardise that.'

He received a watery smile in return. 'Thanks.'

'How long have you been off the dust?' Morgan enquired.

Vandrake threw another nervy look in my direction. As if burned by the action, his eyes hastily slid away again. 'Eighty-two days.'

'That's amazing.' Morgan sounded for all the world like he meant it. 'Who was your original supplier?'

Vandrake swallowed, his Adam's apple bobbing in his throat. His answer was barely audible. 'She was.'

There was no question which 'she' he was referring to. I examined him more curiously. There was nothing to indicate he was lying. Not that it mattered. I already had it on good authority that this pixie-dust stuff was a good thing. It made everything better.

'How did it make you feel? When you were taking it?'

Vandrake took one last swift drag, the end of the cigarette glowing before he dropped it under his toe and stubbed it out. 'What's all this about?'

'Humour me,' Morgan said. 'I'm making a point.' He jerked his head in my direction.

Vandrake's mouth tightened but he still answered. 'I felt like I was flying.' He rubbed his shoulders. 'That ache that's always there? You know the one.'

Morgan nodded. I stared. What ache?

'Well,' Vandrake continued, 'it vanished. The dust made me feel like it didn't matter. That I could be happy here despite...' His voice drifted off and his eyes glazed over momentarily. 'Well, you know.'

'But you needed more, didn't you? Every time you took some, you needed a little bit more.'

Vandrake bit his lip and looked down, toeing the ground. 'I would do anything for some more.'

Morgan's expression hardened. 'Anything for Rubus. Anything for *her*.'

Vandrake nodded, unwilling to look at me again. 'I was an addict.' His jaw clenched. 'I *am* an addict. It never goes away.'

'Thank you. I know that was difficult for you.'

Vandrake raised baleful eyes. I realised, somewhat belatedly, that they were green in colour. A murkier green than my own irises and certainly less vivid than Morgan's but still green. Before I could think about that, he spoke again. 'Can I go now?'

'Of course.' Morgan squeezed his shoulder. 'You take care. And remember I'm always here if you need me.'

Vandrake twisted on his heel and, despite his awkward and tired manner, fled as if the hounds of hell were after him.

Morgan and I watched him go. Once he'd disappeared out of sight, I put my hands in my pockets, ignoring the shiver that was still running across my skin. 'So I'm a drug dealer, that's what you're saying? I've been selling this dust stuff to people all over the city. It's addictive.'

Morgan didn't look at me. 'In essence.'

I raised a shoulder. 'Addiction is bad. But he said himself that the dust made him feel good. Alcohol is addictive and it's a depressant but people still drink it. Legally. Often.'

'Maybe they do,' Morgan answered. 'But bartenders don't withhold alcohol until they can manipulate their customers for their nefarious ends.'

Nefarious ends? I almost laughed aloud. Instead, I swivelled on my heel and looked more closely at him. 'You think I'm evil,' I said wonderingly.

He faced me, his gaze unwavering. 'I think you're a bitch,' he answered.

'Well, gee, don't sugar coat it. How do you know I wasn't simply trying to help the man? Take away that ache he was talking about?'

'Because I know you, Madrona.' Morgan's answer was quiet but firm. 'You keep forgetting that part. I know you better than you know yourself.'

I rolled my eyes. Like that was a difficult feat these days. 'Is that it?' I asked. 'Is show and tell over now?'

His expression was grim. 'Oh no. We're just getting started.'

CHAPTER NINE

Yet again, Morgan took off at a tremendous pace. Initially I didn't bother trying to keep up. My mind was filled with Vandrake. Whether pixie dust was indeed a good or a bad thing, there was no denying the haunted look in the man's eyes – or the fact that he'd been terrified of me. I shook my head to rid myself of the image. Then another thought occurred to me.

Catching up to Morgan, and brushing my hair out of my eyes for the umpteenth time, I broached the subject. 'Do all superheroes have green eyes?'

He halted in his tracks. 'Pardon?'

Maybe it was a stupid question but given the evidence I had to hand, it seemed to fit. 'I've got green eyes. You've got green eyes. Vandrake has green eyes. A guy who asked me for dust back at my hotel has green eyes. That librarian woman, Paeonia – which, by the way, is an even more stupid name than Madrona – has green eyes. Are we all superheroes? Do we all have superpowers?' I considered some more. 'Is everyone with green eyes a superhero or only some of us?'

He stared at me as if I'd grown two horns and started to

belly dance. 'Madrona...' His expression was filled with disbelief. 'Superheroes? Super powers?'

I shrugged, trying to downplay the sudden uneasiness I felt at his incredulous expression. 'What? Come on. You know I did something to time in your pub. I slowed it down. I did that once before after I woke up. And when I was Tasered, I didn't feel anything. Plus you put up that weird barrier thing afterwards so I couldn't get back inside the Metropolitan.' I held up my finger. 'And you can't tell me that everyone in the world gets poisoned by rowan. It's our kryptonite, right?'

For a long moment Morgan just stared at me.

'Jeez,' I said. 'Keep rolling your eyes. Go on. Maybe sooner or later you'll find a brain back there.'

If anything, his incredulity only increased. 'You are something else. You're not pretty enough to be this stupid.'

I scoffed. Game on. 'At least I don't look like a visible fart.'

His eyebrows shot up to his hairline. 'That's a bit playground, isn't it? I'd challenge you to a proper game of wits but it wouldn't be fair when you're unarmed.'

Oh, he was in for it now. 'Playground? That suggests you've been to school when clearly you're not burdened by an abundance of education.'

Something passed across Morgan's face, a shadow that hinted at wistfulness or even longing. I watched him carefully. Nah. I had to be imagining it. His head curved down towards mine until our noses were almost touching. My heart rate picked up and I swear he knew it.

He smiled faintly then stepped back. 'You seriously expect me to believe that you think you're a superhero?' A tiny crease formed in his brow. 'Is that why you came to my pub dressed in a damned cape and mask?'

'No,' I began. Then I grimaced. 'Okay, yes.'

'Rather belabouring the amnesia bit, aren't you?' he

commented. He obviously still believed I was faking my condition. 'And what's that about being Tasered anyway?' His eyes hardened to flinty green chips.

'Gasbudlikins!' I exploded. 'How many ways am I supposed to say the same thing? I'm not lying. I really do have amnesia. And if we're not freaking superheroes, then what are we?'

Morgan merely looked at me with a deadpan expression. 'Say that again.'

I screwed up my face and beat the base of my palms against my temples. 'I've got amnesia!' I yelled in his face. 'I don't remember anything!'

He didn't flinch. 'Not that part. The first thing you said. The first word.'

'Huh?' My anger was still rising and he wasn't helping it abate in the slightest.

'First word, Maddy, what was it?'

'I...' I shook my head. 'I don't know. Gasbudli—'

Morgan snapped his fingers. 'There you go. What does that mean?'

I stared at him. 'What do you think it means? Bloody hell. Shit. Crap. Gadzooks. Fucking...'

'Enough.' He watched me. 'How many other people have you heard say that word?'

'Gasbudlikins? I don't know.' I tried to think past my annoyance. 'No one. So what?'

'Humans don't use that word. It's ridiculously old-fashioned. Even most of us, at least on this side, don't use it any more. You always did.' A fleeting, sad expression crossed his face. 'Even when you were a kid.'

I scratched my head. 'I don't understand anything you're saying.'

Morgan laughed humourlessly. 'I have to hand it to you,

Madrona. When you choose to create a fiction, you really go all in, don't you? You cover every single detail. Even this one.'

I'd just about had enough. Yes, the vexing man had provided me with a few answers but no one should have to put with this kind of prevarication. I was ready to throw in the towel and abandon him right there when he twisted and began heading in the opposite direction. 'You win,' he said. 'Again. We'll go to Castlefield and I'll show you everything. Where all this,' he waved expansively, including both of us in the movement, 'began.' He reached into his pocket and drew out a sleek phone. 'It's me,' he said tersely into the receiver. 'I need a car.'

I watched him, my brow still furrowed. My better nature was telling me to skedaddle – and quickly. Even if it seemed that Morgan harboured some buried feelings for me, it was clear that the better part of him hated me. For all I knew, he'd been behind the golf-course attack. And yet, I didn't think he meant me any real harm.

I had no clue what he was alluding to or what going to Castlefield entailed but I couldn't back away. I had to know everything.

~

'You didn't answer my question, you know,' I said, when Morgan's taciturn driver dropped us off next to an old railway bridge. It had several odd structures in front of it and expanse of green. 'Do we all have green eyes?'

Morgan adjusted his cuffs and murmured something to the driver. 'We do.'

I pumped the air triumphantly. Observation was probably one of my superpowers.

'We are not, however, superheroes,' he added caustically.

'I slowed down time,' I said importantly.

'Which is forbidden.'

I growled impatiently. 'By whom exactly? And why?'

Morgan didn't answer me, unless you count a tut as an answer. He took off while I trailed after him yet again. This was becoming mighty tiresome. At least this time he didn't go far but stopped in front of a brick wall less than a hundred feet away. 'Here,' he said quietly. 'Here it is.'

I looked around. 'Here's what?' I couldn't see anything noteworthy. I supposed it was a pretty area but the wall we were standing beside looked out of place. It didn't fit any other architecture I'd seen and it appeared to have been randomly plonked in the middle of a field. Hang on. If this was Castlefield... 'Is this a castle?' It wasn't very impressive.

Morgan gave me a look that suggested I was a total idiot. 'It's a Roman fort. Or,' he amended, 'it's a replica of a Roman fort.'

I pursed my lips. 'Morgan, if you're trying to tell me that we're time-travelling Romans then...'

'Shut up, Maddy,' he said, not unkindly. 'The Romans were a lot more cultured than history gives them credit for.'

'Roads,' I said.

He cast me another glance, imbued with frustration. 'How can you tell me you have amnesia but know that the Romans built roads?'

'If I knew that then I probably wouldn't have amnesia.'

He sighed. 'Anyway, as I was saying before I was so rudely interrupted, they were tuned in to their world. They felt the power of certain places. Places like this.'

I looked around again. In the distance, an ice-cream van trundled up, its kitsch tune playing loudly for all and sundry. 'Mr Whippy feels that power too.'

Morgan's hands tightened into fists. I grinned. This was fun.

'Even with your supposed amnesia,' he said with barely suppressed irritation, 'you must be able to feel it.'

I nodded sagely. 'That overwhelming desire for a chocolate ice cream.'

'If you're not going to take this seriously—'

I held up my hands. 'Okay, okay.' I paused. 'I really don't feel anything.'

Morgan frowned. 'Rowan,' he muttered under his breath. 'It's affecting you more than I realised.' He beckoned me over and pointed at a spot on the ground. 'Stand there.'

I eyed him warily. It was unlikely that there were landmines but, judging by the look on his face, I couldn't be too sure. He gestured again impatiently and I blew back my hair. 'Okay, okay.' I ambled over and stood on the spot he was pointing at. 'Nope. I don't feel anything.'

Except all of a sudden I did. It was faint and I had to concentrate but it was definitely there. It was like all the molecules in the air were coalescing into a kind of magnet and pulling me forward. There was nothing to be pulled forward into, however, just empty space.

'Now you feel it,' he said softly, although there was an odd light in his eyes that suggested concern rather than triumph.

I raised my hands, stretching them out in front of me. There was a delicious tingle on my bare skin. It wanted me. And I wanted it. Deep longing sprang up inside me, a strange ache that spread along my veins and arteries, hooking into my heart as if it would never let me go.

'I don't understand,' I whispered. 'What is it?'

Morgan didn't answer immediately. With great reluctance, I turned my head away from the invisible force and looked at him. He was slack-jawed and staring. 'You're telling the truth,' he said. 'You really don't remember.'

'As I have said over and over again,' I replied.

'Unbelievable,' he murmured. 'How did it even happen?' He took a half step towards me as if to embrace me then he seemed to remember himself and his arms fell to his sides.

'Morgan,' I said, 'this is not news. I've got amnesia. We know that. What we don't know, or at least what *I* don't know, is what this is. Where *are* we?'

He drew in a deep breath then blinked rapidly as if to recover from the shock of learning what he already knew. 'This is a border crossing between this world and the Fey one. We're not superheroes, Maddy, we're Fey.' I must have looked confused because he elaborated. 'Faeries. We're what the humans call faeries. The Wee Folk. Ten years ago, or thereabouts, something happened. We don't know what or how, but the border closed, effectively trapping all the Fey who were on this side. We can't get back home. We're stuck here. You, me, Rubus, Vandrake. All of us.'

My mouth fell open. No way. 'Let me see if I understand this correctly,' I said. I wondered if I were no longer merely teetering on the brink of insanity but had fallen headlong into the chasm of crazy. 'I'm a faery.' He nodded. 'Like Tinkerbell.'

A look of exasperation crossed his face. 'Not like Tinkerbell. Do you have wings? Are you the size of a thimble?'

I ignored his sarcasm. 'You can't really expect me to believe that I'm a faery. I understand you dislike me intensely but playing around with someone who has a serious brain injury is plain mean.'

'Mean? Madrona, you may have amnesia but you can't keep thinking you're some kind of wondrous superhero. You're more like an arch villain.' His eyes met mine; there was nothing but honesty reflecting back at me. 'You are not a good person. I wouldn't describe you as mean because it's far too mild a term. You're...' he sighed as if casting around for the right word '... evil,' he finished.

I wasn't sure what was harder to believe, that I was supposedly a faery or a bad guy. Either way, emotional self-preservation kicked in and I rounded on him, fists clenched. 'You arsebadger!' I spat. 'What? I'm evil because I didn't play along with your idea of the perfect girlfriend? Because I don't think you're a sex god whose feet I should fall at and worship? Forget scorned women, Morgan. Look at you!'

His eyes narrowed dangerously. 'I'm not referring to what happened between us, Madrona, although that would be reason enough to designate you a bitch and be done with you. You deal in pixie dust. You've created addicts out of hundreds of our kind. You work for Rubus, of all people. If it were up to me, I'd have locked you up years ago.'

'Oh yeah?' I sneered. 'Why didn't you?'

'The truce—' he began stiffly.

'Truce? Ha! That's a laugh. When I woke up on that damned golf course, there was the beheaded corpse next to me of someone who'd obviously tried to kill me.'

Morgan stilled. 'You took someone's head?' His voice was low. 'You killed one of us? But that's impossible. Was it a human, Madrona? Did you kill an innocent human?'

I threw up my hands. 'That's what you're taking from this? Not how am I, or why was I was targeted for execution, but did I kill someone in self-defence? How the hell should I know what happened? I can't remember, as I've told you far too many times already. I think the fact that three ugly goons appeared moments later and tried to shoot me would prove my innocence – and that they showed up at my hotel this morning, no doubt to try again. But, no, *I'm* the evil one. *I'm* the bitch.' I rolled my eyes.

'So a serious attempt was made on your life,' Morgan growled. For the first time since we'd left the library he took hold of me, his hand encircling my forearm in a tight grip. At least it wasn't my other arm; the pain from the cut on my finger was spreading up that limb, sending tentacles of agony through my veins. 'Tell me about it.'

I wrenched away from him. 'Like you care. What the gasbudlikins is the stupid truce anyway?'

He didn't reach for me again. There was no getting away from his expression, however; he was watching me like a hawk. 'It was formed not long after we realised we were trapped here and unable to return home. The humans who own this demesne can't find out that we are here. We all knew that if we didn't re-open the border tempers would flare. There is the potential for … catastrophic chaos if violence between us ensues. It is the one thing that is immutable: no Fey is to seriously attack or kill another. None of us has broken the truce since the day it was declared. In truth, we're physically incapable of it – no Fey can harm another. We all signed on the dotted line and we are all held by it. There are no exceptions.' His voice hardened. 'If someone has found a way to get round the truce, things are far worse than I realised. Were your attackers Fey, Maddie?'

I gestured up at the heavens. 'How on earth am I supposed to know? They were ugly. They didn't look human. They were probably related to each other.' And, I added silently to myself, they were probably working for someone else.

'Usually it's easy to tell, just as it should be easy to tell when you are near a border crossing. It's the rowan. The poison in your system is dampening down your natural instincts and understanding.' His jaw clenched. 'Are these attackers the ones who did that? Did they poison you?'

Unwilling to tell him that I'd done it myself, I looked away. 'Does it really matter?' I said distantly.

'Of course it matters.' His response was harsh. 'If you killed one of us, whether you remember the act or not, then the consequences cannot be changed. If the truce is broken, I will not be able to help you.' Hatred laced his words. 'Don't think Rubus will either, even if you accomplished your … feat under his orders. But if the reverse is true and they attacked you…'

'Like you would care,' I said, stepping away from him to give myself some breathing space. 'You've already damned me. How many – Fey are there?' I wasn't going to use the word 'faery' if I could help it.

'One thousand four hundred and seventy-two,' he answered instantly. 'Most are in the United Kingdom, although some are abroad. The majority of the border points are located here.' He continued to watch me. 'Come with me. I'll get you the nux you need to counteract the rowan's poison. Together we can investigate what really happened to you.'

I took yet another step back. 'And you can ensure justice is served if it turns out I'm the one who's initiated the attacks and broke your truce. You'll be delighted then, won't you, Morgan? Because I'm an evil bitch. I probably deserve it.'

His entire body went ramrod straight at my words. 'Maddy—'

'Forget it,' I said. 'I don't need your help. I'll find some of this nux crap on my own. You can crawl back to your little pub and forget I ever existed.'

'For Fey's sake,' he ground out. 'Will you just come with me? Stop being so bloody stubborn.'

I glared at him. 'Apparently I'm a nasty super villain. I don't need the likes of a goody two shoes like you interfering in my life.'

Then, before he could say another word, I spun away and left him standing. I even managed to resist the temptation to glance back.

CHAPTER TEN

I'd spent more time with Morgan than I'd realised and it was after seven by the time I let myself into Julie's house with her own key. The wisdom of accepting this job, given the irritating green-eyed arsebadger's supposed revelations about me, was diminishing by the second. I was also confused that Julie had permitted access to her home to a virtual stranger. No wonder she was in trouble if she was always this trusting.

The house was surprisingly modest although it was very tastefully done. I pushed aside my concerns about myself and ignored Julie's décor in favour of examining her security systems. There appeared to be very few. Given how pedantic Bodyguard Mark had been about a sealed bottle of pills, it was hard to believe that she only had a simple Yale lock to keep out potential intruders. At least all the windows were closed and properly locked, although when I located Julie's bedroom and saw that it was overlooked by yet another Travotel, I wasn't happy. It wouldn't take an evil genius like me to spy on her in her own home.

I was halfway down the stairs to the ground floor when I heard the front door open and the clickety-clack of high heels on the parquet flooring. I ran all the way down, reaching Julie just as she hung up her coat.

I began with a scolding. 'You don't have any burglar alarms. How can you not have any burglar alarms? Someone could break one of your windows and be inside strangling you before you can reach for the phone. I've counted at least five access points where I could gain entrance within seconds. Seconds, Julie! And this location! There are at least fifty hotel guests across the street who are peering into your bedroom right now.'

She unhooked the scarf from round her neck and smiled. 'Evening, Madrona.'

I frowned. 'Evening. Now, listen, you...'

Julie dropped the scarf, letting it fall into a puddle on the floor, and continued to smile. 'You sound just like Mark. Before we do anything,' she said, 'I need a large G and T.' She waltzed past me into the kitchen.

I followed her. 'Julie, this is serious.'

'Yes, darling, and no one understands that better than I do. But please – it's been a long day and I need a drink.' She opened up a cabinet and took out two glasses, waving them in my direction. 'Ice and a slice?'

I crossed my arms. 'You're paying me to protect you. Alcohol is not a good idea.'

'Mads, alcohol is *always* a good idea. Especially when the scriptwriters change their minds at the last minute and I'm forced to re-learn all my lines.' She tutted before locating a large bottle of gin and pouring triple measures into both glasses. She arched a glance at me. 'You don't mind if I call you Mads? It seems to fit, to be honest, darling.' She retrieved some ice from the freezer before topping up both drinks with a tiny amount of tonic. When she was done she held out one glass to me while taking a gulp from the other one. She smacked her lips. 'Bliss.'

'You may call me whatever you wish,' I said, reluctantly

taking the drink. I took a tiny sip of it, half-choked and hastily put it down on the table top. 'Can we talk seriously about your situation?'

Julie waved a hand. 'Of course, of course.' She kicked off her high heels and sauntered through to the living room. I followed, watching as she settled in a large armchair and tucked her feet up underneath her. When I didn't immediately sit as well, she flung out an arm in the direction of another chair.

'Before we go any further,' Julie said, 'I need you to sign a sort of ... non-disclosure agreement.'

There was something about her voice that instantly put me on guard. '*Sort of* non-disclosure agreement?'

She inclined her head. 'Indeed.' She leaned to her side, lifted up a small wooden chest from the floor and rummaged inside before bringing out a piece of paper. 'Here it is.'

I took it from her. Whatever I might have imagined a typical NDA looked like, it wasn't like this. There was only one line of writing on it: 'I will not reveal the true nature of Julie Chivers, whether by implication, deed or disclosure.' That was it. There was nothing else.

I stared at it, befuddled. I flipped the sheet of paper over but there was nothing on the other side. I looked at Julie, who was watching me very closely, and then shrugged. 'Seems straightforward enough.' Understatement of the century. She'd certainly piqued my curiosity about her 'true nature' though.

'Do you have a pen?' I asked.

Julie didn't move a muscle. 'This isn't that sort of contract.' She delved into her box of tricks yet again. This time, however, she pulled out a needle. Judging by its gleaming tip, it was very sharp.

I recoiled in my chair. 'Wait just a goddarned minute,' I said. Maybe I'd gotten ol' Julie Chivers wrong from the start.

‘Relax.’ She held the needle up. ‘What? You think I could hurt you with this? Darling, don’t be ridiculous.’

Given that my arm was aching constantly from a barely visible nick to my finger, I wasn’t about to take anything for granted. ‘Maybe you should explain,’ I said, without taking my eyes off of her.

Only the faintest tremble to her hands betrayed her nervousness. Somehow I liked her better knowing that she wasn’t as confident as she appeared. ‘All this does,’ she said, ‘is prick your finger. It will draw only the tiniest amount of blood, which you then use to agree to the contract.’

I schooled my face into a deadpan mask. ‘You want me to sign in blood. It sounds like something the devil might request.’

Julie was no longer smiling. ‘I can assure you that I’m not the devil. Your blood simply offers me greater ... certainty ... than a mere signature can do.’

‘Did Mark do this? Did he sign in blood?’

She inclined her head. ‘He did. As did the others before him.’ She sighed. ‘I would explain further, Mads, but until you sign the contract I’m unable to do so.’

More unwilling rather than unable, I thought. Even so, Julie was interesting me more than enough for me to agree – but there was no way I would let a strange needle pierce my skin. I was keen to find out more but I wasn’t going to compromise my own safety, not when the ache in my arm was testament to just how dangerous a small cut could be.

Casting my eyes downwards and using my unwounded hand, I ran my index along the edge of the contract. I hissed at the brief flare of pain as the paper did as I’d intended then I pressed the small bead of blood underneath the writing.

‘You’re even more cautious than I appreciated,’ Julie commented. ‘That’s good.’

No, I was capable of learning from my mistakes. I didn’t

have the chance to tell her that, however, because my attention was wholly caught by the contract. There was an odd smell of burning coming from it and, from the point where I'd smeared my blood, a single wisp of white smoke appeared. I gaped and threw the contract onto the floor just as the bloody blot vanished and my own name appeared.

'That's...' I stared. 'That's...'

'A crude magic of sorts,' Julie provided helpfully.

I flung wary eyes in her direction. She simply looked relieved that I'd 'signed' on the dotted line, so to speak.

'What are you?' I breathed. She didn't have green eyes so she couldn't be Fey like me. Or so I supposed.

'Have some of that gin,' she advised. 'You're going to need it.'

I didn't need telling twice. I gulped down the entire contents of my glass, draining it to the dregs. Then I dropped it on to the side table next to me. 'Time to 'fess up.'

If I'd been expecting a chatty preamble, I was mistaken. Julie raised her glass to me and, before taking another sip, said, 'I am a vampire.'

The only sound in the room was the ticking of the small clock on the mantelpiece. Julie lifted the glass to her lips and finished off her gin. I just waited.

'You know,' she said finally, 'I've done this seventeen times. Never have I had a reaction like yours.' She leaned forward and repeated, 'I'm a vampire.'

I nodded. 'I heard you. I was expecting more.'

She raised a plucked eyebrow. 'More?'

'More explanation.' If I was going to give any credence to the idea that I was a faery, I could hardly be taken aback that Julie was a vampire. And she hadn't questioned my assertion that I was a superhero; she deserved the same respect she'd granted me. As long as she didn't grow fangs and try to bite me, of course.

'Unless I've forgotten more than I realise, vampires can't go out during the day or they burn up in the sun. They can't drink anything other than pure blood. They're pale and cold and,' I hesitated, although there was no point in beating around the bush, 'dead. None of the above seems to apply to you.'

'Where does all this knowledge about vampires come from?' Julie asked. Her expression was patient and I sensed she'd had this conversation several times before. At least seventeen times before .

I scratched my head. 'Uh, I've got amnesia, remember? I assume I've heard about vampires from horror stories.' I tried to think. Did vampires exist across the Fey border? Who knew? 'Count Duckula, perhaps.'

A trace of a grin flashed across Julie's lips. 'Everything you know, or think you know,' she amended her words, 'or think you remember or don't remember, is nothing more than propaganda. Vicious lies designed to wipe my kind off the face of this planet. A campaign of pure genocide has been waged against us. That is why I have to go to such lengths to keep my secret safe.' She pointed at the floor, where the contract still lay. 'The blood you have signed there will bind you forever. If you even think about revealing what I've just told you, you will suffer and all those of your own blood will suffer along with you. You will die – and not pleasantly or quickly.' She licked her lips. 'You're welcome to try. Others have in the past and it didn't go well for them.' Julie sighed. 'It's not a threat. It's simply fact. And, alas, a necessary evil.'

I shrugged. 'Hey, I get it. I still have questions, though.'

'Do I need to drink blood to survive? Yes.' She waved her glass at me. 'But I do enjoy other beverages, as well as food. You already know about the Valium. I don't need to kill to obtain the red stuff, Madrona. There are eight pints of blood in the average human body. I don't know about you but I couldn't drink eight pints of beer.'

I couldn't be sure but I reckoned that, if challenged, *I* could. I decided it wouldn't be sensible to say so. 'Do you want *my* blood?' I asked.

She shook her head. 'No. You're my bodyguard, not my chef. I get a pint delivered every week from the local hospital. They think I have aplastic anaemia so it's no problem to get hold of it. And a pint a week is more than sufficient for my needs.'

I considered this while trying to prioritise my next questions. 'How old *are* you?' I coughed. 'I mean, do you age?'

'I'm 173 years old. I stopped ageing when I reached my fortieth birthday.' Her face took on a distant expression. 'That was some time ago.'

I frowned at her. 'Is it wise being an actor then? Especially on television? Surely people will notice sooner or later.'

She smiled. 'Advances in plastic surgery, not to mention Botox, mean I can get away with it for some time yet. I am aware, however, that there will come a time when I have to stop. It will be an easy matter to alter my appearance.' She touched her hair self-consciously. 'Although I will miss being blonde.'

'Do you have a soul?' I asked.

Her smile turned into a laugh. 'Do you?'

Good question. I grimaced and leaned over to grab my glass. 'I need some more gin,' I said.

Julie stood up. 'I knew I liked you.'

~

It took some time – and several more gins – but I finally managed to get the full story out of her. And I'd thought *my* life was complicated. It turns out that vampires are born, not made. Several hundred years ago there were thousands of them scattered across the globe. The paranoia of the Middle Ages, however, did them few favours. Even the slightest hint of anything untoward – such as a smear of blood about their lips, more animals going missing than usual or weakened damsels with blood loss, and they would be outed, rather stupidly, as witches. Vampires were strong but burning at the stake would kill them just as surely as it would anyone else. Not all of them were circumspect about their … ethnicity, either. In the end, confiding their secret, even to a select few, proved to be their undoing. Vampires, it turned out, were an endangered species.

'As far as I'm aware,' Julie told me, with only the slightest waver in her voice, 'there are now fewer than fifty of us across the globe. I should be able to give you exact numbers but I've not heard from several old friends for some months and I fear the worst has happened.'

I leaned forward. 'What do you mean?'

She fiddled with the hem of her skirt. 'Despite our best efforts to hide our existence from the world, the damage was done centuries ago. There are people today who know of us and who seek to either destroy or entrap us. These hunters are the same people who have used literature and the media to transform us into the monsters that the world now believes us to be. I'm no more evil than you are.'

According to Morgan, that meant she was pretty darned evil. The NDA I'd signed only worked one way though, so I wasn't about to reveal that little titbit. Not yet. 'So holy water?'

'No effect.'

'Crucifixes?'

'Nothing.' She fixed me with a steely stare. 'All part of the propaganda machine that works against us. If God Himself despises us, then so should the rest of the world. Those bastards were clever. They took some of what was true and twisted it for their own ends. For example, it is believed that I cannot enter another's home without permission but, in fact, the reverse is true. I have no serious security measures in place here because no one can enter unless I give them express permission. In here, I am safe.'

'You could just stay in here then.'

Her mouth tightened. 'What kind of life is that? In many ways, liberty is more important than life. I won't be made a prisoner in my own home.'

Her words sounded accusatory and I held up my palms to appease her. 'I get it.' I paused. 'Sunlight...'

'Not a problem.'

I gave her an arch look. 'Can you turn into a bat?'

'Don't be ridiculous. I don't sleep in a coffin either.' She shuddered. 'I like my memory-foam mattress and my four-poster bed, thank you very much.'

I grinned. Fair enough. 'So that man who attacked you—'

'A vampire hunter.' She grimaced. 'Lately they've taken to abduction rather than assassination. I imagine their motives are nefarious, that they wish to trap rather than kill us. Maybe to experiment on us with torture. Either way, there is at least one group of hunters who know what I am and are doing what they can to get hold of me. That's why I need you. They won't dare attack a television studio and they can't come at me here. It's only when I'm out and about on the streets and in public that I am truly in danger. You questioned my choice to maintain such a high public profile? Well, in truth, that is all that is keeping me safe. While people recognise me and I'm well known, the hunters have less opportunity to come after me.'

I mulled this over; it did make a kind of sense. 'How many of them are there?'

'The hunters? Three, that I know of. There may be more.'

She sniffed. 'I've eluded them so far but no one is infallible. Sooner or later, my luck will run out.'

'The letters you told me about,' I said, 'and the animal body parts.'

Her mouth turned down. 'Those parts are true. The hunters are trying to rattle me.' She grimaced. 'Unfortunately, it's working. And you see now why I can't go to the police.'

Yeah, that was a non-starter. I wasn't surprised Julie was rattled. Nothing about this situation was good and, so far, I couldn't see many advantages to being a vampire. In fact, it truly sucked. I smiled slightly at my own pun. 'You know,' I told her, 'not all the media nowadays is against you. A lot of vampires have been cast in a more positive light in recent years. Vampires are sexy.'

Julie sniffed. 'Where do you think the funding for those new films and books came from? We have wealth, Madrona. But wealth only takes you so far.'

Indeed. 'So you only need me when you're outside? I don't have to stay here in this house?'

She smiled. 'No,' she agreed, 'you don't have to. I get lonely, though. It will be nice to have a companion. Men like Mark are all very well but there's not much conversation to be had with them. I could do with some female company and I get the feeling you and I are going to get on well.'

I raised my glass in her direction. 'Do you drive to work? Alone?'

'I do.'

'That has to stop,' I said in my best strict-teacher voice. 'That's a weak link in your security chain.'

'My car is very visible and the route I take is busy. If they tried to attack me in public, others would step in and help. The world is full of good Samaritans and I'm too well known.'

'All the same,' I told her, 'apart from when you're here or

actually on set, I will be with you at all times. That's my condition.'

'You're not afraid to be with me?'

I shook my head. Frankly, after all that I'd learned about myself, I wasn't sure I was afraid of anything.

CHAPTER ELEVEN

If I'd hoped that the gin-induced pounding in my head when I woke in Julie's guest bedroom the next morning would take my mind off the spreading pain from the cut on my finger, then I was very, very wrong.

Agonising threads of discomfort were spreading across my shoulder and collarbone. Simply turning my head was becoming painful. I might have snubbed Morgan's offer of some nux to counteract the rowan poison in my body but if I didn't find some soon, I'd be crawling back to his door and pleading with him for help. My joints were growing stiff and, when I sneaked a look at the cut itself, the foul rotting scent and sickly-green pus made me recoil. I gave myself a ten-hour deadline. Find nux before Julie finished work tonight or lose my pride, self-esteem and ego.

After wrapping the wound tightly so that it was protected and the gangrenous stench didn't seep out, I got dressed and headed gingerly downstairs.

Julie was already sitting at the breakfast bar in full make-up, sipping from a delicate china cup. Initially I thought it was coffee but when I got closer, I realised I was very wrong.

'You took the news so well last night,' she said, 'that I didn't think you'd mind if I partook of a little of the red stuff.'

I watched her take a sip. The blood stained her lips but, oddly, I didn't feel nauseated. I congratulated myself for having a stomach of steel. Decapitated corpses, witnessing the drinking of blood and even copious amounts of alcohol – it appeared nothing could make me vomit. 'Do you heat it up first?' I asked, curiosity getting the better of me.

'It's much tastier when it's warm.' She smacked her lips then arched an eyebrow as if daring me to retch.

I shrugged in response. 'Whatever floats your boat.'

'Would you like some?'

I smirked. 'I'll pass, thanks.'

She took another sip and smiled. 'So, I promised you some help with the amnesia problem.'

'I'm not sure you *can* help,' I said honestly. 'Not unless you have a magic memory potion tucked away along with all that blood.'

'I could try bopping you over the head to knock those brain cells back into action.'

We shared a grin. 'If I thought that would work, I'd hand you the mallet.'

Julie chewed her lip thoughtfully. 'Is there anything you've come across that's been familiar in any way?'

'I feel like Manchester is familiar. I know my way around even if I don't remember specific streets or buildings,' I admitted. 'So I must have lived here before.' Morgan's face flashed into my mind. 'And there are people I've met who know me. Or knew me,' I amended.

'You know, darling, your face just took on the strangest expression. Are we talking about someone special?'

'There's a man.'

Julie laughed. 'There's always a man. Is he good looking?

Upright? The sort you want to wrap his arms around you and always keep you safe?'

I sighed. 'Yes, yes and yes. But he won't do any of those things. He hates me.'

'Why on earth is that?'

'Something to do with a guy called Rubus. As far as I can work out,' I said, carefully avoiding any mention of the weird Fey shit, 'I betrayed Mr Sex On Legs by running to Mr Evil.'

Intrigued, Julie leaned forward. 'Mr Evil?'

'Not his real name, obviously.' I winced in frustration. 'Some guy called Rubus who I've not yet met but who doesn't appear to be the nicest man in the world.' I laughed bitterly. 'That's an understatement. Everyone seems to think he's the devil incarnate. Because I supposedly work for him – or maybe even sleep with him – I'm the same by default.'

'Do you think this Rubus is the devil?'

'All the evidence seems to point in that direction,' I said glumly. 'I've not heard a single good word about him.'

Her eyes held mine. 'It's my experience that there's rarely smoke without fire. You might do best to avoid this Rubus fellow altogether.'

'I'm certainly not trying to seek him out,' I told her. 'I have enough complications in my life without adding an alleged super-villain to the mix. I gather I'm pretty villainous too, but there has to be a line somewhere. The reaction that people have to Rubus whenever his name is mentioned is bloody scary.'

'Then avoiding him is definitely the best course of action. Normally I'd say you should make up your own mind rather than listening to gossip, but it sounds as if you don't need any more problems.'

I nodded, feeling better for the conversation. 'What time are we leaving for the studio?'

Julie glanced up at an old-fashioned clock hanging on the

wall. 'Now would be good.' Draining the last of the blood, she stood up. 'Are you ready?'

I nodded and followed her into the hallway. She checked her reflection in a large hallway mirror and patted her hair before smiling at me and pointing at her reflection. 'Another thing the books got wrong,' she murmured.

'I'll never believe anything I read again,' I told her. Then I caught a glimpse of my own face in the mirror. Truth be told, if anyone were a shoo-in for the living dead it would be me. My complexion was pale, my freckles stood out in sharp relief and my hair looked matted and unkempt. I made a vague attempt at smoothing the frizz down; if anything, I made it worse. It was lucky I wasn't trying to impress anyone.

'I'll drive,' Julie announced as we reached her car, which was parked in the small garage attached to her house. 'I need you to go through my lines as we travel.' She tossed me a dog-eared script. 'That's the trouble when you're on television three nights a week,' she muttered. 'Too many damn words to learn. I acted before, you know. In the twenties. Just stage stuff, of course. There weren't many films being made back then. At least with the theatre, you only have one script to learn.' She tutted irritably to herself.

As we drove, I scanned the sunny street, searching for anyone watching Julie's house. If there was anyone, they were keeping a low profile; all I saw were a few tired people on their way to work.

I flipped through the script as a thought occurred to me. 'Do the hunters know that all the vampire myths are – well, myths? Or do they think you can't go outside in the sun?'

'I'm on television, Mads. *St Thomas Close* usually shoots during the day. I think the fact that I can withstand sunlight is well and truly out of the bag.' She paused. 'Although I have to admit that they tend to try and attack me at night.'

'How many times have they tried?'

She revved the engine, speeding up to avoid a red light. 'Too many to count.' Despite her calm mask, I could sense the underlying tension. She might have evaded capture – or worse – until now but that didn't mean she wasn't scared.

'I won't let them get you,' I said quietly. I meant it too and not just because she was paying me – although that helped.

'Thank you. I appreciate the sentiment.'

I drummed my fingers against my thigh. 'You know, there's one question you've not answered. How do they know? How do these hunters know what you are?'

For a long moment she didn't answer. When she did, her eyes were distant. 'The simple answer is that, like many of my compatriots, I shared my secret with the wrong person. Even though I knew what had happened before, and even though I'm young by vampire standards and have history to guide me, I made the same mistake. The complicated answer is that I fell in love with the wrong person and my name and likeness ended up on the wrong list. My own personal real-life soap opera.' Her jaw tightened. 'It was a long time ago. Now, I need to practise. Start when my character, Stacey, walks into the hairdresser.'

I saluted. I knew when a change of subject was required. 'Yes, ma'am.' Finding her first scene, I began to read the lines. '*Good morning, Stacey*.' I glanced up. 'Hardly Shakespeare, is it?'

Julie rolled her eyes. 'It's a soap opera.' She shook her head slightly and deepened her voice. '*Tom told me you were out with my husband last night. Is it true?*'

'Yeah, it is true. And you know what else is true? He loves me.'

'You're lying!'

'No, I'm not. The best part of all this is that I don't give two figs about him. I'm only with him because I know it will wind you up.'

'Cue audience gasps,' Julie muttered.

I looked at her. 'You seem annoyed.'

She made a face. 'I'd quite like to play the villain for once rather than the wronged, innocent wife. After all, vampires are always being painted as villains. Sometimes I think I should play to type. And Stacey is just so *good*. She has a lot of fans and people love her but it gets rather monotonous always being so upright and morally good.' Then she laughed. 'Don't go getting any ideas. That's not the vampire in me talking. Not really. That's the actor. Bad guys are more fun to play.'

'Why?' I half-listened while skipping forward to see what happened next in the script.

'Your typical bad guy moves the plot forward. Good guys are weak because they wait for things to happen to them rather than the other way around. Not to mention that all drama is conflict. Villains create that conflict. The people watching at home might be rooting for Stacey to take her revenge on Lisa for what she's done, but they'll relish every moment of Lisa's actions. The entire show would be pulled off air in a moment if it weren't for characters like Lisa. *St Thomas Close* needs them more than it needs characters like Stacey.'

'There's a catfight at the end of this scene. That's exciting at least.' I turned the page. 'Wait. Is Hector your on-screen husband?'

'Yes.'

'He interrupts the fight! And look!' I jabbed at the words on the page. 'He believes Lisa when she says you started it. She's horrible!'

Julie took her eyes off the road for a moment to look at me. 'See?' she said. 'You're more fascinated by evil Lisa than by perfect Stacey.'

'I'm on Stacey's side though,' I protested. 'I want her to win.'

'Sure you do. You also want to see her suffer first.'

I opened my mouth to argue. Then I realised she was probably right. Shaking my head in dismay, I read on. My amnesiac self knew enough about pop culture but nothing about this programme so I'd probably never watched it before. That was definitely a mistake I planned to remedy. After I'd solved all my other problems.

~

I stuck around on set long enough to glare at the production crew and actors as well as to satisfy myself that Julie was as safe as she could be. It would be just my luck if she got herself vamp-napped on my first day on the job. It probably wouldn't be all that great for Julie either. Still, given that even she had to plead with the studio security to allow me in, and that there was a minimum of entrances and exits, I couldn't see how she was in danger here. Besides, I had to respect that she'd been at this hunter-avoidance business a lot longer than I had and was fully aware of her vulnerabilities and strengths.

Borrowing her car with the proviso that I'd pick her up again at seven o'clock on the dot, I drove back towards Manchester city centre. It seemed that if I wanted to get confirmation or repudiation of Morgan's assertions – as well as some much-desired nux – the man to find was this Rubus fellow. I'd start with Mike Timmons, the Travotel manager. He'd mentioned Rubus so he must have a good idea where I could locate him. I was almost certain that he'd alerted the golf-course goons about my presence in the hotel so they could try and kill me again. This time I'd have the element of surprise on my side; even if I ran into the would-be assassins, I'd be more prepared.

I indicated left to leave on the next slip road, checking my mirrors as I did so. It was just as bloody well. A boy racer in some showy red sports car appeared from nowhere, undertaking me. I narrowly avoided slamming into his side and the family saloon behind me narrowly avoided crashing into my arse.

'Gasbudlikins!' I slammed on the horn. The only response I got was a tanned arm thrusting out from the driver's window and flicking me the finger. Then he accelerated away.

For the briefest moment, I stared after the disappearing car. A typical superhero would catch up to him, force him to stop in a safe place and remind him pointedly of the rules of the road. I had no idea what a typical faery would do. I did, however, have a very clear image in my head of what a villain would do after such a slight. Bad guys move the plot forward, I reminded myself. Well, I was going to move this arsebadger's plot forward.

Speeding up, I gripped the steering wheel and focused, keeping the red car in sight. He wasn't stupid enough to run the red light at the next crossroads so I caught up to him quickly enough. Music blared out, some thumping, tuneless idiocy that I supposed passed for a song. He deserved some come back for forcing everyone to listen to that rubbish. My guts tightened. I had to time this perfectly.

In the split second before the traffic lights flicked to green, I altered time. It was becoming easier to manage the more I did it. This time I felt the smooth transition as the road rager's seconds turned to sludge whilst mine remained normal. Then I veered out on the hard shoulder in front of him, effectively blocking his path. A moment later, time returned to normal and his oh-so perfect vehicle smashed into the back of mine with a tremendous sound of crunching metal.

For a few seconds I watched in my mirror as he sat dumbstruck in his car. He had the sort of tanned smooth skin and overly large forehead that were annoying all on their own. I paid close attention to his expression, noting the exact moment when it changed from shock to grim determination. He opened his door and got out, anger vibrating in his shoulders.

There was no doubt in my mind that he'd find it easy to shout at me. He'd use the fact that I was a slightly built female with unkempt hair to try and intimidate me with his maleness. As if. All the same, this would be far easier if I were a large burly bloke. Preferably with a swarthy beard and biceps.

I waited until he was almost at my car door and got out. When he caught sight of me, his face altered and he hesitated. Then he pulled back his spine and glared.

'You crashed into me!'

I cocked my head and regarded him. 'No,' I said calmly. 'You crashed into *me*. You hit my rear. Not only is the liability yours, but the fault is yours.'

His brow creased for a heartbeat as if something were confusing him. Then he pursed his lips and shook off whatever was bothering him. 'That's bullshit,' he blustered. 'You ... you came out of nowhere.' He swung his head from left to right as if searching for witnesses who didn't exist to prove his claim.

'I think you weren't paying attention. Give me your insurance details and we can settle this properly.' It occurred to me, rather belatedly, that I didn't know whether *I* had any insurance. It didn't matter; this wasn't about the money, it was about the racing arsebadger getting his come-uppance. 'In fact, given that you're clearly a menace on the roads, we should probably just call the police.'

As expected, his face paled dramatically. No doubt he had some form of contraband in his wanker-tanker that he didn't want the police to find. Drugs, probably. Even though I was supposedly a drug dealer myself, I didn't have any sympathy for him. He should have thought of that before he drove like a maniac and almost killed three people. Although it was tempting to pop out one of his eyeballs or demand his firstborn as retribution, given his reaction to my mention of coppers this seemed like the best way to go.

'We're not calling the fucking police,' he hissed. His fists clenched.

Here we go: this was where he would step forward and threaten me. There would be numerous epithets – bitch, whore, whatever – and he'd use his size to tower over me and force me into submission.

I upped the ante myself and took the first step, closing the gap between us. Huh. He was shorter than I'd realised. 'Why not?' I enquired, the very picture of calm, cool and collected.

The man's face contorted, a furious red flushing his neck. 'I'll give you money for the repairs,' he muttered. 'We don't need to involve anyone else.'

I blinked. I hadn't expected such a fast climb down. I was almost disappointed. 'Really?' I asked. 'You'll just give me a wad of cash?'

He looked from the damage at the back of Julie's car to the damage on his. 'Yeah. Like you said, it was my fault. I've got money in the glove box. Hang on.' He twisted on his heel and got into his car, as if fiddling around to find the money. A second later, he started the engine and swerved round both me and Julie's car in a bid to escape.

He hadn't appreciated quite how much damage had been done to his own vehicle. He barely got fifty metres away when his car came to a juddering halt and smoke started to pour from his engine. Once again he got out. He kicked the tyres and started to yell inarticulately at the sky. Either he was a supernatural creature who had the power to talk to animals or he was having a very, very bad day because he'd only just started when a pigeon flapped overhead and let loose, splattering both him and his smoking sports car with gross white liquid. He screeched and then shouted even louder.

I walked to the back of Julie's car. It was dented, to be sure, but the damage looked fairly superficial to me. She could dock my wages but it would be worth it. I shrugged, got in, drove the short distance up to the still-bellowing arsebadger and popped my head out of the window.

'Tell you what,' I said, interrupting his tirade, 'you pay more attention to how you drive and we'll call this quits.' He was lucky I was in a good mood. I was an evil villain, after all.

He opened his mouth then apparently thought better of answering, snapped it closed again and nodded mutely. I watched him and decided I should make sure. Leaving my own engine running, I got out of the car again and opened his passenger door, ignoring the smoke still billowing out of the front. While the feckless man stared at me, I reached into his glove box. There was, alas, no money but there was a small plastic bag filled with at least a dozen white pills that I doubted he'd got on legal prescription. I ignored them and found his driver's licence.

He stomped towards me. 'What are you doing?' he shouted, finding his voice.

I read the details on the small card. 'Julian Mayweather,' I said aloud. '23 Grand Bellock Road, Manchester. Date of birth...' I paused. 'Wow, you look younger than you really are. Do you use Botox?'

His steps faltered. 'What do you want?' he whispered. 'What are you really after?'

'I told you,' I said pleasantly. 'I want you to be a better driver.' I waved his driver's licence in the air before tossing it in his direction. 'If not, I know where I can find you. I might just pop in from time to time to make sure you're behaving.'

I reached up and patted him on the shoulder. He flinched in response. That was weird. It made an odd kind of sense that people who knew who I was were afraid of me – or at least of my connection with the mysterious Rubus – but this guy didn't know me from Adam. Yet I'd still managed to terrify him into submission with very little effort. It had to be my demeanour, I decided. Yep. I was evil through and through.

Whistling, I returned to my car and closed the door before pointedly clicking my seatbelt into position. It was important to abide by the laws of the land. Then I checked my rear-view mirror and started: the face I'd started to get used to wasn't looking back at me. I was no longer Madrona of the pale skin, freckles and mousy brown hair; the face in the mirror was that of a swarthy man with a bushy beard, harsh eyes and, when I glanced down at my body, the most enormous bulging biceps.

CHAPTER TWELVE

It was strange. I still felt the same. I still sounded the same. When I parked Julie's car, got out and tried to lift it, my pathetic lack of strength was the same as ever. Most of my upper torso and right arm were still in agony from the poisoned cut on my finger, so that hadn't changed along with the rest of me. Neither did I feel like a thirty-something man and, when I scratched my chin, my skin felt as smooth as usual. Yet, in the mirror, I still looked like a thirty-something Hell's Angel, with a ridiculous scratchy beard, who should know better. Apart from my eyes, that was. They were still a bright Fey green despite the hard light which shone within them.

Not taking anything for granted – after all, Julie might have bewitched her car mirrors along with the blood-magic imbued NDA – I went into a public toilet in the nearest shopping mall to double-check my reflection. Yep: I was still a burly male. No wonder the red-car arsebadger had seemed intimidated; I looked like a brute. I even had several missing teeth and a cauliflower ear. The attention to detail was extraordinary.

Undoing the zip on my jeans, I peered down. Well, you would, wouldn't you? A squat, ugly penis, surrounded by coarse black pubic hair, hung there. I jiggled my hips and the penis jiggled in turn. I was reaching for it, hoping to experiment to see how hard it was to aim correctly while peeing standing up, when the door opened and another woman entered. Comically, she froze and gazed at me open-mouthed before letting out a tiny squeak, whirling away and skedaddling as fast as her high heels would let her. I followed quickly, zipping myself up again. It wouldn't be wise to find myself on the wrong side of the law for indecent exposure and entering the ladies' restrooms when I was, apparently, a man.

It was obvious what had happened: I'd stumbled across more of my superhero – or rather Fey – powers. I'd wished I could look like a swarthy man and now I did. The trouble was that I had no idea whether I could change back again. Amusing as this body was, I had zero desire to look like this in the long term. But it didn't matter how hard I concentrated; I couldn't seem to change myself back. I wondered if the genuine owner of my new body was now walking around somewhere looking like me. I had no idea how any of this worked.

While I didn't want to stay like this, I *was* beginning to enjoy it. I had to concentrate on walking in an appropriate fashion, strutting with my groin pushed out in front of me and my arms swinging. People took one glimpse at me and veered away. I was no longer the Madhatter; now I was the Mad Man – and, as Julie had suggested, it was far more fun playing the villain than the hero.

I swaggered down the mall's concourse. A small child wearing a pink frilly dress dropped her lollipop as I passed and started to cry. Her mother put out a protective arm to guard her against me. Even the security guard in front of one of the more well-heeled shops appeared intimidated. I could get used to this.

I looked around. If Morgan thought I was evil – and if I

looked evil – then, darn it, I was going to be evil. A girl needed to have some fun, after all.

I wound out of the mall and headed down the street towards the Travotel. As I passed a row of parked cars, I thumped each one, setting off various car alarms. Their piercing shriek was remarkably gratifying. I swung left and entered the hotel, marched straight up to the front desk and leaned against it. I allowed myself a brief sweep with my eyes. No sign of any ugly goonies – not that they'd have spotted me even if they were here. There was some advantage to looking like a slightly pinker version of the Incredible Hulk.

Although I recognised the woman behind the desk, she obviously didn't recognise me. 'Good morning, sir,' she said with a forced smile. 'How may I help you?'

'I want to see the manager.' The voice that came out of my mouth was entirely my own. Ah. Clearly it was only my appearance that had been altered. No wonder the red-car arsebadger had looked so flummoxed when I'd first spoken. I deepened my voice to a hoarse, gruff tone and tried again. 'Get me Mike Timmons.'

She blinked rapidly, revealing her nervousness. 'Do you have an appointment?'

I smiled at her and displayed my lack of good dentistry. 'No. Tell him...' I paused and thought about it. 'Tell him Rubus is here to see him.'

'He's very busy,' she began.

'Look, lady,' I said, enjoying myself immensely. 'I want to see Mike Timmons and I want to see him now. When he hears that I'm waiting, he won't be happy.' I made a shooing motion. 'Go and tell him.' I checked my watch, realising too late that I wasn't wearing one, although the Rolex I'd taken from one of the McNasties was still in my pocket. Then I simply growled, 'He's got five minutes.'

Her eyes widened. I could tell she desperately wanted to tell me to piss off but fortunately, afraid of what I might be capable of if refused, she decided to do as I asked. She turned away and opened the door leading into an office behind her.

I leaned over the desk and saw a nice pen on the other side. 'I'm having this,' I declared to no one in particular, swiping it and placing it in my pocket. I looked round. Unfortunately no one was in the lobby so my theft went unnoticed. Being evil was only really fun when other people were around to be horrified. Perhaps I could find an animal shelter and kick some kittens in front of would-be adopters. Then I grimaced; I was evil but I wasn't *that* evil.

The receptionist re-emerged. She kept her distance, even though the desk was already acting as a barrier between us. 'Mr Timmons will be out shortly.'

Again I checked my invisible watch. 'He's only got three minutes and twenty seconds,' I said, making it up as I went along, 'before I kick up some hell.' I paused. 'Make that three minutes and ten seconds. Nine seconds. Eight seconds.' This could go on for some time.

Towards my left there was a cough. I turned in its direction, spotting the man himself. 'You ... you're not Rubus,' Timmons stammered.

I pasted on a gruesome smile and stalked towards him, my arms held out wide. Before he could do anything, I drew him into a massive bear hug, squeezing him tightly so that all the air was pushed out of his lungs. 'Appearances can be deceptive,' I murmured in his ear. After all, if Rubus and I were both Fey, it stood to reason that Rubus could alter his appearance just like I had. I could be him, regardless of how I looked.

When I eventually released Timmons, he sprang backwards. 'I'm so sorry. It's been a long time. I didn't recognise you immediately.' He was virtually bowing and scraping at my feet. At least my ploy was working. 'Come,' he said. 'I'll show you to my office.'

I let him lead the way round the back of reception into a small, dingy room with only a tiny window to provide some natural light. Once inside, I stepped past him and sat at his desk. If he was thinking about arguing, it didn't show on his face; he simply took the chair opposite.

'To what do I owe the pleasure?' he asked, twisting his hands in his lap.

I lifted my legs onto his desk and crossed them at the ankle after kicking away some papers that were in my way. 'Before we get into that,' I drawled, trying to remember to alter my voice, 'do you recognise me now?' I had to be sure before I fully relaxed; those McNasty bastards might still be around.

Timmons swallowed, his Adam's apple bobbing in his throat. 'Rubus?' he asked tentatively. 'But obviously wearing a glamour.' He swallowed again. 'A very effective glamour, I might add. I've not seen one so well thought out before.'

I regarded him thoughtfully for a moment, absorbing the word 'glamour' and wondering whether he was telling the truth about its effectiveness or merely massaging my ego. Either way, I had to take full advantage of this situation while Timmons still believed that I was big, scary Rubus. Whoever Rubus was, I knew that Timmons was afraid of him. I could work with that.

'It has come to my attention,' I said gruffly, 'that you recently had dealings with one of my ... employees.'

Timmons' green eyes flickered. 'The Madhat— uh, Madrona. She was staying here, yes. But she sought me out, not the other way around. I would never approach one of your Fey, Rubus.'

'Really?' My voice was flat. 'So you didn't go to her room and demand that she gave you some dust?'

'No! I wouldn't do that!'

Lying arsebadger. 'Madrona is a much-trusted employee. She asserts quite the opposite.' I regarded Timmons with a steely eye. 'Is she lying then?'

'I...' He loosened his collar and coughed. 'Um...' His face fell. 'I just wanted some dust.'

'Indeed.'

'I'm sorry.'

I nodded. 'As you should be. I can't abide liars.' Taking a stab in the dark, based on what else I'd learned about this strange Fey society, I raised an eyebrow. 'I see you're also lying about your name.'

'It's not a lie!' he protested. 'The Fey know who I am. I couldn't use my real name here. I'd never be taken seriously! Not by the humans anyway.'

'Hmmm.' I tried to look as if I knew exactly what he was talking about. 'You real name being...'

'Begonius.'

Yeah, okay. I could see why he'd changed it. I didn't have time to comment, though, because Timmons looked wildly from side to side and hastily interjected with an explanation of his own. 'We're supposed to maintain a low profile. We're supposed to keep our true selves quiet.'

'So we are.' Maybe that was why altering time was frowned upon. With the proliferation of CCTV cameras in this country, any untoward or inexplicable action could be flagged up by powerful humans. Given what Julie had revealed about the vampire hunters, it made sense. The Fey probably possessed zero desire to be hunted down in the same manner. 'Well,' I continued, 'you still lied to me. You also alerted others to Madrona's presence.'

Timmons' panic flared further. 'What? No! I didn't tell anyone she was here!'

'Then why did three gargoyles show up at her room moments after she left?' I spat, watching his reaction carefully.

'Three what?' He paused. 'Wait. The Redcaps. They were here for her?'

What the gasbudlikins were Redcaps? Some other sort of supernatural being? Maybe humans didn't exist at all; maybe everyone living here was something else entirely. I wasn't sure I'd met anyone normal since I'd woken up on that bloody golf course. I sucked in a breath and tried to focus. 'Who were they?' I demanded. 'Who were these Redcaps?'

He shook his head, terrified. 'I don't know! I'd never seen them before! They showed up, ran through the hotel and then left. They were nothing to do with me, I promise! I didn't even connect them to Madrona.'

He wasn't the brightest star in the sky – unless he frequently had grotesque creatures sprinting through his hotel during the day. But it seemed that he was telling the truth. He was too scared not to. Shame.

'It doesn't change the fact that you lied. We'll have to find a way for you to make it up to me.'

Timmons' eagerness was pathetic. 'Of course, of course! I'll do whatever you want. You're so amazing, Rubus. I'll follow your lead. Just tell me what to do and I'll do it.'

Ick. I had the feeling that if I asked him to lick my shoes, he would. I tapped my mouth as if thinking deeply on the matter. 'How about some nux?'

Momentarily befuddled, he stared at me. 'Nux?'

'Yes.' I drifted a lazy hand through the air. 'Give me some nux and I can be persuaded to forget this little matter.'

Timmons' growing puzzlement transformed abruptly. He stood up, pushed his chair back and glared at me. 'You're not Rubus!' he accused.

Gasbudlikins. 'Of course I am.'

'No, you're not. Rubus wouldn't come to me for nux. You're her! You're Madrona!' He pointed at me. 'You thought you could fool me!'

To be fair, I *had* fooled him. Just not for long enough. 'Now, listen—'

He shook his head in sudden, stubborn defiance. 'Has Rubus excommunicated you? Is that why you're here? Because I'm not helping one of his enemies.' His mouth tightened. 'No way. And how the hell are you maintaining that glamour? No faery – apart from maybe Rubus or Morganus – can keep up a spell of that intricacy for more than five or ten minutes. What *are* you?' He said this last part as if I were a slug that had crawled into his cornflakes.

'Stronger than you,' I answered. 'Obviously.' I sighed. 'Fine. If you won't give me any nux then tell me where I can find Rubus.' This other Fey who everyone kept mentioning couldn't be that bloody scary. And no doubt I'd have to meet with the man sooner or later, especially as I supposedly worked for him.

'I'm going to tell Morgan about this,' Timmons or Begonius or whatever he wanted to be called said in a high-pitched whine.

I gritted my teeth, suddenly irritated. 'Morgan Shmorgan.' I yanked my legs down from the desk and stood up before leaning across and grabbing Timmons' collar. 'I need nux,' I hissed.

'I don't have any!' he yelled in my face.

I raised my hand to backhand him. I wasn't intending to actually strike him he still staggered and clutched his face as if to protect his middling good looks. 'You can't do this. You can't hurt me. The truce...'

I was getting mightily fed up of being told what I could or could not do. 'I don't give two hoots about the stupid truce,' I said. My grip tightened on him, my fingers digging through the material of his shirt and into his skin.

Timmons began to shake. If this was what most Fey were like, it was a wonder we'd survived this long. 'You're not a good person at all,' he whispered.

I rolled my eyes and wished I didn't feel sorry for the ridiculous man. He'd tried to intimidate me when it suited him but now he was a blubbering wreck. He was the worst kind of bully, using his own fear to manipulate those weaker than himself while brown-nosing anyone stronger. I might be evil but at least I was trying to be honest with myself. 'No,' I said. 'I'm not a good person.' There was a strange wrench in my stomach. 'But they say only the good die young. I'd rather be bad and live longer.'

Timmons cowered. I was highly tempted to slap him properly. Waterboarding was an option. I glanced back at his desk; maybe I could use the stapler on his hamster-like cheeks. Or pull out his fingernails. There had to be a pair of pliers around here somewhere.

'I'm sorry,' he whined. 'I don't have any nux. I don't know where Rubus is. All I wanted was some dust, a little pick-me-up to keep me going. The ache is so bad. I've not had dust for months and when I saw you were staying here I thought you'd come to sell me some. I'm sticking to the rules. Don't hurt me.' He covered his face with his hands. 'Please don't hurt me.'

Good grief. Forget kicking kittens, this was like throwing sharpened daggers at a defenceless baby. I cursed to myself then gently pressed Timmons back into the chair. 'You need to grow a spine,' I told him sternly. 'What kind of Fey are you?'

'The good kind!' he sobbed.

'Then act like it,' I snapped. 'When we first met, you virtually threatened me to get what you wanted. Then, when you thought I was Rubus, you grovelled like a worm.'

'I don't understand. What do you want from me?'

I pulled his hands away from his face. 'I want you to be yourself. If you need dust, go and get some bloody dust. If you want to be a good faery, be a goddamned good faery. Don't compromise yourself or your morals.'

Timmons stared at me. 'Huh?'

'You feel the ache for home. Of...' I struggled with the words '...Fey Land. Everyone feels that ache. We all miss it.'

Tears filled his eyes. 'It hurts.' He clutched at his chest. 'It hurts in here.'

'I know,' I soothed. 'But you're not alone. Meet with others. Form a support group or something. Draw strength from each other.'

'Yes.' He bit his lip and nodded vigorously. 'Yes, that's a good idea. A support group. I can do that. People would like that. Other Fey would like that.'

'You need to stand up for yourself, too. This is your office, Begonius. You shouldn't have let me sit in *your* chair in *your* office.'

'I thought you were Rubus,' he mumbled.

'So? Even if I were, I'm still on your turf! No one will respect you if you don't stand up for what is yours.' I waggled my finger at him. 'Not in a mean way that compromises who you are, but in a way so that you're not trodden all over. It's not rocket science.'

Timmons gazed up at me as if I'd grown horns. 'You're not as horrible as people say you are. You're not as horrible as I thought you were, either.'

Gee, was I supposed to say thanks? 'Maybe,' I said gently, 'you shouldn't cross people who have horrible reputations. Yes, there's a truce but it doesn't mean bad stuff can't happen.' I hesitated. 'I don't suppose you've heard about anyone getting their head chopped off?'

He recoiled. 'What?'

'Or anything more about those three ugly guys who are trying to kill me? It wasn't a coincidence that they came here. What did you say they were? Redcaps? What the hell are Redcaps anyway?'

If I thought he'd been looking at me strangely before, it was nothing compared to now. 'What on earth is going on with you?'

I sighed, unwilling to display my vulnerabilities. 'Believe me, that's what I'd like to know.' I ran a hand through my hair. 'You really don't have any nux? Or know where I can find Rubus?'

He shook his head. 'No. Rubus finds you, not the other way around.'

There was something ominous about that statement that I chose to ignore. 'Where else can I get nux from?'

Timmons' brow creased. 'Are you alright? You're asking some very strange questions.' I narrowed my eyes ever so slightly. He apologised. 'Sorry. The only other person I know who has nux is Morgan.'

My heart sank. Typical. That was how my life rolled these days: the only people who could help me find the antidote I desperately needed were a man I couldn't remember and couldn't find, and another man who despised me and everything I stood for.

Noting my expression, Timmons raised a shoulder. 'Morganus, I mean. And you and he...'

'Me and Morgan what?'

There was a knock on the door. Without waiting, the receptionist put her head round. 'Is everything okay?' She didn't look at me. I applauded her bravery in interrupting; Timmons could learn a thing or two from her.

'It's fine, Mindy,' he answered.

'Good.' She hesitated. 'There's a couple at the front who are complaining about the water pressure. And they said there was a cockroach in their bed. They want to see you.'

Timmons grimaced. 'I'll be right out.' He turned at me. 'I should go.' Then he bit his lip. 'May I go?'

I sighed. 'Yeah.' It was clear that he didn't have much to offer me. There were plenty of gaps he could fill in but he didn't know anything substantial. Gasbudlikins. Being evil was a lot harder than it looked. And if there were cockroaches in this hotel, it was high time I made an exit. Yuck.

CHAPTER THIRTEEN

Spotting a smoker as I exited the hotel, I squared my shoulders and stomped over. So far I'd resisted the lure of nicotine but at that moment I really needed a cigarette.

'Give me a fag,' I growled at her, in my best bad-guy voice. I wasn't yet done with being evil, I decided. What I needed was an argument with a complete stranger. Or fisticuffs. That would make me feel much better.

The woman, wearing a flowery dress and looking as if she'd just stepped out of a posh garden party, ignored my glower and smiled. 'Of course. I know what it's like when you're desperate for a puff.' She dug into her bag and pulled out a pack. 'Take a couple.'

I stared at her. Couldn't she tell I was a villain? To all intents and purposes, I was a large, ungainly man who needed a shave and had a dangerous glower. She had no right to be this nice to me. Unless she was trying to give me lung cancer. It was a slow revenge, to be sure, but it would work in the end.

'Thanks,' I muttered. 'I just need one.'

'No problem.' She continued to smile at me. It was eerie.

Taking her lighter, I lit the cigarette with my good hand and inhaled deeply. Almost immediately, I choked. My body may well have been craving nicotine but clearly I'd gone long enough without smoking for the nasty side effects to hit me. Light-headedness over took me and the taste in my mouth was like ash. I made a face and dropped my hand with the cigarette in it.

'You don't really want it, do you?' the woman said. 'Just stub it out. I won't be offended.'

I gazed at the smoke curling up into the air then flicked her a glance. 'Why are you being so nice to me?'

She shrugged. 'You look like you're having a bad day. And it's nice to be nice.'

'I'm trying to be nasty,' I admitted, surprising even myself with the disclosure.

She ground out her cigarette. 'When you're nasty, people are nasty back. And you don't think you deserve anything better.' I must have looked astonished because she gave a brief laugh. 'Been there, done that, had the therapy,' she told me. 'Whatever's going on in your life, at least you're alive. Rise above the shit.' She smiled again. 'Nice talking to you.' With that, she strolled away, leaving me staring after her with an open mouth.

Shaking my head, bemused, I discarded the cigarette and shambled along the pavement towards the main street. It was looking more and more likely that I'd have to crawl back to Morgan with my proverbial cap in hand. Quickly, too. I was fairly certain that the pain was getting worse. Most of my chest now ached, as well as my hand and arm, and my thoughts were becoming sluggish. Maybe that was why I was such a pathetic excuse for both a villain *and* a superhero; I clearly wasn't working to capacity.

I huffed as I walked along the road. Was it possible to be amnesiac *and* have an identity crisis at the same time? Sure, I couldn't remember anything about myself but you'd think I'd instinctively know whether I was good or bad and act accordingly. Unfortunately, it appeared that life wasn't as straightforward as it was in soap operas.

I rounded the corner, narrowly avoiding a collision with a pair of loved-up teenagers and almost losing my balance in the process.

'The bigger they are,' the boy snickered, 'the harder they fall.'

I spun round, prepared to give him my best villain glare. Unfortunately the action only served to make me dizzy. As the kids wandered away laughing, I doubled over, trying not to vomit. This was ridiculous. How could I maintain a stomach of steel when faced with gruesome sights but feel the need to upchuck when I simply turned round too quickly? I did my best to hold in the contents of my stomach but it was a losing battle. Moments later, a stream of yellow bile splashed onto the pavement. Bleurgh.

Feeling like death I straightened up, taking my time in case my stomach protested again. My skin was clammy. But every cloud has a silver lining: the rowan-induced pain, which had been spreading for days, appeared to have vanished. Perhaps the nausea and vomiting were a result of my body expelling the poison by itself. If I'd made myself throw up on the golf course, I'd probably have been right as rain. No doubt Morgan was trying to put the wind up me by harping on about nux. Ha! Who needed it? Or him? I could manage perfectly well on my own. I'd have jumped for joy if my current body weren't so cumbersome.

I continued on my path, weaving in and out of the growing number of pedestrians. Most of them gave me a wide berth, which was just as well. My breath was probably about as ripe as a warthog's morning fart right now. There was also an annoying buzzing in my ears. It was probably a side effect of walking around in this body. I'd get over it.

Although it had been blazing sunshine not long ago, the sky had darkened considerably. It was darned cold too, and I kept shivering. I should try that charity shop again and see if they had Godzilla-sized jumpers. Autumn wasn't here yet but this was still England – world champion at grey and chilly.

I turned left onto the next street, realising as I did so that not only were there more people around but that many of them were looking at me strangely. A few looked scared – as they should – but most appeared concerned. That wasn't how this was supposed to go. I'd have to remind the world who I was.

Throwing back my head, I let out a loud, fake, villainous laugh. 'Mwahahahahahaha!' Oddly, it didn't make the other pedestrians run away. If anything, they looked even more worried.

A small boy tugged at his mum's hand. 'Is the big man alright?'

I swivelled my eyes towards him. 'I am fine,' I boomed. Even to my own ears, my voice sounded overly loud. 'And,' I added, 'I am not a man. I'm a woman.'

The boy's mother glared at me. 'Stay away from us,' she said in a low voice.

'Mummy...'

'The man is drunk,' she told him. 'Even though it's only eleven o'clock in the morning.'

I frowned at her. 'I'm not drunk. And I already said. I'm not a man. I'm a woman. Well, technically, I'm a faery.' I raised myself up onto my tiptoes and flapped my arms. 'See?'

The woman grabbed her son and the pair of them walked hastily away. A braver woman stepped up to the breach. 'Are you okay, sir? Would you like me to call you an ambulance?'

'You can call me that if you like,' I said. 'It's not my name though.' My knee inexplicably gave way and I stumbled down to the pavement. 'Hey!' I protested. 'Who pushed me?'

There was a murmur from the growing crowd around me. 'Call the ambulance,' someone said. 'He's obviously taken something. He could hurt someone if we leave him like this. Look at the size of him!'

'I'll hurt you,' I muttered. I braced myself, trying and failing to get back up to my feet. If anything, it was even darker now than it had been before. I glanced up at the sky. 'Is it night time?'

'Uncle! There you are!' A blonde woman appeared in front of me, reached down and pulled me upright. I blinked at her. She looked oddly familiar but I couldn't quite place her. 'Sorry everyone,' she said. 'He's on strong medication. He escaped from our house before anyone noticed. I'll get him home.'

'Will you manage? Are you sure?' asked another passer-by.

'I can still call an ambulance,' someone else suggested.

'No, no, it's all good,' she trilled. 'I'll be fine. So will he. I just need to get him back to bed.'

Her face swam before me, blurring in and out of focus. Hang on a gasbudlikin minute. 'I know you,' I said. 'You're Jodie. You work for Morgan.'

A flash of surprise crossed her face then she bit her lip and nodded. 'That's right. I'm your niece, Jodie. Come on. I'll take you home.' She pulled at my arm with surprising strength.

My legs felt like ten-ton weights but Jodie was so briskly business-like that I decided to play along. I stumbled beside her while she pulled out a phone from her pocket. 'It's me,' she muttered. 'I'm in the high street just down from St Peter's Church and I've got a problem.' She glanced at me. 'A big problem.'

'That's because I'm the Big Bad,' I informed her airily. Then my gaze snagged on something else. Across the street, staring at us, was another familiar figure. It was the tall Amazonian woman who I'd been sure was about to shoot me on that first day. 'Hey!' I said. I pulled away from Jodie and turned in the woman's direction. 'Hey!' I waved my arms. 'I'm here. Come and get me!'

I stepped off the pavement to walk towards her. A moment later, Jodie yanked me back, just in time to avoid the double-decker bus trundling towards me.

'Who are you?' she hissed. 'Are you one of Rubus's men?'

'I...' My stomach lurched and the world darkened even further. I lifted a hand to my head and rubbed it. 'I don't feel very well.' I felt myself swaying.

'Fuck,' Jodie swore. 'Just hang on. Try to...'

'Look,' I said, pointing. 'There's the pavement.' Then it rushed up to meet me.

~

There was a swirl of voices above my head but it was far too much effort to open my eyes. Then it occurred to me that playing dead might be the best thing I could do. I was vulnerable enough; until I knew who these people were and what they wanted from me, I wasn't going to move a muscle.

'I don't recognise him. There's no database anywhere with his picture in it, either foreign or domestic.' The clipped male accent wasn't one I recognised.

Given what he'd said, I must still be wearing my Hell's Angel body. The thought that the second head blow had returned my memory filled me with hope but it only took a second or two to realise that nothing had changed in that department either.

'There's no doubting that he's Fey.'

'Have you ever seen a Fey that size? I certainly haven't. He's a bloody monster.'

There was a delicate sniff. 'When I came across him, he was telling half of Manchester that he was a faery.' That was definitely Jodie. 'I thought you lot were supposed to keep that part secret.'

'We are.' At this new voice, I had to force myself to keep my breathing even. It stood to reason that Jodie had taken me to Morgan – she did work for him after all – but it was still jarring to know he was standing over me. 'He's been poisoned with rowan though. His whole body reeked of it. Leave it untreated for too long and it can cause dementia.' Huh. He'd not mentioned that little fact to *me*. I wondered whether that was deliberate or not.

There was a sharp intake of breath from the other side. 'Rowan? It's too much of a coincidence that the Madhatter bitch was poisoned with rowan too.'

Morgan's answer was sharp. 'Don't call her that.'

'Do you think she did this?'

What an arsebadger. Why would I go around poisoning other faeries? I almost raised my head to snap at the suggestion but fortunately Morgan was already there. 'No,' he answered. 'There's no reason to suggest she did.'

There was a brief pause. 'Has anyone checked the border? Did he come through? Is—'

'It's still blocked.'

Disappointment coloured every word of the response. 'Shit. You're sure? Shit.'

'We should wake him up. Question him and find out who he really is and what he knows. Throw some water on him or something.'

'No need,' Morgan answered. 'He's already awake.'

Gasbudlikins, that man was vexing. Yielding to the

inevitable, I opened my eyes, propped myself up on my elbows and gazed round at the room. I definitely still felt woozy. Better though; I was sure I was better. I clocked the one and only exit – blocked to me at the moment – and the lack of weaponry, which could be both a good and bad thing. Then I turned my attention to the people.

Four pairs of eyes stared back at me: Morgan's ice-green chips; an older looking gentleman wearing a morning suit, of all things, whose racing-green cravat matched his irises; a middle-aged woman with lighter green eyes which were watching my every breath, and Jodie's baby blues. No prizes for guessing who wasn't Fey then.

'Who are you?' Morgan asked. There was no censure in his tone but it was clear he wasn't going to be my best friend just yet.

I didn't answer immediately. I wasn't yet sure how to tell him who I really was. If he'd struggled to believe that I had amnesia before, how could I get him to believe that I looked like a hairy wrestler now? Timmons had already suggested it was next to impossible to maintain a glamour for any length of time.

While I debated the best way to approach the truth, my captors were growing impatient. 'Listen, matey,' Cravat Man hissed, 'we've given you the nux antidote you needed. Your system has all but flushed the rowan out. You owe us. Now tell us who you are and where you've come from.'

I brightened. Finally, some good news. I'd barely had time to digest it properly, however, when the Fey woman broke in. 'This is a waste of time. Unless we test him properly with a truth draw, we'll never know whether he's telling us the truth or not. It's not like one of Rubus's Truth Spiders but it'll still work.'

'Viburna, just wait. You...'

She crouched down beside me and took my hands. Maybe she wanted to dance or something. That was a nice thought – until my skin began to tingle unpleasantly. 'Hey!' I exclaimed.

Morgan's eyes narrowed though he didn't say anything. He simply crossed his arms over his broad chest and continued to watch me.

'What's your name?' Viburna asked, her words soft and melodic.

The tingling sensation increased. I tried to pull my hands away but Viburna was much stronger than she looked. She kept a firm grip on me and continued to stare into my eyes.

'He's resisting,' Cravat Man muttered.

'Tell us your name,' Viburna repeated.

I licked my lips. It felt as if the answer was being tugged out of me against my will and, for that reason alone, I forced my mouth to stay closed.

Cravat Man stared at me. 'Try something else. A different question.'

Viburna's fingers stroked my skin. 'Where have you come from?'

Beads of sweat broke out on my forehead. She was obviously using some sort of nasty Fey magic on me. Frankly, that was just rude. I'd have told them the truth by now if they hadn't started treating me like an enemy prisoner. Maybe.

'He knew my name,' Jodie butted in. 'He must belong to Rubus.'

'Is that true?' Viburna asked. 'Are you one of his?'

I continued to resist. So much for the damned truce Morgan kept talking about. It was taking every ounce of energy I had to stay quiet; this was torture in all but name. No wonder all these Fey arsebadgers were so miserable and tense all the time if they had this kind of crap to put up with.

'He's strong,' Cravat Man said. 'Try harder.'

Viburna gritted her teeth. 'I *am* trying.'

'Let me try.' Morgan moved down and took Viburna's place. She released my hands and I expelled a breath, relief cascading through me as the compulsion to talk was lifted. Then he took my hands and the pressure returned. This time it was even stronger.

'Who are you?' he asked, his voice silky smooth.

My lips opened. I bit back the word. It was sheer stubborn will holding me back now. I was really struggling but I wasn't going to give in. Not like this.

Morgan's green eyes held mine. 'Who poisoned you?'

I couldn't hold it back any longer. The word fell out of me in a rush of air. 'Madrona.'

He dropped my hands as if he'd been burned.

'See?' Cravat Man said. 'I told you that bitch was behind all of this.'

I yanked my hands back, placing them behind my body as if that would help me. 'You absolute idiots,' I spat. '*I'm* Madrona. I poisoned myself by touching a poisoned sword. Not my finest hour, I admit, but I didn't know any better.'

All four of them stared at me in shock. I was only just getting going.

'You call me evil?' I hissed, addressing Morgan in particular. 'You lot dragged me here against my will and began interrogating me like we're in Guantanamo Bay. I've not done anything wrong! How dare you try and pull information out of me like that? It's ... it's...' I searched for the correct word. 'Impolite!'

While the other three continued to stare at me open-mouthed, Morgan leaned back on his haunches and regarded me carefully. 'You're certainly not on the side of good, Madrona,' he murmured. 'If indeed that's who you are.'

I almost howled in exasperation. 'I've got amnesia! Apparently I'm Madrona – everyone keeps telling me I am – but I don't know for sure. And I tried to be bad. I've spent all crappy day trying to be the villain you think I am. It's not worked.' My voice was rising. 'You know why it's not worked? Because I reckon that I'm not the bitch you keep telling me that I am. I've not met this bloody Rubus you keep talking about. I bet he's a damn sight nicer than you lot. He can't be much worse. So I theoretically sell some pixie-dust drug shite to some faeries to make them feel better. Big bloody deal! At least I've not tried to drag answers out of someone with some stupid truth-spell thing. I almost died out on the street an hour ago and now I'm trapped in this ridiculous oafish body. None of this is my fault! Stop being such an arsebadgering bastard and let me go!' I glared at him for extra effect.

All Morgan did was take a step back. He did not, however, take his eyes off me. 'Yeah,' he said slowly. 'That's Madrona.'

Jodie's lip curled. She might have been doing a good impression of disdain but I could tell she was nervous. 'You told me that you guys could only keep up glamours for a short period of time. If that's your ex, how come she still looks like that? It means any of you could pretend to be someone else whenever you wanted.'

Morgan's head tilted. 'I wasn't lying to you before, Jodie. No Fey had ever been able to maintain a glamour for more than a quarter of an hour.'

Her arms flailed in my direction. 'Then how is she doing it?' she screeched.

'Good question.' He raised an eyebrow at me. 'Madrona?'

My glower only increased. 'Do I look like I have any answers? Everything that happens to me only gives me more questions! I don't want to look like this! I want to look like me!'

Morgan glanced at Viburna and Cravat Man. 'Well,' he

drawled, 'the wind *did* change direction earlier today. Maybe she's stuck in that form forever.'

My glower abruptly transformed into a gape. 'What the hell? Are you telling me that I'm trapped like this? That I'm going to look like a brutish, muscle-bound prat with a Santa Claus beard for the rest of my days?'

He shrugged. 'You could shave.'

'You...'

Morgan held up his hands. 'Relax. I was only joking. The wind's got nothing to do with it.'

'Then what does?' I demanded. 'Why do I still look like this?'

Recovering slightly from her shock, Viburna spoke up. 'It could be the rowan poisoning,' she said doubtfully. 'It might be preventing her from returning to her normal appearance.'

'Or,' growled Cravat Man, 'it might be one of those dust concoctions. Who knows what Rubus has been adding to his bloody drugs?'

I'd had enough. I got to my feet, dusted myself off and sniffed. 'I don't know who any of you people are. Unless you're planning to keep me here against my will, I'm leaving.'

It irked me beyond belief that Morgan merely looked amused. 'You're not a prisoner. I should point out, however, that if Jodie hadn't noticed your shenanigans in the centre of town and called us, it's highly likely you'd be dead by now. The rowan was working its way through your body faster than I'd realised. We saved your life. And if you want to know how to return to your normal body, we can help you with that too.'

'Why?' I asked suspiciously. 'You obviously hate me. Why would you want to help me?'

He put his hands in his pockets. 'I never said I hated you.'

'*I* hate you,' interjected Jodie. Then she seemed to regret her words and took a step back. I smiled at her. I liked people who told the absolute truth. Unfortunately, my expression only seemed to scare her even more.

Morgan's mouth flattened. 'Perhaps it's best if the three of you leave. I'll deal with Madrona.'

'We have questions,' Cravat Man said.

Viburna nodded. 'Lots of questions.'

'Yeah?' I sneered. 'Well, I don't have any answers.'

Morgan sighed as if we were a bunch of squabbling children. He might have been right. 'Answer three questions, Maddy. You owe us that much for giving you nux. As an added bonus, I'll help you get rid of the glamour.'

I drew in a deep breath. 'Fine. But I was telling the truth. I might not be able to answer your questions. I don't know very much.' I lifted up my chin and gazed at the others. 'And they leave. It's just you and me.' I glanced at him. 'Not because I like you or trust you, or anything like that. I've just had enough of the sniping and the staring.'

Cravat Man stepped forward. 'Why you...'

Morgan moved in front of him. 'Deal.'

'We're going to find out what you say anyway,' Viburna said. 'He'll tell us.'

'Great,' I returned. 'Bully for you. I'd still like it if you left. Too many freaks and not enough circuses.'

Viburna glared; in fact, all three of them did. They really didn't like me very much.

'Go,' Morgan said.

Jodie pouted slightly. 'But—'

'It's for the best.'

The three of them gave me their own special brands of dirty looks, which were amusingly identical, and started to leave. I could hear Viburna and Cravat Man as they walked away.

'How the hell is she maintaining that glamour?'

'Fucked if I know. And how did she resist the Truth Draw?'

Easy: I was simply a superior being.

Morgan stared at me. 'You've built up a resistance. There's only one way that could happen and that's if Rubus used his Truth Spiders on you.'

I shuddered. I didn't really want to know what a Truth Spider was. I yanked my gaze away from his as something else occurred to me. I pushed past Morgan and went after the unfortunate trio. He lunged for me, his hand encircling my wrist. I stopped in my tracks but called out, 'Jodie?'

She turned and looked me, wariness written all over her face. 'Yes?'

'Thank you.' I coughed. 'For helping me out in the street. You didn't know who I was but you still came to my aid.'

She seemed surprised. 'I knew you were Fey,' she muttered eventually. 'You have the eyes. And you were shouting up and down the street that you were a faery.'

I winced. I didn't think I'd really been shouting. 'All the same,' I said, 'thank you.'

She stood there for a moment before pursing her lips and shrugging. 'You're welcome.'

I closed the door with my foot and moved back, eyeing Morgan. 'You're still holding me like I'm about to run away with your family jewels.'

He didn't let go; instead he watched me, his expression shuttered. 'You keep surprising me,' he commented.

I rolled my eyes. 'Even evil drug-dealing bitches can be polite.'

His response was quiet. 'I deserve that.'

I looked away. 'Why is Jodie here anyway? She obviously knows about all this faery business. Why is she allowed to know the truth?'

'She was in trouble and I helped her. My identity was

revealed in the process. If you want to know more, you'll have to ask her. It's her story to tell.'

That was remarkably gentleman-like of him. 'Fair enough.' I waggled my index finger at him. 'Be careful though. Talking to humans about their real ethnicities didn't help the vampires.'

Morgan blinked. 'Vampires?'

The briefest flash of pain rattled through me. So that was Julie's NDA in action, I thought faintly. Morgan frowned and I shook my head in dismissal. 'Never mind,' I said quickly. 'Just me being crazy.' I beamed at him. 'Let's get this show on the road. I've got places to be and people to meet. Not to mention that my balls are really itchy. How do you guys deal with that all the time? It's so annoying.'

Morgan looked faintly disgusted. 'You're right. The sooner we both get what we want and you get out of here, the better.'

CHAPTER FOURTEEN

'So,' Morgan drawled, once we were sitting on chairs in a more civilised manner than when he'd been trying to force me to talk on the floor. 'When you say you tried to be a villain today, what actually did you do?'

I glanced at him archly. 'Is that one of your three questions?'

'No. I'm simply trying to establish how much time I need to spend cleaning up whatever other disasters you've created.'

I folded my arms. 'There were no disasters. No one was hurt.' I sniffed pointedly. 'Apart from me. So you have nothing to worry about. Let's stay focused on the here and now, shall we? How the gasbudlikin hell do I get back to my normal body?'

He rubbed his chin. 'It would help if I knew how you ended up like this. Did you choose that particular body based on someone you saw?'

'No.' I shrugged. 'It was an unconscious deed. I didn't plan on looking like this. I just had a passing thought that a certain situation would be easier to deal with if I were a burly man. When I looked in the mirror, I was.'

Morgan didn't even twitch. 'You didn't have to concentrate to make the change?'

'Nope.'

'You didn't feel any pain or alteration in your physiognomy when it happened?'

'Nope.' I paused. 'Physio-what-omy?'

He rolled his eyes. 'Never mind.'

'So what's the magic word?'

Morgan looked me up and down. 'Magic word?'

'You know. To transform me back. There must be a special word or something so I can return to normal.'

He let out a bark. 'The last thing you'll ever be is normal, Maddy.'

I beamed at him. 'Thank you. But, really, come on. What do I say?'

Exasperated, he muttered something under his breath. 'There's no abracadabra. We're not wizards, Maddy. We're Fey.'

'So you keep saying, but I don't really understand what that means. I don't know what I'm capable of or how being Fey makes me different from everyone else on this planet. And if Fey Land is so amazing, why on earth did we all leave it in the first place?'

Morgan ran a hand through his hair. 'The history is complicated. And it's not Fey Land – we don't come from a theme park. The name of our homeland is Mag Mell. It's not even a separate place, it's a mirror image of here. Just more...' he cast around as if searching for the right word '...natural.'

That made no sense. 'Pardon?'

'In essence, Mag Mell – and us by extension – are more attune with nature. Both there and here.' He flicked a hand at me. 'Your name is Madrona.'

'So I'm told. It's a stupid name. Everyone from Fey Land, I mean Mag Mell, has stupid names. Apart from you. At least Morgan is vaguely sensible.'

'It's Morganus actually.'

Oh. I'd already known that. 'So Morgan for short? Can I call you Mo?'

He tutted. 'A madrona is a type of flowering tree. Viburna, who you just met, is named after a type of hedgerow. Opulus's namesake is a rose.'

Cravat Man? He certainly hadn't been sweet enough to be named after a flower, even if it did have sharp thorns. I was beginning to see a trend, though. 'And Morganus? What kind of plant is that?'

'A morganus isn't a plant.'

I raised my eyebrows. 'What makes you so special?'

'I'm not special,' he grunted. 'Let's move on.'

Hang on. 'What's a morganus?'

'It's really not important.'

'If it wasn't important,' I drawled, 'you would have told me.' I flicked back my hair before belatedly remembering that I still didn't have enough hair to flick back. 'Go on. What's a morganus?'

Morgan clenched his jaw. 'Antigulareus Morganus is a small sea creature.'

From the look on his face there was more to it than that. 'What kind of sea creature? A whale? A dolphin? A shark?'

'A snail,' he said stiffly.

I let out a crow of laughter. 'You're named after a snail?'

'The sea snail is a very noble creature.'

'Mm-hmm.' I pressed my lips together and tried to keep a straight face.

'Moving on...' Morgan said.

A small giggle escaped me. I choked with the effort of trying to hold back but it was no good. Before too long, I was doubled over. 'You're named after a snail.' I laughed harder. 'Is that because you're very slow? Or because you're very small?' I held up my pinky, crooking it to indicate what I was referring to.

'You're being ridiculously childish.'

I gasped for breath. 'You're named after a slimy snail!'

He folded his arms and glared. 'The coil on a sea snail's shell is extraordinarily elegant. The spiral is also a vital part of all nature. It forms the very basis of mathematics. The Fibonacci sequence is mirrored on certain shells. The golden ratio of maths is expressed through the humble sea snail.'

I wiped away the tears from my eyes. 'Yep. Sure.'

Morgan sighed. 'Madrona, do you want to hear about Mag Mell and the Fey or don't you?'

'Sure.' I nodded, trying to bring myself under control. 'Speak on, Snail Boy.'

The throbbing muscle in his cheek gave away his irritation. 'I'm so very refreshed and challenged by your unique point of view.' He glowered. 'As I was saying, Mag Mell is not a separate world. It's more like an extension of this one, or vice-versa. Both demesnes are intrinsically linked, not that the humans know that. What happens here affects Mag Mell. Fey were regularly dispatched here to ensure that the environmental damage caused by the onslaught of technological advances was not too great. We would minimise the effects, which would minimise the mirrored damage in Mag Mell, which in turn would keep the human demesne equally healthy. It's a symbiotic relationship.'

'It sounds,' I said, recovering from my giggling fit and beginning to appreciate that this was actually rather serious, 'that all this was in the past. We don't do anything now for the environment?'

His answer was flat. 'Very little. Not because we don't want to but because we can't. When the border crossings closed, we were effectively shut off from our own power source. There is next to nothing we can do, even as Fey, without the invisible ties and links to Mag Mell. Without our interference, and without Mag Mell's continued support, the damage here is getting worse.' A grim note entered his voice. 'No doubt the reverse is true in Mag Mell. We cannot tell because we have been unable to communicate with anyone there for a decade.'

I examined his sober expression. 'What happens if the borders never re-open?' I asked softly.

Morgan raised his shoulders. 'We don't really know. The humans may discover ways to maintain a better balance on their own. They are trying to improve their ways. Or our lack of ability to interfere may lead to total catastrophe. We can't really tell – no one knows what the future will bring. Many of us still try to mitigate the effects of the border closures and influence the humans to look after their world.'

'I'm guessing,' I said drily, 'you're referring to people like yourself.'

He inclined his head although there was nothing self-congratulatory about the look on his face. 'There are other Fey who choose to live their lives selfishly, uncaring about what might happen next.'

I eyed his expression. 'You mean Fey like me, don't you?'

'I was referring more to those like Rubus. But,' he said heavily, 'yes. Fey like you.'

'Because I work for Rubus.'

Morgan gave me a brief nod. 'You do.'

I mulled this over. There was more to Morgan's disgust for me than simply hatred of my drug-dealing ways, even though I was beginning to think that they were bad enough. Credit where credit was due – he certainly possessed an admirable streak of selflessness. 'We still have access to magic, though. I altered time.' I pointed at my large body. 'I look like this.'

'Fripperies only,' he told me. 'Those sort of tricks aren't meaningful. Not in any earth-shattering way. Not unless you over-use them anyway.' His eyes took on a distant sheen. 'We used to be able to encourage growth, affect the seasons when necessary and dampen down pollution. That's the reason why most of us are located here, in the centre of the country, rather than in the south in London. Not that it makes much difference any more. Now all we can do is a few parlour tricks while pining physically and emotionally for home.'

I swallowed. Any taunts or irritation had gone from his voice; all that remained was a deep melancholy. No wonder I'd turned to dealing drugs.

'In any case,' Morgan continued, 'that is why it is such a surprise that you have been able to keep the glamour for so long. Without setting foot in Mag Mell, our abilities are severely hampered and much diminished. If I hadn't seen you maintain this body shape for so long, I wouldn't have believed it.'

'Under normal circumstances,' I asked, 'how would I change back?'

'You would wish it and it would be done.'

I nodded slowly. 'I wish to be myself again,' I declared loudly. Nothing happened: no earthquake, no crack of thunder. When I looked down at my hands and heavy thighs, I was still an overly large man. I grimaced. 'This was fun to begin with but I'm getting tired of it now.'

'Viburna was probably right. The rowan poisoning is why you've stayed that way for so long. It's the only thing that makes any sense.'

'But,' I pointed out, 'you said you'd given me nux while I was out. I should be alright now.' I was aware that my voice was rising. 'But I'm not alright!'

'Stop panicking,' he said briskly. 'You'll be fine. You just need a reminder of who you are.'

'I've got bloody amnesia!' I yelled. 'I don't remember who I am!'

He smiled, which did little to make me feel better. 'Not that sort of reminder.' He stood up and walked towards me, beckoning me to my feet. 'I have a plan,' he said.

'A good plan? A plan that will work? A plan that I will enjoy?'

His smile turned rueful. 'You'll probably enjoy it more than I will.'

I frowned. 'What's that supposed to mean?'

'Come closer,' he instructed.

I gave him a wary look. 'Why?'

His lips curved upwards. 'You'll have to trust me,' he murmured.

I was tempted to turn tail and run; instead I fought against my better instincts and did as he asked. It was gratifying to realise that in this body, at least, I towered over him. It was also rather pleasant to be close enough to inhale Morgan's scent. 'Mmm,' I sniffed. 'Did you bathe just for me?'

He gave a mild snort. 'You certainly didn't do it for me. You smell like a trucker who's been on the road for a month.'

'Right now,' I retorted, 'I *am* that trucker.'

He smirked. 'Close your eyes. This will go easier on both of us if we're not looking at each other.'

More suspicion flared up inside me. 'What...?'

'Just do it, Madrona,' he said. 'For once, just do as I ask.'

Wondering what the hell he was up to, I closed my eyes. I was still half-expecting to receive a no-holds-barred smack in the mouth. Instead it was something else entirely which brushed against my lips.

I leapt backwards, opening my eyes and staring at him. 'What are you doing?'

Morgan sighed. 'I should have thought that was obvious.'

'Is that why our relationship didn't work out?' I demanded. 'Because you're actually gay?'

'If I were gay, Maddy, then believe me when I say you wouldn't be my type.'

I put my hands on my large hips. 'And why not?'

'Stop complaining. This is far harder for me than it is for you.'

'You kissed me!'

He gazed at me patiently. 'Yes. I'm attempting to remind you of who you are. I'm telling your body that you're not this man but that you're Maddy. A heterosexual female faery.'

'I know that's what I am!'

He smiled. 'Yes. But right now your body and your magic believe otherwise. If I'm right, this won't take long. Just let me kiss you properly and we'll be done with it.'

My eyes narrowed. 'You're assuming that my body will respond to yours, that the feeling of your lips against mine will make me feel like a woman again because of your superior, awe-inspiring masculinity.'

'It's not an assumption. It's not arrogance either.' His gaze remained on me. 'It's simply fact. Regardless of anything else between us, I make your toes curl.' For the first time since I'd met him, his grin had an edge of wickedness. 'My kiss makes you wet.'

'Not in this body,' I retorted, though I couldn't deny the zippy turmoil in the pit of my belly. 'But fine. Do your worst.'

'No, Maddy. I'll do my best.' He stepped up to me. This time both of us closed our eyes – and I kept mine closed. Somehow it seemed safer that way.

To begin with, Morgan's lips were light, barely pressing against mine. I couldn't help wondering what this was like for him, snogging another man who was both a foot taller and a foot wider than he was. The strangeness of the situation meant that it took me a few moments to relax. As soon as I did, however, Morgan must have felt it because he increased the pressure of his mouth while his hands moved to my shoulders, gripping me lightly. My lips parted.

The moment I could taste him properly, all rational thought flew away. His heady masculinity absorbed me, his stubble brushing against mine. I could feel myself involuntarily pressing my body against his. Before I begin to wonder how uncomfortable this would be if my current body were to get an erection, the air around us shifted. It would have been all but imperceptible except for the change in our heights. Suddenly, it was Morgan's whose head was curved down towards mine rather than the other way around.

I inhaled deeply, opening my eyes to see his emerald irises gazing into mine with satisfaction.

'It worked,' he said. 'It didn't even take very much.'

'We should keep going,' I breathed. 'Just to be sure.' I reached up, coiled my arms around his neck and raised myself up onto my tiptoes. I was going to enjoy this.

Morgan reached up, unhooked my arms and stepped back. 'I don't think so.'

His rejection was akin to having a bucket of icy water flung over me. As if drenched, I sprang back and rubbed my arms. 'Yeah. You're right.' Gasbudlikins. Without looking at him directly, I returned to the chair, sat down and busied myself examining my body. Everything seemed to be in order. Until I looked in a mirror, I couldn't be entirely sure but it seemed that all my limbs were as they should be. I pulled at the neck of my T-shirt so I could glance down at the bare skin of my torso. My breasts were back. Hello.

'I never thought I'd be glad to see my bra,' I muttered. I reached down for my waistband to check my other parts.

Morgan coughed pointedly. 'Perhaps you should do that later,' he said. 'When you have some privacy.'

I shrugged, still avoiding looking at him. 'I don't mind.'

His answer was quiet. 'I do. Everything appears to be in order. I wouldn't worry.' He nodded to himself, all business-like. 'My plan worked.'

'I started out with nothing,' I whispered, 'and I still have most of it left.' Almost unconsciously I brought my fingers to my lips. Then I shook myself. Wakey wakey, Maddy.

'Right,' I said. 'Come on then. What are your three questions? What do you *really* want to know?' The faster I did what I had promised, the faster I could get out of here with some scraps of dignity left. I looked up, my gaze finally meeting his. His expression was inscrutable.

'I will know if you lie,' Morgan said.

I pursed my lips. 'This is where our relationship goes wrong. You immediately assume the worst. Lying hadn't even crossed my mind. I have no reason to lie to you.'

'You don't know what I'm going to ask.'

Unless it was about Julie – which would be impossible because he couldn't know anything about her – then I was a completely open book. Mr I'm-Too-Good-To-Be-Turned-On-By-That-Evil-Bitch-Even-When-She's-Panting-For-Me was entirely too untrusting.

'Go on then,' I said. 'Ask. I won't lie.'

Morgan took a deep breath. 'When you woke up with amnesia, explain to me exactly what you saw and exactly what happened.'

Easy. 'I opened my eyes and there was a dead body next to me. I knew he was dead because his head had been cut off,' I added helpfully.

Morgan's expression remained unreadable. 'Was he Fey?'

I tried to think. Had he had green eyes? It had been night time and I wasn't even sure his eyes had any colour to them. 'Uh, I don't know. I honestly don't. He could have been.' I offered a helpless shrug. 'His skin was kinda green. Anyway, I worked out I was on a golf course. I also found a sword underneath the dead guy's body. I touched the blade and...' I held up my now-healed finger. There was no trace of my earlier wound. 'Well, you know what happened with that.'

'Describe the sword.'

I bit my lip. 'It was long. With a pointy bit at the end.'

Morgan rolled his eyes. 'Really? Is that the best you can do?'

'I'm not a sword expert. Or at least I don't remember being a sword expert. It was just a damned sword. What does it matter?'

He stood up and walked to a bookshelf, glancing along the row of spines before pulling a leather-bound book out and flicking through the pages. Then he walked over to me and pointed. 'Did it look like this?'

I glanced at the page. There was a photo of a sword displayed in black and white on the left-hand side. 'Yes. That looks like a sword. The weapon I found looked like a sword.'

'You're being deliberately obstructive,' he snapped.

'I'm really not. Pointy weapons obviously aren't one of the things in my vast repertoire of knowledge. I was also,' I reminded him, 'somewhat traumatised and concussed.' Concussed anyway. Morgan shook his head in annoyance. 'Does it really matter?' I asked.

'This is an example of a sword belonging to a bogle,' he said, as if that explained everything.

'And a bogle is...?'

'Technically, a faerie. They're trapped here just like we are but they're not part of the truce. Neither do they tend to have much power, or to care what Fey like us do. They're bad-tempered but not typically violent.'

'Except they carry around swords,' I said, pointing out the obvious flaw in his last statement.

'Bogles use their swords to destroy things, not people.'

'Well, that didn't work out very well for this bogle,' I muttered. 'Anyway, this is good news. If bogles aren't part of the truce, it doesn't matter whether it was me that killed him or not.'

Morgan gave me a long look. 'It doesn't matter if you murdered a living being?' he enquired, ice dripping from every word.

I grimaced. That came out wrong. 'What I meant was, even if I did cut off his head – and I'm not saying that I did – I've not broken the truce. And if I did behead him, it was probably in self-defence.' I was aware that I was digging myself into a deep hole here but I couldn't help it; my mouth had a mind of its own

Morgan turned away and returned the book to its original position. 'The truce doesn't work like that. As Fey, we can't hurt another. But bogles and other creatures are lesser faeries. They're not included in the truce.'

'What?' I screeched. 'How the gasbudlikins is that fair?'

Morgan ticked off his fingers. 'They have a lot less power than we do. Many of them are native to this demesne, not to Mag Mell. Typically, they're not violent.' He looked at me. 'And no one ever said life was fair.'

'I think not being able to defend myself is stretching that concept to extremes.'

He shrugged. 'You walked away. The bogle didn't.'

'If you're going to keep judging me, I'm going to feel less inclined to tell you everything I remember.'

'You promised,' he said, without a trace of emotion. 'Carry on.'

I gritted my teeth. At least Morgan's manner was reminding me that I disliked him. Intensely. As dispassionately as possible, I described the rest of that night, leaving out no detail. If he wanted to know everything, he could know everything. I failed to see how I could have acted any differently and still survived.

'The three men who attacked you,' he said once I'd finished. 'What exactly did they look like?'

'Ugly.'

'Be specific,' Morgan instructed. 'It could be important.'

I shrugged. 'Pull the CCTV from my Travotel if you really want to know. They went there to try and find me as well.'

Morgan stiffened. 'Which Travotel?'

'The one where Mike Timmons is manager. Or Begonius, if you want his real name.' At Morgan's look, I added, 'And no, I didn't know there was a Fey in that hotel before I stayed there. It was a coincidence. Timmons had nothing to do with the McNasties either. I checked. After I persuaded him to talk, he told me they were Redcaps. So,' I said gloomily, 'it's not just the odd bogle that wants my blood. I suppose you're going to tell me that I'm not allowed to kill Redcaps either.' I rolled my eyes in disgust.

For a moment, there was silence. 'Is he alright?'

'Who? Timmons?' I glared at Morgan. 'Are you asking because you think I cut off his head too?'

'I'm just—'

'He's fine,' I interrupted. I was beginning to get mightily tired of all this. 'Are we done?'

'I'm simply trying to ascertain exactly who attacked you. It might be important.'

'*Might* be? I'm glad you're taking such an interest in my welfare.'

'You forget, Madrona,' Morgan said, his voice dangerously soft. 'We're not friends or allies.'

'Or lovers,' I added.

'Or lovers,' he repeated. 'I am interested in what happened to you because it might have repercussions for the rest of us.'

I shouldn't have been surprised or disappointed. He wasn't being rude; to him, I was simply insignificant. I sighed, stretching my arms out behind my head. As I did so, the fabric of my T-shirt grew taut. Morgan's eyes drifted unwillingly down to my breasts. 'Hey,' I said softly, 'my face is up here.'

He jerked his gaze back up again. 'I apologise,' he said almost instantly. 'That was unbelievably rude.'

It was; it was also unbelievably gratifying. Maybe he wasn't quite as cold to my continued existence as he wanted to pretend. 'Forget about it,' I said. Because I wouldn't. I reached into my pocket and tossed the Rolex watch to him. 'If you're so intent on tracking those arsebadgers down, maybe that will help. I took it from one of the attackers.'

Morgan turned it over in his hands. 'This is expensive,' he said.

'All three of the Redcaps were carrying a lot of money. Whatever they are and whoever they work for, they're paid well.' At least that was something. I didn't want to think of myself as a cheap date.

'May I keep this?'

I inclined my head. I'd been going to pawn it for more cash but I didn't actually need the money. Handing it over without a grumble made me appear a better person than I was. 'Go ahead. What's your next question?'

Morgan pocketed the watch and glanced at me. His green eyes didn't flicker. 'Have you been in contact with Rubus since the golf course?'

'No.'

'Phone call? Text? Email?'

'I took the word "contact" to encompass all of those,' I said drily. 'I don't even know what Rubus looks like.'

There was a gleam of satisfaction in Morgan's eyes. 'Good.'

'Last question,' I said. I checked the clock on the wall. 'And just as well. I've got a job to go to.'

His brow furrowed at that. 'If your life is in danger, you are welcome to stay here.'

I snorted. 'And end up stabbed in the back by you or your cronies? I'll be fine. Thanks for the concern. Ask your last question, Morgan.'

'The truce—'

'Yeah, yeah.' I stood up and made a show of brushing away invisible dust from my clothes. 'Ask now or forever hold your peace.'

He stayed silent for so long that I thought he wasn't going to say anything at all. Then he inhaled deeply and looked at me. 'When I kissed you just now, how did it make you feel?'

I met his gaze. 'Like I couldn't imagine life without you,' I answered simply. His expression shuttered. 'Now may I go?'

'You may,' he bit out.

I curtsied and headed for the door, walking out without a backward glance.

CHAPTER FIFTEEN

The sun was already setting when I walked out of the Metropolitan. It was fortunate that I was parked in the mall car park nearby; I didn't have any time to waste if I was going to get back to the television studio to pick up Julie. I no longer had pedestrians scattering in my wake either – yep, I obviously looked like myself again.

I was almost at the front entrance to the mall when I felt something – or rather someone – brush against my elbow. I whirled round, my stomach tightening in anticipation when I saw who it was. Standing there, with her head tilted and a wary expression on her face, was the statuesque Amazon woman. I checked her eyes. They were green all right.

'Hi,' I said.

Her face tightened. 'Hi? Is that all you have to say to me?'

I took a step backwards, scanning her up and down. I was as certain as I could be that she wasn't carrying any weapons. Judging from the size of her, however, her body was a lethal weapon all on its own. 'What would you like me to say?' I asked carefully.

She put her hands on her hips and glared. 'How about an explanation about where you've been for the last four days? Maybe you'd like to add why you ran away from me when I spotted you in the street. Maybe you'd like to include what the hell you've been doing with Morganus. You came out of his bar! What were you doing there? Did you have anything to do with the large man they dragged in there? He collapsed in the street after yelling to half the damn world that he was a faery. He was nothing like any faery I've ever seen. Is he still alive?' She stared at me. Then she leaned forward and drew me into a hug. 'I've been worried sick, Mads. Rubus is acting weird. You're acting weird. Just what is going on?'

Listening to her was like listening to a steam train. She barely stopped for breath. I could only focus on one thing at a time. Using her last words, I licked my lips and fished tentatively for information. 'You work for Rubus,' I said.

She blew out air. 'That's no reason not to talk to me, Mads! You work for Rubus too!'

I examined her face. There was no doubt that she was severely pissed off but as far as I could tell, she was genuinely worried about me. 'We're friends?'

Her eyes widened with sudden dread. 'Oh no, Mads. What have you done?' she whispered.

I tutted. 'It's not like that. Well, I don't think so. I'm afraid I don't know who you are.'

Her expression altered. 'What the fuck?'

'I've got amnesia. I don't know who you are but I don't know who I am, either. Not beyond what other people have told me. I woke up on Friday night in the middle of a golf course with a bunch of ugly guys trying to kill me. Redcaps. Or so I'm told.'

Her mouth dropped open.

'Perhaps if you told me your name, it might jog my memory,' I said.

She continued to stare at me.

'Or not.' I shrugged. 'And I'm sorry I ran away from you the other day. I thought you were about to pull out a gun and shoot me. I've been having that kind of week.'

She didn't twitch. She didn't even bloody blink.

'Were you planning to kill me?'

Nothing. I raised a hand and waved it in front of her face.

'Hello?'

Her tongue darted out and wet her lips. 'Sorry, Mads,' she whispered. 'I've got to go.' She turned round and started to walk away.

'You didn't tell me your name!' I yelled after her.

She didn't respond. I debated whether to go after her. She obviously knew things that even Morgan couldn't tell me but if I didn't get to Julie's car in the next five minutes, I wasn't going to make the pick-up in time. The actress might seem harmless but she was still a vampire. It was probably a good idea if I kept my promise and fulfilled the job I'd been hired to do. I grimaced: evil villain or angelic superhero or simply amnesiac numbskull – there was no excuse for tardiness.

~

I made it with about twenty seconds to spare. Unclipping my seatbelt, I turned up the radio full blast and leaned back in the driver's seat to relax just as Julie waltzed out of the gates and waved. Abandoning my all-too-brief moment of meditation, I clambered out to meet her.

'Hey!' She sauntered over, flipping a pretty scarf emblazoned with bright colours round her neck. 'Have you been waiting long?'

'Ages,' I said. 'I didn't want to be late on my first day so I made sure to get here with plenty of time to spare.'

'Sorry to keep you waiting, darling.'

I waved a hand airily. 'No problem. It's what I'm here for.' I dangled the keys in front of her. 'Do you want to drive or shall I?'

'I will. I thought we might take a detour on the way home. A friend of mine is having a little soirée. I promised I'd drop in.'

I frowned at her. 'You didn't mention it this morning.'

'I only heard about it at lunch.' Julie peered at me. 'Do you mind?'

'No. But if I'd known I could have scoped out the place beforehand.' I rather liked the idea of marching around someone's house so I could check out the exits. Maybe I should invest in an earpiece and a pair of sunglasses to look the part.

Julie just laughed. 'Honestly, the likelihood of anything happening is next to nothing. We're talking scones and cups of tea, not vampire hunters with stakes.'

Hmm. It struck me that if you wanted to bring down a supposedly all-powerful un-dead being, you'd want to do it when she least expected it. Still, I supposed a party would pass the time of day.

'How's your day been, Madrona? Anything exciting happen?'

Erm... 'I'm sure your day was more interesting than mine.'

Something in my tone of voice must have given me away because Julie shot me a sharp, knowing look. 'I doubt that. Have you remembered anything yet?'

I sighed. 'No. My mind is still drawing a total blank.'

She patted my hand. 'Not to worry. You'll remember something sooner or later. I could always smack you several times on the head and try to beat it out of you.'

'Tempting. Maybe another time.'

She grinned. 'Then let's hit the road.' She turned to the car, her glance snagging on the back. 'Did you have an accident?'

I winced. 'It's a long story.'

She offered me a bemused look. 'I thought I was the only one who regularly had fender-benders. We have even more in common than I'd realised.'

Somehow I doubted that.

~

It was no wonder that she often had car accidents; Julie drove even more haphazardly than she had in the morning. There were several occasions when I was sure we were going to collide with other cars. Even the red car arsebadger this morning would have been no match for her.

Clinging onto any solid surface I could find I cringed, squeaking every time we had a near miss. 'Julie,' I said in a strained voice, 'perhaps you ought to slow down.'

She swerved round a bus. 'Why? Life is much more fun in the fast lane!'

I was beginning to get an inkling as to why Bodyguard Mark had been so humourless: Julie's driving had probably knocked all of the fun out of him. When she reached into her pocket, pulled out her pill bottle and swallowed a couple of Valium before accelerating even harder, I actually gulped.

'Won't your fans think less of you if they know you're a road demon in disguise?'

'They love it! I write blogs about my exploits. It's one of the things I'm known for.'

The brake lights on the car ahead flashed red. Julie only just slammed on her own brakes in the nick of time. 'I'm going to need hazard pay,' I muttered.

Another car drew up on our left, also slowing as it met the

traffic. As soon as it was level, the person inside honked their horn. The window scrolled down and a head popped out. 'Stacey! I love you!'

Julie opened the passenger window using a button on her side. 'I love you too!' she shrieked. Then the traffic moved and we pulled away.

'You're nuts,' I said, shaking my head like a disapproving schoolteacher.

'The truth is that I drive like this so that any hunters following me are unlikely to keep up.' She frowned. 'Although they always manage to find me sooner or later.'

'Your personalised number plate might have something to do with that,' I grunted. 'Along with the fact that you don't hide your identity and people scream at you whenever they spot you.'

'Those people also help keep me safe,' she reminded me. 'Even if the hunters catch up to me, they wouldn't dare hurt me when my fans are around.'

'So you keep saying.' Judging by the rabid look on the driver's face when he'd stuck his head out of the window, I wasn't quite so sure.

Fortunately, once we pulled off the motorway onto a quiet country lane on the outskirts of the city, Julie did slow down somewhat. We continued for another couple of miles, passing a few fields of sheep, until she veered off into a driveway leading up to a grand old country house.

'Am I supposed to come in with you?' I enquired when thankfully we parked and I was able to escape the confines of the car. 'Or should I loiter out here and look dangerous?'

'We're perfectly safe, darling. You're free to come inside with me or freeze your tits off out here. It's your choice.'

She had a point; now the sun was down, it was rather cold. 'I'll come in,' I murmured.

Julie beamed. 'Excellent. I can't wait to show you off!' She strolled away, pushing open the door and entering without so much as a knock.

I followed her indoors, marvelling at the impressive interior. It might have been an old building but it oozed charm. Dried lavender lay artfully in pretty bowls on the sideboard and the rustic oak floorboards gave the place a homely feel. Whoever Julie's friends were, I liked them already.

At the end of the hallway, hanging over a small table, was a large painting. The scene it depicted wasn't anything extraordinary: a small waterfall cascading down a rocky hill, with verdant hills in the background. It spoke of little more than a fantastical pastoral imagination. Glancing at it, however, made my chest ache strangely. I rubbed at the spot. It was less painful and more ... hollow.

'Mag Mell,' I whispered. Finally I understood the sense of loss and abject homesickness that I'd been told about. I examined the painting more closely. Had a Fey painted this? Was it the home I couldn't remember?

'Madrona?' Julie asked. 'Is everything alright?'

I pressed the base of my palms to my temples. 'I might be remembering something. The painting...' My voice trailed off as my hungry eyes took in every detail.

'You know this place?' She looked at the painting.

'I think it's the atmosphere of the painting rather than the painting itself,' I murmured.

She smiled. 'It makes sense. You're a creative at heart. Now come on. Let's party!'

My brow creased as I dragged my eyes away from the picture. 'I thought you said this was tea and scones?'

Her mouth curved into a wicked smile. 'I did, didn't I? There might be scones. And Alice knows how to make the best Long

Island Iced Tea this side of the Atlantic.' She turned to her right and opened a door. 'Cooeeee! It's me!'

There was a loud, delighted chorus of welcomes. I walked in, remaining close to Julie's heels. You never knew when danger was around.

Ten minutes later, it was clear that the only danger was that I might slit my wrists through boredom. Julie's friends were nice enough but you can only listen to tales from the frontline of make-up artistry and waxing before your eyes start to glaze over. Spotting a crumpled packet of cigarettes, I begged one from the overly-coiffured man they belonged to and headed outside. The male body I'd glamoured myself into might not have enjoyed his morning cigarette but perhaps this one would be better. It couldn't be any worse than what was back inside. Yeah, I thought morosely, it looked like I was as much of a bitch as Morgan had suggested I was.

I lit the cigarette and inhaled. The taste wasn't any nicer and the same light-headed sensation overtook me but I was determined to finish it, if only to delay having to go inside. The last thing I wanted was to open my big mouth and offend someone. Normally I wouldn't care but I didn't want to lumber Julie with fallout from my lack of thoughtfulness.

I gazed at the trees then, deciding that the view wasn't providing me with any more entertainment than Julie and her friends, ambled round to the back of her car. Perhaps I could kick the dents out and save a trip to the garage.

I crouched down, attempting to pull on the bumper and straighten it out. The metal sighed but didn't look any different. Cursing, I hunkered down further in a bid to curl my fingertips underneath and gain a better purchase. It was that action that allowed me to spot the slim grey box attached to the under-carriage.

There was nothing in my pathetic brain that suggested I knew much about cars but I was pretty certain that the box did not belong there. Scooting my body underneath, and with my heart in my mouth, I examined it more closely.

There were no visible wires and no blinking lights or give-away countdown timers. It was probably too small to be a bomb; when I pulled it gently away from the car, it fitted too neatly into the palm of my hand.

Pushing myself out, I used my fingernails to dig into the hard plastic edge and open the box. Inside was a small, neat green motherboard. With a sinking sensation, I realised what it was: Julie's vampire hunters kept on finding her not because of her celebrity status or her flashy car; their methods were far more prosaic – and far more sinister.

The sensible thing would be to attach the device to one of the other cars parked nearby. It would fool the hunters into tracking someone else. Unfortunately it might also mean that someone else ended up getting hurt. I wasn't completely heartless.

The only positive thing right now was that she'd assured me the hunters avoided attacking her in public. There were far too many people inside for them to make a move here, regardless of how isolated the house was. I comforted myself with that thought, but all the same I raised my eyes to the dark horizon and scanned it. Fear trickled uneasily down my spine. Unwilling to ignore my gut instincts, I centred myself and focused. There had to be something useful in these Fey skills to help me out. Concentrate, Madrona.

I stiffened. There. Over to my left and hiding amongst the trees, someone was watching. I closed my eyes and listened. My hearing sharpened, honing in on the precise area. When I blocked out everything else, it was a wonder that I'd not noticed the watcher before. Even from this distance, I could hear a regular heartbeat, unworried by stress or adrenaline. I could also hear the waiting arsebadger's breath. Someone was out there. And there were no prizes for guessing what – or rather who – they wanted.

CHAPTER SIXTEEN

'She's obviously very strange. Bring Mark back. I don't like the way that girl looks at me.'

I whirled into the room, ignoring the fact that Julie's friends had been gossiping about me – and not in a good way – and stalked over to where she was sitting. 'We're leaving,' I growled. 'Now.'

Julie blinked. 'But darling, we've barely just arrived.'

'I told you she was strange,' someone whispered behind my back. 'Who'd want a bodyguard like her? She could use some more muscles. Or brain cells, at the very least.'

I half-turned my head. 'Your gene pool could use some more chlorine,' I snapped.

The whisperer jerked. He obviously hadn't expected me to overhear him. Frankly, that just made it worse; if he were going to insult me, then he damned well better have the balls to do it to my face.

Julie rose to her feet, her mouth twitching. She was clearly more amused than offended that I'd insulted her friend. 'Mads, darling. Have a cocktail. Everything's fine.'

I met her eyes. 'It is not fine,' I told her, trying to convey what was going on through facial expressions .

Some of my alarm sank in. Her face paled. 'There are lots of people here.'

'Maybe they've changed tactics since the last failed attempt,' I said.

Julie swallowed.

'What's going on?' Alice, the hostess, also stood up. 'Julie, is there a problem? Should we call the police?'

I glanced at her. 'Julie has some rather ... over-eager fans,' I said. 'Stalkers, if you will. One of them is outside. The police are aware of his existence but won't make a move until he has broken the law. I'd prefer it if he never got that chance. It's safest for Julie – and for the rest of you – if we leave right now.'

At my words and my grim tone it wasn't just Julie who looked frightened. At least Alice managed to keep it together. 'Of course,' she nodded. 'Is there anything we can do?'

'Just stay here and don't go outside until we're well away from the house. He'll follow us, not you. As long as you keep out of sight you'll be okay.' I took Julie's arm and propelled her out of the room.

'You're an excellent liar,' she murmured in my ear as we marched back out of the house. 'Is it a hunter who's waiting outside?'

'In the trees over to the right,' I answered. 'But don't look, and walk normally. We don't want him to know he's been rumbled.' Whoever the hunter was, he'd know I'd found the GPS tracker but he had no reason to worry that I'd rumbled him.

Julie pasted a smile on her face. 'No one followed us here,' she muttered with gritted teeth. 'No cars were behind us and this evening was organised at the last minute.'

I faked a grin in return. 'Your car has a tracking device on it.'

I heard a sharp intake of breath. 'Then shouldn't we take someone else's car?'

I shook my head. 'No. I have a plan.'

'A good plan?'

I grimaced slightly and didn't answer, simply opened the passenger door and beckoned her in. 'Buckle up,' I instructed. 'I'm driving.'

For once, she didn't argue. It was just as well; somehow I didn't think that Long Island Iced Tea and a car chase were natural pairings.

I headed to the driver's side, started up the engine and withdrew the tracker from where I'd left it. I tossed it into her lap. 'Hang on to that for now.'

She stared at it as if it were a snake. 'Shouldn't we throw it out of the window?'

'Not yet,' I cautioned. I glanced at her. 'I'm not sure if what I'm doing is the right thing, Julie. But you've been looking over your shoulder for too long. We need to turn the tables on these hunter bastards so that you're safe once and for all.'

'How are we going to do that?'

'Right now,' I said, accelerating away from the house, 'they don't seem to think you're dangerous, regardless of your vampire ethnicity. We need to change that. We need to make them so afraid of you that they won't dare to come near you again.'

'I'm not sure I like the sound of that, darling.'

I braked, stopped the car and looked at her. 'If you want, I can take you back to the safety of your house right now. The hunters won't be able to enter and you'll be fine. Until the next time. Or the time after that. Or whenever. You said yourself that it's only a matter of time before they manage to get hold of you. They got damned close the other night.' I gazed at her. 'We can do that, if that's what you prefer. At the end of the day, you're the boss.' I licked my lips. 'Or we can change things and take control. We can stop them from bothering you ever again.'

Her eyes widened fractionally. 'How on earth are you going to manage that?'

My answer was quiet but determined. 'By making them so afraid of you, that they'd rather sell their own mothers to the bogeyman than come within a hundred miles of you.'

'But I'm not scary, Madrona. I'm a cuddly vampire, not an evil vampire.'

I held her gaze and bared my teeth. 'But I'm not cuddly.'

Julie shivered. Actually shivered. Then she nodded, albeit with some reluctance.

I started the car again. Excellent. If ever there was a time to really be an evil bitch, then this was it.

~

The last place I wanted to end up was back on the busy motorway. These quiet country roads were just what any self-respecting villainous mastermind would wish for. Therefore, instead of continuing straight, I turned right into an even narrower road. When the hedgerows on either side started to close in and the road tapered into a single-lane track, I pumped the air with my fist. This was perfect. I flicked the headlights onto full beam until I found what I wanted then I stopped the car and reversed a hundred feet or so.

Julie placed a manicured hand on my arm. 'Is this really the best spot?'

I grinned at her. 'Hell, yes.' I killed the headlights and turned off the engine. 'Take the GPS tracker. Just up there, there's a gate leading into a field. You go up and wait there. I'll deal with everything else from here.'

'It doesn't seem entirely sane,' she said, doubt colouring her voice.

'I'm the Madhatter, Julie. I don't do sane.' I reached across and opened her passenger door. 'Now go.'

She skittered off, heading for the gate I'd pointed to. She'd be off the road and safe while I dealt with whatever was to come. I watched her slim figure until it was swallowed up by the darkness, then I got out of the car and selected my own perfect spot to wait.

Strategically speaking, I wasn't sure I could have done better. Julie's car was waiting at the apex of a curve in the road. Without its lights on, anyone coming up behind wouldn't know it was there until it was too late. As they'd already be following the GPS tracker, which was a short distance ahead with Julie, they would be driving cautiously but still moving. They'd crash into the car and I could take full advantage of their resulting surprise and distress. Honestly, it was a wonder that I'd not yet been snapped up by the human security services or the Fey equivalent of SWAT. Even with crippling amnesia, I was clearly a natural at this sort of thing.

Choosing to wait behind the car rather than in front of it, where I might get hurt by flying metal and glass, I pressed myself into the hedge. Then, with the same focused energy that I'd utilised back at the house, I listened. A smirk of triumph flashed across my face when I heard the distant engine.

I didn't have long to wait. Whoever was after Julie was hot on our tail and gaining speed. The engine noise grew louder and louder. I held my breath and hunkered down. A motorbike passed me. Collision in four. Three. Two— The bike came to a screeching halt.

What in gasbudlikins had just happened? How had they known the car was there? My mouth twisted. I didn't have time to fret over it now, though; for Julie's sake, I had to act.

I sprang away from the hedge and sprinted forward, just as

the biker disembarked. I tightened my muscles, praying that I'd recovered enough to alter time again. When the very molecules in the air seemed to hum, I knew I'd achieved what I needed. All the same, I didn't slow down. While the biker remained frozen, trapped by the time change that didn't affect me, I ran up the road, arms outstretched. I would do whatever was needed.

The gap closed. He was a safety-conscious vampire hunter and wore a helmet so unfortunately his head was off limits. I aimed for his chest instead, more than prepared to wind him before ripping out his lungs entirely. My hand thrust out – and then the biker lashed out, caught me on the shoulder and flipped me hard onto my back. My spine bounced off the road and agony shot through my limbs.

The biker loomed over me. Perhaps if I truly were a superhero, I'd have been able to get up but the pain was too much. No matter how hard I willed it, I couldn't make myself move quickly enough. There was only time for one thing.

'Run, Julie!' I screamed. Then I braced myself for the end. Make it fast.

The biker flipped up his visor. Familiar green eyes blinked down at me. 'Who's Julie?' Morgan enquired. 'And what on earth are you doing?'

My mouth dropped open. All I could do was stare. Morgan tutted loudly and presented his hand. I reached up, allowing him to help me up. As soon as I back on my feet, however, I shook off the pain and grabbed the lapels of his leather jacket. It was almost impossible to believe that he was involved in all this but I wasn't about to deny the evidence in front of my eyes.

'You,' I hissed. 'All along it's been you? Impressive. That's one way to avoid detection. Blame me for being the bad guy when all along you're the one who's really the face of evil.' I tightened my grip. 'Just tell me why, Morgan. Why do you want her so badly?'

He watched me with a blandly curious expression. 'I really don't have the faintest idea what you're on about, Maddy. What fascinates me is that you think you can best me in a fight.' He glanced down my hands, which were still gripping his jacket to the point where my knuckles had turned white.

'I'm very motivated,' I snarled.

He pursed his lips. 'Go on then. Give it a shot.'

A deep growl rose in my chest. I swung at him, throwing as much force behind the shot as I could. Unfortunately he ducked, and my momentum almost made me fall over.

'Don't bother trying to mess with time again,' Morgan added, looking amused. 'It won't affect me. And as I'm certain I've already mentioned, it's forbidden.'

I launched myself at him. I'd show him forbidden. Yet again, however, he sidestepped. When I whirled back round to face him, he was examining his fingernails as if he were bored. 'Have you had enough yet?'

I shook my head vehemently. 'I'm not going to let you take Julie. I don't care who you are or what it takes to stop you. It's not going to happen, Morgan.'

Morgan dropped his hands and his expression changed. 'I don't know who Julie is, although I assume from the number plate that it's her half-destroyed car you're driving. Is she your new employer?' He frowned. 'If she's not Fey, I don't care who she is. I'm not interested in her, Maddy. I'm tracking *you*.'

'You stuck that thing underneath her car in order to follow me? Bullshit.'

Morgan's head tilted. 'What thing? I tracked you from this.' He reached forward and his fingers brushed my shoulder. I flinched, staring as he picked out a little white thread between his forefinger and thumb. 'Dandelion fluff,' he said. 'It travels by its own nature. All it takes for a Fey to find it is the original plant, the mother, so to speak. She told me where you were. I placed the fluff on you when you were unconscious in my pub. If that annoys you,' he shrugged, 'I don't care.'

I stared at him. 'You talk to weeds?'

He smiled faintly. 'It's less of a conversation and more a – sensation. It wouldn't occur to most Fey to use the dandelion in this manner.'

'You're trying to tell me that you're not "most" Fey.' I snorted.

'That's right.' He kept his eyes on me. 'I'm not.'

'Why?' I bit out, still disbelieving his motives. 'Why follow me?'

'Rubus.' A muscle clenched in Morgan's jaw. 'He's going to be missing his favourite minion. Sooner or later he'll come looking for you to bring you back into the fold. I have decided I don't want that to happen.'

'Why not?'

Morgan's gaze shifted slightly. 'There is enough pixie dust on the streets as it is. We don't need you working for him again and spreading even more about.'

Interesting. I was sure that Morgan was lying about that last part; everything else seemed to be true. He wasn't interested in Julie at all. Gasbudlikins. That meant... I cursed and started to run.

'Julie!' I yelled. 'It's alright! Come back!' I sped past her empty car towards the gate where I'd instructed her to wait. Damn it – she wasn't there. When I'd first shouted, she must have taken me at my word and gone. Then another chilling thought struck me. I spun round, ready to call Morgan, but he was already there, watching me with a concerned expression. 'Were you there?' I demanded. 'Were you in the trees watching the house?'

'I haven't been to any house. I've been a good three-quarters of an hour behind you because I had some other business to take care of before I came after you. Otherwise I wouldn't have used the dandelion, I'd have just followed the car. It's hardly inconspicuous.'

Someone else had been watching. Julie's hunters were out there and she was all alone. I'd totally and completely fucked up.

'Julie!' I bellowed. 'Julie!'

Morgan caught my arm. 'What's going on?'

'I don't have the time or the crayons to explain it to you.'

He rolled his eyes in exasperation. 'Maddy...'

I opened my mouth to answer but before I could there was the flash of lights from around the corner, followed by a high-pitched screech of rubber and the horrific sound of a collision. Someone had just crashed into Julie's car. It was either an unfortunate farmer working late or a vampire hunter. I'd lay money on the latter.

I abruptly switched direction, running back towards the cars. Whoever was inside had not been driving all that fast. There were no flames but there was a considerable amount of twisted metal. As the driver started to haul himself out with a dazed expression on his face, my insides hardened. I recognised him.

None of this was about Julie; I'd dragged her into my own mess, whatever it was.

'Redcap,' Morgan said in an undertone as the hapless arse-badger stumbled into the road.

My fists tightened as I watched the large, bald freak raise his eyes and finally spot us. 'Redcap who tried to shoot me just a few nights ago,' I muttered. 'On the golf course, right after I woke up with this blasted amnesia.'

'You,' the bastard in question growled, his attention wholly on me.

I stretched out my arms and grinned unpleasantly. 'Me.'

We smiled at each other nastily. And then all hell broke loose.

The Redcap barrelled towards us, head and shoulders down. I braced myself for the impact but Morgan shoved me out the way and raised his fists. With considerable dexterity, he held one up in front of him as a defensive manoeuvre and used the other to smack the side of the Redcap's head. Both of them crashed to the ground with a heavy thud.

I sucked in a breath, leapt on top of them and started pummelling the Redcap's back. Despite the pathetic lack of strength in my arms, I must have hurt him because he hissed and momentarily abandoned his efforts to smoosh Morgan into the tarmac.

The Redcap rose up and flung me off his back. 'I've been hoping we'd meet again,' he said.

Breathing hard, I faced him. 'Aren't you the lucky one?'

'Lucky indeed. You won't walk away from me this time. This fight is mine.'

'Over my dead body,' I snarled.

He bared his teeth at me in a smile. 'That can be arranged. Your blood will stain this road tonight.'

Fortunately, Morgan took that opportunity to kick out. His foot connected with the Redcap's leg and brought him down to the ground again. In one lithe movement, Morgan sprang upwards and towered over his victim. 'I don't want to hurt you,' he said, 'but I will if that's what it takes.'

The Redcap grinned evilly and reached inside his coat pocket, drawing out a gun. I heaved in a panicked breath and jumped towards Morgan, knocking him out of the way in the nick of time. The Redcap fired a shot, missing my ear by centimetres. Morgan cursed and lashed out, trying to kick the gun out of his hands.

I reached down inside myself, drawing on the same time-altering magic that had served me so well up until now. The long day had obviously affected me adversely, however; although I could feel the magic pulsating through me, I couldn't pull on enough tendrils to have an effect. I tried harder.

'So you've thrown your lot in with this bitch, Morganus?' the Redcap said, clutching tightly onto the gun. 'Bad move. We'll stop at nothing to get her and her boss. We're willing to sacrifice everything. Are you?'

Morgan gave a snarl in response. He reached down for the wily arsebadger, hauling him upwards. 'What do you mean?' he demanded, just as the Redcap loosed another shot and I managed to bring together enough time-magic to spark up.

The world slowed. The bullet glistened in the night air; I could see that the Redcap had found time to coat it with rowan poison to end both Morgan and myself. It was heading directly for Morgan's heart.

Without thinking, I ran the few steps back to Morgan and grabbed him to move him out of the way. Morgan flashed me a quick, green-eyed look; as he'd said, he was unaffected by the sluggish time bubble I'd created. I collided with him, which altered his grip on the Redcap. I pushed Morgan out of the bullet's way just as he heaved the Redcap upwards. The Redcap's body sailed overhead and the gun fell out of his hands.

I could already see that it was wrong. My interference had made Morgan's body twist so that when he threw the Redcap, the angle was off. In terrifying slow motion, the Redcap spun through the air and I knew that he would land badly. So did Morgan. Both us whirled, grabbing at the flying body in a bid to turn it.

We were too late. The Redcap slid out of our grasp and landed on the hard road. Head first. There was a sickening crack and then everything went still.

CHAPTER SEVENTEEN

I edged over to the Redcap's body, wary in case he would try to get back up again. I shouldn't have been concerned; his pupils were fixed and dilated and he was no longer breathing. I muttered a curse under my breath.

'He's dead,' I said to Morgan, accusingly. 'I wanted to question him.'

Morgan wiped the blood off his face and walked over stiffly, trying not to show that he was in pain. He stopped next to me and stared down at the Redcap's body. 'Fuck,' he swore, before turning away. 'His neck is broken. There's not much that will kill a Redcap but breaking their neck will do it.'

'Does this mean that you've now broken the truce too?' I enquired. 'Will the same terrible fate meet you as well as me?'

'Redcaps aren't Fey,' Morgan said. 'They're not included under the terms.'

'How convenient. They're obviously not human, though. If he's not a faery, what is he?'

Morgan was silent for a second. 'They're probably akin to what humans would define as ogres. They have their own demesnes. By all accounts, it's a grim, grey place. A group of them were here when the borders closed and they were trapped just like us.' He looked at me. 'What have you done, Maddy?'

I stared back at him. 'What the hell do you mean? It was you who dealt the killer blow.' I didn't mention that it was my interference that meant the blow went wrong. I didn't need to.

Feeling sick because of the Redcap's abrupt death, my mouth spat out words before I could stop them. 'Don't start castigating me again. This isn't all my damned fault.'

His green eyes flashed. 'That's not what I was referring to.'

'Then what?' I demanded.

Morgan sighed and ran a hand through his hair. 'I know this guy,' he said. 'And I know who he works for.'

When he didn't immediately elaborate, I demanded, 'Well? Who?'

'Rubus, of course,' Morgan answered. 'But if he works for Rubus, why is he trying to hurt you? Why is your own employer after your blood?'

I wondered how many times I was going to have to remind him that I had amnesia. Honestly, the man had a worse memory than I did. 'I don't know, do I? Besides, if this truce that you keep harping on about is in place and is so damned important, Rubus can't be trying to kill me.'

Morgan didn't take his eyes off me. 'Not with his own hands. But he could hire someone else to do the deed for him.'

'Oh for goodness' sake. Did no one think about this loophole when they set up the truce?'

'Normally Fey possess more honour than to abuse the system like this.'

'Not enough honour to manage without the damned truce in the first place,' I snapped back. 'Besides, you've spent every conversation we've had telling me that I'm not honourable and neither is Rubus. Couldn't someone have foreseen this happening? And why would my boss want to kill me? I'm supposed to be one of his best employees!'

'That's exactly what I want to know,' Morgan said. Oddly, he didn't appear all that perturbed.

Rolling my eyes in vexation, while acknowledging to myself that I was beyond glad it was Morgan I'd found first rather than the enigmatic Rubus, I stomped over to the Redcap's wrecked car and peered inside. His phone was on the dashboard, displaying a small map. I scooped it up and examined it. A red flashing light at the top of the screen was moving slowly away. So it *was* the Redcap arsebadger who placed the tracker on Julie's car. She was clearly still on the run – and still had the tracker with her. At least I'd be able to find her.

Taking the phone with me, I tramped off to Julie's vehicle. Morgan watched me as I twisted the keys and tried to start the engine. It spluttered and coughed.

'That car's a write off,' he called out over the noise.

'No, it's not,' I muttered. I tried the key again. It was going to work because I willed it to do so. I thumped the dashboard. 'Start, damn you!'

'Madrona,' Morgan sighed. 'It's done for. We can take my bike and find your friend. You'll have to leave the car here for now.' He waggled his phone at me. 'I'll get my people to come and clear the road so there are no more accidents.'

I ignored him, still intent on getting the stupid car to do what I needed it to do, but no matter how much I wanted it the arsebadgering piece of metal wasn't going to spring back to life.

'Fine,' I said through gritted teeth. I got out and glared at him.

As if he were out for a Sunday stroll, Morgan ambled to the hedgerow and straightened his motorbike before hooking his leg over it. Then he grabbed the helmet and held it out to me. 'Here,' he said. 'I think you need this more than I do.'

'My brain is already damaged,' I informed him sniffily. 'Keep it.'

He didn't blink. 'Put on the damned helmet, Maddy.'

'Now you're concerned for my safety?'

Morgan didn't bother responding. I sighed and walked over, taking it from him and squeezing it down over my head. Inhaling deeply, it occurred to me that this was clearly part of his devious master plan. Now all I could smell was Morgan, all around me. Well, just because he smelled divine didn't mean I was going to fall to the ground and worship at his feet. I was made of far stronger stuff than that.

'Get behind me and put your arms around my waist,' he instructed.

I did as bade me. Good grief, his body was strong and wide and comforting. Without even thinking about it, I leaned against him. Okay. I'd worship him if he wanted me to.

'You don't need to cling quite that tightly,' Morgan murmured. 'I'm good at this.'

I didn't relax. In fact, I tightened my hold, enjoying the heat of his body against mine. Mmmm. Snuggly. 'If you say so,' I answered. I inhaled again. I could get used to this.

Apparently yielding to the fact that I was going to hang onto him like a limpet, Morgan switched on the bike's engine. 'Which way?' he asked.

How was it possible for someone to come out of a brutal fight to the death and still smell so good?

'Maddy!' he said sharply. 'Which way?'

I shook myself. He doesn't want you, I reminded myself. And Julie needs rescuing from a field. I raised the visor and glanced at the phone. 'Straight ahead,' I muttered. 'Then take the first right.' At least Julie was on foot and hadn't got very far. I pressed myself against Morgan's back. I'd have to take my comfort where I could get it.

He revved the engine and took off along the narrow road before turning where I'd told him to. I had to admit that he was right; he was indeed a good bike rider, maintaining a careful speed and not veering too close to the looming hedgerows. At one point a fox bounded out in front of us. Without missing a beat, Morgan slowed, nimbly driving round it so it was free to scamper back to the undergrowth in safety. When we picked up Julie, I'd have to point out to her that she should take note of the benefits of careful driving.

I wondered how we were going to fit three people on the back of the bike. Maybe I'd end up walking back after all.

Using the map, I directed Morgan to the left. Julie's red blip was still moving but very slowly now. She appeared to be taking a cross-country route. That was sensible for avoiding scary vampire hunters but it was less useful when her bodyguard was trying to catch up with her.

I tapped Morgan's arm. 'Stop here,' I told him. 'I think she must be in that field.'

He did as I asked, pulled the motorbike neatly into the side and turned off the engine. Reluctantly, I slid off the back. I was going to miss the warmth of his body. I yanked off the helmet and pointed. 'She's that way.'

'Who is this Julie exactly?' Morgan enquired. 'And what do you do for her?'

'She's a soap star,' I said. 'I'm her bodyguard.'

He snorted in disbelief. 'Bodyguard? Since when?'

'Yesterday.' I located the gate and hopped over it, my feet squelching in mud as I landed.

'You thought that someone was trying to attack her down a quiet country lane? When you're a drug-dealing faery who was almost killed just a few nights ago?'

I shrugged. 'People are out to get her too.'

'What people?'

Uh... 'Stalkers.'

'Stalkers plural?'

'She's very famous,' I answered stiffly. 'Are you coming with me to fetch her or are you staying here?'

He leaped over the gate with far more grace than I'd managed. 'Coming with you, of course. I'd hate to think you'd get attacked by a crazed cow.'

I glanced round the dark field. 'Sheep,' I said. 'Not cows.'

Morgan squinted. 'It's unusual for sheep to be bunched together like that unless they're being herded. I don't see any sign of a woman either. Are you sure she's in this field?'

I glanced at the phone. 'According to this, she is.' I held it up. 'She's still moving.'

'Maddy,' Morgan said, 'no one's there.'

My stomach tightened. 'Of course she's there. We just can't see her yet.' With that, I took off and jogged towards the flock. None of the animals appeared to be sleeping but that was probably because Julie's presence had woken them up. She was going to be there, I told myself; she'd be sitting next to one of the sheep and chatting away to it whilst swigging from a hip flask. I was prepared for her yelling at me for being a useless bodyguard but I wasn't prepared for her not to be there.

Scanning the field desperately, my eyes finally alighted on a huddled figure beside a clump of trees. Breathing a sigh of relief, I headed straight for it, narrowly avoiding a collision with several sheep.

'Julie!' I exclaimed. 'I'm so sorry! I...' My voice trailed off. It wasn't her. What I'd thought was a person was nothing more than the stump of a tree. I looked down at the phone again. According to the map, she was less than twenty metres away. Then my eyes snagged on one of the sheep that was straying away from the others. In its mouth was a small grey box.

I darted over. The sheep, startled by my approach, dropped

it almost immediately and ran off. I ignored it and picked up the tracker. Maybe Julie had dropped it by accident and was still somewhere around here.

I opened my mouth and yelled. 'Julie! It's Madrona! Where are you?'

My voice echoed back. I spun round, continuing to search. Trying to stay calm, I centred myself, digging down for the same sensitive hearing I'd used back at the country house. All I could hear, however, were the shallows breaths of dozens of sheep. No one else was here.

Then, over in the far corner, Morgan raised his arm. 'Here,' he said, his voice grim.

I sprinted over to join him. Snagged to a post was a scarf. Even in the gloom, I immediately recognised it as the brightly coloured one that Julie had been wearing. I stared at it, my heart sinking into a dark chasm of despair. While I'd been snuggling into Morgan and enjoying myself, the vampire hunters had nabbed her.

CHAPTER EIGHTEEN

It didn't take long to re-orientate and re-group. The Redcap, who was lying dead out on the road behind us, had been surprised to see me. He was also one of the trio who had attacked me on the golf course that very first night. Whatever his motives had been then, it was clear that it wasn't me he'd been after tonight. While we'd faced him down, his two buddies had circled round and grabbed Julie from the front. It was a strategic action I should have foreseen. There was no point berating myself about it, however. I could wallow later; right now there were far more pressing matters.

'You said that the dead Redcap worked for Rubus,' I said to Morgan. 'Are you sure about that?'

He watched me, obviously not entirely sure what was going on but understanding that it was serious. 'Positive.'

'Would he ever work for himself or for someone else at the same time?' I asked, wanting to avoid making another stupid mistake.

Morgan shrugged. 'Anything's possible.'

I nodded, although that information wasn't really all that

helpful. 'And where,' I asked through clenched teeth, 'would I find Rubus right now?'

'He has various hideouts,' Morgan said. 'He switches between them to avoid the likes of me repeatedly trying to shut him down.'

I kept my breathing even and steady, although my heart rate had ratcheted up several notches. 'You must have an idea about where he is. If you were following me, you must have thought about following him too.'

Morgan barely moved. 'He's wise to my actions and he's a slippery bastard.'

'You wouldn't hurt him because of the truce though.'

'No,' he answered. 'But I could still make life difficult for him if I knew where he was. He's secretive, Maddy.' He ran his tongue over his teeth. 'Do you think he's abducted your new employer to piss you off? Because if that's the case, attempting to rescue her has to be a trap. Rubus is certainly capable enough – and mean enough – to try something like that. And don't forget that the Redcap's presence means he's been trying to kill you.'

'Mmm.' Except Morgan didn't know what I did about Julie – and I couldn't tell him. Her abduction might have nothing to do with me at all and everything to do with her vampiric ethnicity, especially given McNasty Number One's reaction to my presence. Either way, I was going to raise hell to get her back. I folded my arms and met Morgan's gaze with a hard-eyed stare.

He sighed. 'Hang on. I'll make a call or two and see if anyone's seen him recently.'

I bit out a thanks and strode back across the field, ignoring the sheep that scattered in my wake. Morgan walked with me, muttering into his phone. By the time we reached the far gate again, he'd put the phone away.

'You have an answer?'

'A possible answer – but it's dangerous. You should let me handle this. Humans are out of bounds and Rubus will pay dearly for involving them. This is something I should deal with.'

Except Julie wasn't human. Not to mention that she was my responsibility. 'Just drop me off at the place, Morgan. Then you're free to go on your merry way. Thank you for your help so far.' My words were stiff and angry.

Although the sentiment wasn't directed at him, his eyes flashed at me through the darkness. 'What Rubus does or doesn't do is as much my business as it is yours,' he sniped. 'I'm not leaving you to deal with him on your own.'

'This is my problem, not yours.'

Morgan laughed humourlessly. 'Where you're concerned, it's always my problem. Besides, if Rubus has kidnapped a human, his time is up. Drug dealing and stealing you is one thing, but messing with the people on this demesne is entirely different.'

I stared at him. 'Stealing me? I'm not an object, Morgan. And whether I can remember them or not, the choices and decisions that I've made in the past were mine.'

He put his hands in his pockets. 'You were mine, too.'

Half an hour ago I might have been flattered. 'I don't have time for this caveman bullshit.'

'Then,' he bit out, 'stop arguing with me and let's get a move on.'

I gritted my teeth. Right now it wasn't as if I had much choice.

~

The address that Morgan had managed to finagle out of whoever he'd spoken to was in a quiet corner of Salford Quay, a recently re-developed area of the city. The building wasn't as highly stylised or well refurbished as the others, however. It was shadowed by a glittering high-rise residential structure and it was barely noticeable. It wasn't rundown *per se* but it paled into comparison with its neighbours. I bet plenty of passers-by wandered past without giving it a second glance. It was ideal for a hide out.

Morgan stopped the bike on the corner opposite and we gazed across at it the same assessing look in our eyes. The building was shrouded in darkness and there wasn't a flicker of life visible from any of the grimy windows.

'Tell me about him,' I said quietly. 'What do I need to know about Rubus that I can't remember?'

For a long moment, Morgan was silent. I wasn't even sure if he'd heard my question and I was about to repeat it when he finally spoke up. 'He's bullish,' he said. 'Likes to get his own way and is overly concerned with how others treat him. By which I mean that he expects to be venerated for who he is. If he doesn't receive the respect that he thinks he deserves, his temper flares up quickly.'

'He doesn't sound as if he has much of a sense of humour,' I commented.

'No,' Morgan agreed quietly. 'He doesn't. But as much as he acts like a brute who's quick to anger, don't underestimate him. He's not stupid and he likes to play the long game. There was once a Fey who insulted him when we were back in Mag Mell, laughed at him when he tripped and fell. Rubus pretended to laugh it off like it was all a big joke. Ten months later, when that same Fey petitioned to be allowed to cross over here to retrieve some mugwort to help his sick daughter, Rubus made sure his petition was denied.'

'So he's high up then? In Fey Land? I mean, Mag Mell,' I corrected.

'Yeah.' Morgan's mouth tightened. 'Or at least he was.'

If there was one thing I'd learnt about myself over the last few days, it was that I possessed a sharp tongue. 'I'm surprised that I chose him,' I mused. At Morgan's sideways glance and brief, annoyed flush, I hastily explained. 'If I've learned anything about myself it's that I don't tend to keep my mouth shut. I can see how that could annoy someone with a short temper and a large ego.'

'Rubus has a jealous streak,' he murmured. 'Even when we were kids, it was the same. Whenever I had something, even if he'd shown no interest in it, he immediately wanted it.'

'You grew up together?'

Morgan's jaw clenched. 'He's my brother.'

I stared. 'You didn't think to mention this little fact before?'

'It's why I have as much right to confront Rubus over what he's done to your new boss as you have,' he said stiffly, without looking at me.

I swallowed and plucked at the hem of my T-shirt. 'Did I betray you with him?' I asked, suddenly nervous about the answer.

All I received in response was a tight, barely noticeable nod. Gasbudlikins. No wonder Morgan despised us both.

'Maybe you're too close to all this,' I said. 'Maybe you should stay here while I check out the building.'

'You're not going in there alone,' he growled. Both his tone and his expression were implacable.

Arguing felt like a waste of time. 'Fine then,' I said. 'Let's do this.'

'What's the plan?'

I turned to him and bared my teeth. 'March up there and break down the door, of course.'

A faint glimmer of amusement lit his eyes. 'Of course.'

I hopped off the bike and Morgan followed. My shoulders were tense; there was no denying the knot of anxiety in the pit of my stomach. But I had no choice – I had to do this. I strode across the street, blood roaring in my ears and Julie's scarf wrapped tightly in my hands. As soon as I reached the large steel door, I kicked at it. The metal reverberated loudly. I scowled and tugged at the handle. Morgan reached down and placed his hand on mine.

'Allow me,' he murmured.

Reluctantly, I stepped back. He touched the door, his palm flat against it and he murmured something under his breath. A moment later, he tried the door again. This time it slid open easily.

My eyes narrowed. 'That's a neat trick.'

'One you're adept at, as well,' he told me. 'I'm sure you'll be breaking and entering all over the place once you get your memory back.'

'You really don't have a very high opinion of me,' I muttered, although given what I'd learnt that was hardly surprising. I stepped over the threshold,

Morgan hesitated at the doorway. 'No ward,' he said, as much to himself as to me.

I glanced back. 'Ward? Is that what you put on the pub to prevent me from entering?'

He nodded. 'They need to be refreshed every six hours if they are to remain effective against Fey intrusions. For someone like Rubus, I'd imagine they're a foregone conclusion.'

I swung my head round and searched the cavernous, dark interior. 'You don't think he's here.'

Morgan grimaced. 'I'm beginning to doubt it.'

I curled my hands into fists and nodded. Whatever Rubus had been to me, I wasn't going to let him get away with abducting Julie. 'Even if he's not here, there might be clues as to where he's gone. We should still look.'

'You actually sound reasonable, Madrona,' Morgan told me. 'It must be time to up my medication.'

I let out an unladylike snort. 'Yeah, yeah. Save it till later.' I pointed. 'I'll go right if you go left.'

Morgan nodded agreement. 'Yell if you need help.'

My eyes flashed at him. 'Ditto. I'm perfectly prepared to come and rescue you if you need it.'

He offered me a half smirk before turning and melting away to the side. I took a deep breath and headed in the other direction. Coming, Rubus. Ready or not.

The corridor was desperately dingy, with the sort of melodramatic cobwebs hanging from the corridors that looked like they'd been manufactured in a factory for a Halloween party. I stopped in my tracks, my feet refusing to continue. I scanned the cobwebs. It didn't look like there were any spiders hiding in them. I told myself that the webs were too large to be real and that I shouldn't be surprised if I rounded the corner and was attacked by a plastic skeleton. My heart rate slowed. That was better. Come on feet.

Shuffling to the corner, I peered round and was confronted with a vast space of nothingness. The place didn't look like it had been touched in months. At least there were no giant spiders scuttling towards me. Telling myself that appearances could be deceptive, and that I had to look beyond what was on the surface, I edged forward. Given that I left no footprints, the warehouse was certainly cleaner than it looked on first inspection. I sniffed the air delicately. There was a definite eau de mould clinging to the air but, if I weren't mistaken, there was something manufactured about it. Rubus wanted incomers to believe that this building had been abandoned for months. There must be a reason for that.

Moving forward silently, I swung my head this way and that. There were a number of doors on the left-hand side and nothing but empty space to my right. No prizes for guessing which direction I should head in, then. I tiptoed over.

'What's behind door number one?' I whispered, before pushing it open.

I was immediately assailed by the stench of death. Covering my nose and mouth with my sleeve, I eyed the small space. There was nothing there apart from the tiny corpses of three rats. I pursed my lips and hunkered down.

Obviously I was no veterinary expert but it looked to me as if they'd not been dead for long. They weren't rotting; in fact, their bodies were remarkably intact. I bent down further. On the dark brown fur of one of them, I saw something sparkly; it was as if the rat had rubbed itself in a bath of glitter before expiring. Interesting. I extended a finger to poke the corpse and investigate further but before I could do so, something poked me.

I almost screamed out of shock, not fear. I managed to stifle the sound and whirled to confront my assailant. When I saw Morgan, I bared my teeth. 'Don't bloody do that!' I whispered angrily. 'At least give me some warning that you're behind me.'

'I did,' he whispered back. 'Anyway, you need to stay quiet.'

I rolled my eyes. That's exactly what I'd been trying to do. I glared at him and pointed at the rats. 'They look fresh,' I declared. 'And the one on the right has something glittery in its fur.'

Morgan barely glanced at it. 'Dust.'

'It's not dust. Dust doesn't glitter.'

He sighed. 'Pixie dust. The sort *you* sell. The sort that makes addicts out of perfectly normal faeries so you can bend them to your will and...'

I held up my hand. 'Alright. I get it.' Talk about harping on. I eyed the rat. 'Is dust that dangerous? Would it have killed these animals?'

'In large quantities it might have.'

'It means Rubus was definitely here,' I mused.

Morgan raised an eyebrow. 'Or you were.'

My glare intensified. 'I…'

He lifted his hand and placed his index finger against my lips. 'Hush. I told you that you have to be quiet.' He pointed behind us.

My eyes widened. 'Someone's there?' I twisted round and crept out, this time heading away from the doors and into the cavernous space. I couldn't see anything, no matter how hard I looked.

I was about to tell that to Morgan when I realised that, yet again, it wasn't sight that I should be relying on. Somewhere above and to my right, there was the sound of quiet but regular breathing. I froze. My glance fell on a set of banister-less stairs leading up to a mezzanine floor. I turned to check on Morgan but he wasn't looking at the stairs. He was looking at me.

'Rubus?' I mouthed.

He shook his head. 'Human,' he mouthed back. 'Male.'

I grimaced. Not even a faery. That was unfortunate. This would have been a whole lot easier if Rubus had left one of his minions behind so we could torture them for information. One of his *other* minions, I amended. All the same, the human might possess some information that could prove useful. I was confident I'd be able to wheedle something out of him.

I'd have a better chance of handling this situation quickly and without a fuss if I were on my own. I indicated to Morgan that he should stay put. He frowned at me. I gestured more vigorously. Morgan's eyes narrowed but he indicated that I could go ahead. If there was any trouble, he wouldn't be far behind and he possessed the skills to eavesdrop on anything I said. He'd be neither out of the loop nor shooing me off into immediate peril. The man had to chill out and stop being such a worrywart. Besides, I might not have had all my faculties or understood all my powers but I was still the Madhatter.

Keeping my footsteps as light as a mouse scurrying past a slumbering cat, I headed up the stairs. Whoever was up there, I had no desire to wake them up until I understood the lay of the land and what I was up against. Our sleeping beauty might indeed be human – but humans could be dangerous.

When I reached the top of the precarious staircase, I remained on the balls of my feet as I tiptoed forward. I allowed myself one quick glance backwards. Morgan had moved to the foot of the stairs and was watching my every move, his arms folded and his expression inscrutable. I flashed him a cheesy grin and a wave. When that didn't elicit a reaction, I pasted on my best evil-villain stare and glowered at him instead. I couldn't be sure but I thought I spotted the glimmer of a smile in return.

Re-focusing, I looked around. The gentle wheezes were coming from the corner of the room to my right. Although the monstrous spider webs remained in evidence here, hanging from various corners and with numerous dead insects caught in their lethal threads, I still felt like the area was cleaner than it should be. Given his attention to detail, it was obvious that Rubus was a canny bastard. For some reason, that thought comforted me. Whatever my reasons had been for abandoning Morgan to be with his brother, I'd not saddled myself with a complete nincompoop even though the evidence thus far was to the contrary.

I snuck along, ignoring the damp piles of ancient newspapers and the mouldy cardboard boxes. There weren't any dead rats up here; maybe the giant spiders had eaten them. I scowled at myself for thinking that and tried to maintain regular breathing and stay relaxed. That didn't mean I wasn't ready for a fight.

As soon as I reached the doorway, I flattened myself against the wall. A mirror to peer round the corner would have been handy. Once all this was done and dusted, I was going to organise a proper handbag for myself with the things a girl really needed to get through her day. Without any equipment to hand, I'd just have to rely on myself. I tilted my head and squinted round.

The room was more comfortable than I'd expected, given the rest of the building. There were no cobwebs and definitely no small animal corpses. Whoever was sleeping inside had taken the time to spray some sort of potent air freshener liberally around the room. A flowery scent still clung to the air, masking the unpleasant smells from outside. There was a small table with a chair propped up next to it, and a dog-eared paperback sitting on top. The slumbering man wasn't curled up in a corner and trying to sleep on a hard floor; he had a proper mattress with clean-looking sheets and two plump pillows. I half expected Laura Ashley curtains and a fur throw to come into view.

Satisfied that there was a lack of weaponry in the room, unless there was a gun underneath the pillow, I examined the man. All that was currently visible from beneath the pristine cover was a shock of tousled brown hair. I couldn't see anything of his face from this angle. He was on his belly and definitely fast asleep.

I peeled away from the wall and went in. Three steps into the room and I trod on a creaky floorboard; to my ears, the noise was painfully loud. Fortunately, the man didn't move. He was still sleeping. I breathed out.

Chiding myself for making a rookie error, I took more care. I sidestepped away from the plank of wood and sidled up to the mattress, then I stood over the prone figure. This was very Zen in both its simplicity and peacefulness. It was almost a shame that I'd have to ruin the picture.

I bent my head, catching a glimpse of the man's face for the first time. It was in profile and he was slack-jawed, with a faint line of drool dribbling from the corner of his mouth onto the pillow. I recognised him instantly. I bunched my hands in fists and clenched my teeth. What were the chances, I thought grimly, that Dave from the Metropolitan bar was the same human who was here? I glared at him angrily. Then I reached down and slapped him hard on his exposed cheek.

He shot bolt upright, nostrils flaring and eyes wide. 'Wh – what?'

I didn't give him a chance to recover. My fingers curled round his throat and I hauled him upwards, slamming his body into the nearest wall and pinning him there. Well, go me. It appeared I did have some strength to call on when I needed it.

Dave blinked, the sleep vanishing from his eyes. 'Who the fuck are you?'

'Like you don't recognise me,' I snarled.

He stared at me, nervous tics starting up all over his face. 'No, I don't! I promise I don't!' His breathing was coming fast and shallow. 'You look a bit familiar but...'

I held up my hand. 'Enough.' His babbling was irritating and I belatedly remembered that I'd been wearing my Madhatter superhero costume the last time we met. Maybe I could use his lack of memory against him. 'The last time we met,' I hedged, 'was with Rubus.'

If I'd thought he'd been scared before, it was nothing compared to now. 'R- Rubus?' he stammered. 'You were there when he gave me the stuff and told me what to do?'

Gasbudlikins. The idiot couldn't have been more vague if he'd tried. 'Of course I was,' I snapped. 'Do you still have the stuff with you?'

I could feel him shaking under my fingers. 'Some. I've sold most of it. But Rubus said I could! It was mine to sell! Has he...' He swallowed. 'Has he changed his mind?'

I'd started this conversation aggressively and it seemed that now I had no way forward other than to ratchet up the level further. I cursed to myself and squeezed my fingers round his neck slightly. Dave whimpered. 'No, he's not changed his mind. But he wants to know who you sold it to.'

Dave's arms flailed. 'There were lots of people!' he protested. 'I don't know their names. I don't ask for that sort of thing. They wouldn't trust me if they thought I was keeping records. The police are clamping down on any sort of shit to do with spice. Besides, anonymity works both ways.'

I looked into his eyes; I didn't think I was imagining that his pupils were dilated. Dave might have given a good impression of a stand-up citizen when I met him a few nights ago but it was clear that he was little more than a drug addict. Perhaps a drug dealer too. Who knew? It was almost like we were kin. 'Spice,' I said slowly. It didn't mean much to me but I doubted it was for cooking clandestine curries.

'There's a high demand for it! I told Rubus he should have given me more. Just because his lot don't take dust very often doesn't mean that my lot and spice are the same.'

I absorbed this information without easing my grip on this sorry excuse for a man. 'Rubus wants me to make sure that you're keeping to your side of the bargain. He wants to make sure you've not forgotten.'

Dave looked around him. 'I'm here, aren't I? I promised I'd stay and keep an eye on whoever showed up.'

'That's one thing,' I purred, hoping my gamble would pay off. 'What about the rest?'

He swallowed, his Adam's apple juddering nervously in his

neck. 'I did the rest too! I went to that bar. Nothing happened. I didn't even see the guy he'd been talking about.'

'You might not have noticed him,' I said, silently urging him to say more.

'A green-eyed, muscled bloke who looks just like Rubus but with more hair?' Dave asked. 'I'm hardly likely to miss him.'

It was definitely Morgan that Dave was talking about. So what was the motive? Why would Rubus send a human to keep an eye on his own brother? 'He was there,' I growled. Then, for good measure, 'Your instructions were very clear.'

'I couldn't follow him if I couldn't find him! I've not used your sparkly shit on him yet. I was going to go back tonight and try to get him but I'm not Superman. I don't have super powers.' When he mentioned the superhero, his eyes flared. He looked more closely at me and I saw the cogs in his dim brain turning. Enough of that. I shook him hard, causing just enough pain for him to close his eyes. That would have to do.

'Where's this sparkly shit you were going to use? You'd better still have it or there will be consequences.'

'It's in my bag,' he muttered, thankfully still unwilling to open his eyes and look at me.

There was a creak from the same floorboard that had almost given me away. I knew without turning that it was Morgan. For once renouncing his cat-like tread, he walked over and grabbed a faded backpack. I was impressed by his ability to look intimidating; I'd have to practise that thunderous expression later.

When Morgan rummaged inside the bag and pulled out a small glass vial filled with something glittery, his face grew stormier. Even I almost flinched.

'What else did Rubus tell you to do?' I said, my voice low and threatening and very close to Dave's ear.

'That's it!' He paused and flicked open his eyelids. Fortunately my expression must have been pretty scary because he closed them quickly again. 'Wasn't it? I didn't think there was anything else.' His panic was rising. 'Have I forgotten something?'

I extended the index finger of my free hand and softly grazed Dave's cheek. He cowered even more. 'No,' I said. 'It seems like you've covered everything.'

He breathed out in relief but I wasn't done yet. 'You have fucked up, though, Davey boy. Big time. You should have given Rubus's lookalike the sparkly shit by now.'

'I told you! I couldn't! He wasn't there. I've been every night.'

'You've been distracted, though. You went with friends. You tried to pick up women.'

Dave's body tensed. I had to be careful; he was already close to putting two and two together and I couldn't afford for him to do that. I released my grip on his neck and used my hand to cover his eyes.

'I'll tell you what,' I murmured. 'I quite like you, Dave.' I ignored the sharp look Morgan gave me. 'I'm going to help you out. Rubus will be furious when he finds out you've not done as he commanded. He's been nice to you until now but when he gets angry... Well, let's just say you don't want to be in his vicinity when that happens.'

'Oh God,' Dave whispered. 'Don't let him hurt me.'

I smiled. 'The only way he won't hurt you is if he doesn't know how badly you've screwed up.' I paused, as if giving serious thought to the matter. 'So I tell you what. I will take the dust. I will give it to the man in the Metropolitan. As far as Rubus will know, you did exactly as you were asked.'

Dave licked his lips. 'You'd do that?'

'As I said,' I told him, 'I like you. You'll find a way to make it up to me later.'

'Yes.' He nodded vigorously. 'I will. I promise I will.' He hesitated. 'What's your name? So I know who I owe?'

I shot a quick look at Morgan. He shrugged impassively. Uh...

'It's Stacey,' I said.

Dave jerked. 'Stacey? But normally you lot have names that are all, like, weird and stuff. Your name is really Stacey? Like that character on *St Thomas Close*?'

Another of Julie's fans. That was interesting. 'Yes,' I told him. 'Just like her. But not quite as nice.' I leaned in and licked his cheek. Of everything I'd said and done, that action scared him the most. 'Stay here,' I said, 'until you hear otherwise.'

'Yes. Yes, Miss Stacey, I will.'

Morgan was already moving out of the room. I reached carefully for the power inside me, unable to afford Dave catching another glimpse of my face. Time slowed to sluggish heartbeats. I lifted my hand away from Dave's eyes and spun away. By the time the earth's rotations returned to normal, Morgan and I were both striding out of the warehouse and back into the night.

CHAPTER NINETEEN

Morgan's fingers drummed against the handlebars as he drove. His body had been rigid for miles. I wasn't even convinced that he had a destination in mind; it seemed as if he were simply driving aimlessly around the empty streets. It was only when the familiar sight of the fake Roman fort came into view that he brought the motorbike to a halt.

'You didn't ask the human where Rubus is now,' he said, after he'd turned the engine off and glorious silence returned to the night.

I shrugged. 'There was no point. That would have given away my position and my identity and there's no chance that he knows where your brother is. Rubus would not have been stupid enough to tell a guy like Dave where he was going to be.'

Morgan swung his head round to look at me. 'You say that like your memory has returned,' he said. 'Like you know exactly what kind of person Rubus is and how he acts.'

'Sorry to disappoint you,' I replied. 'I still remember nothing. But I've learnt over the last day that someone like Rubus wouldn't tell someone like Dave where he's spending his time.'

Morgan's mouth tightened but it was obvious he grudgingly accepted my words. 'I can't believe he thought that sending a human to spike me with pixie dust would work.'

I slid off the back of the bike so I could face him. 'It didn't have to work,' I said quietly. 'I don't think Rubus cares whether you have dust in your system or you don't. What he wants is for you to be distracted. Maybe he was hoping you'd kill Dave and have to deal with the consequences. Or maybe that you'd spend the next week turning the city over to find out what's going on. It's a smokescreen. Rubus is up to something and wants to make sure you're nowhere near the action.' I gave a derisive snort. 'Hell, he's abducted Julie. We *know* he's up to something.'

'Why do you think that?'

'Because,' I answered without meeting his eyes, 'it's what I would do if I needed you out of the way for a while.'

A muscle ticked in Morgan's jaw but he didn't respond. 'You altered time again,' he eventually said gruffly, without looking at me. 'How many times have I told you that's forbidden?'

I rolled my eyes. 'Dave was on the verge of remembering who I was. I couldn't let that happen.'

'He's the human you came with to my pub.'

I nodded. 'I met him on the street about ten minutes before we walked in. There's was nothing nefarious going on. It was just a coincidence.'

Morgan sniffed. 'You mean the same sort of coincidence as Rubus kidnapping your new boss?'

I had to admit that looked shady. 'I haven't lied to you, Morgan. I don't know any more about that than you do.' Unless the fact that Julie was a vampire was an issue – but surely that wasn't related to all these coincidences.

'There's no other reason why Rubus would have taken her unless it was something to do with you.'

'Maybe he's a big soap fan. Maybe he never misses an episode of *St Thomas Close*.'

Morgan ground his teeth in exasperation.

I sighed. 'I'm telling you the truth, Morgan. I appreciate I might not be the good person I thought I was. I appreciate you have very good reason to despise me. But my connection both to Dave and to Julie is nothing more than coincidence. There is nothing more to it than that, unlikely as it may seen.'

'You're right,' he growled. 'It's completely unlikely. In fact...' His voice trailed off and his brow furrowed. He looked at me, his green eyes all but pinning me in place. 'Tell me again about when you woke up on the golf course.'

I ran a hand through my hair. 'What does that have to do with anything? I've already been through it.'

Morgan shook his head. 'You told me what happened. You didn't tell me how you felt.'

I failed to see why that was important but as long as Morgan wasn't pointing his finger at me, or hauling me in for torture and interrogation because I supposedly knew more than I was letting on, I figured I shouldn't complain.

'Well,' I drawled, 'I certainly didn't feel all zip-de-do-dah. That's hardly a surprise.'

'Stop being difficult, Madrona.'

He could be a patronising bastard when he wanted to be. I put my hands on my hips and injected as much sass into both my body and my voice as I could. 'I'm actually very easy to get along with, once you learn to worship me properly.'

Morgan muttered something inaudible before raising baleful eyes. 'Be specific. How did you feel exactly? I want to know everything.'

'Do you?' I dropped my voice to a low seductive husk. 'Is that what you really, really want, Morgan?'

He gazed back. 'Yes,' he said, his tone flat.

Gasbudlikins. I sighed. 'Fine. I felt sick.' I raised my eyebrows. 'I wasn't actually sick but I definitely felt nauseous.

My ribs were sore, as if they'd been cracked. My legs were stiff and it was difficult to walk at first, although that eased off later when people started shooting at me. Then, of course, I cut myself on that stupid rowan-coated sword.' I shrugged. 'We all know what happened next.'

Morgan remained watchful. 'Anything else?' he prodded. 'Anything at all?'

I tried to think. 'I had a bad taste in my mouth. Like wet dog or something.'

He nodded. 'Get on the bike.'

I cocked my head. 'Why?'

'Because there's a woman we need to see about that wet dog,' he told me.

'Julie is still missing. Rubus still has her. I don't have time for games, Morgan.'

'This is far from a game. And unless you have any bright ideas about how to find either of them, quit complaining and get on the damned bike.'

I crossed my arms. 'You know,' I said in an overly sarcastic voice, 'I really can't imagine for the life of me why I left you. Not at all. I mean, it's *so* much fun having you ordering me around all the time, or withholding information just because it suits you. I just love snapping to your every order and fulfilling your every whim.'

He swung his leg off the bike and stepped towards me, until our toes were almost touching. 'Believe me, Maddy,' he said, 'if you were fulfilling my every whim then we would not be having a conversation.'

I matched his intense gaze. 'Then, tell me, Morgan. What would I be doing instead?'

He shook his head, exasperated, then returned to the bike and turned the key. Yet again, the engine roared into life. 'I'm already visualising duct tape over your mouth,' he muttered. Apparently he thought I couldn't hear him.

I shrugged. 'Sure, if that floats your boat. You can tie me up too, if you wish. Handcuffs are fine.' I held out my wrists. 'Then you can have your wicked way with me.'

'Don't tempt me.'

Somehow I didn't think it was a sexy game he was considering; it was probably a cold, damp prison cell and gloopy porridge three times a day. Giving up on trying to flirt, I pushed my hair out of my eyes. 'Is it going to take long?' I enquired. 'This little visit of yours?'

'No. It might even be worth it.' He bared his teeth in a crooked smile. The contents of my stomach did an annoying little flip-flop.

'Fine,' I muttered. I got back on the bike. 'Onwards, good knight!'

'I can get hold of duct tape if I really need it, Maddy.'

Yeah, yeah. I sighed. This would be a far more entertaining chat if I didn't keep thinking of Julie, who was probably wrapped in duct tape at this very moment. Whatever Morgan was up to, I sincerely hoped it was going to lead to something – for her sake.

~

If I'd thought that Rubus's abandoned hideout was depressing, I hadn't been using my imagination enough. Morgan stopped in front of a ramshackle hut near the canal and wasted no time in striding towards it.

I gaped after him. 'You can't seriously tell me someone's inside there.'

'Someone's inside there.'

'Well, you can't go in. You won't fit.'

'I'm going in,' he flung out over his shoulder. 'I strongly suggest you come with me.'

I stared at the hut. 'Into that? A strong gust of wind will blow it over. Not to mention it's the size of a broom cupboard.'

'Well then, you should be happy. It means it'll be a short visit.' Morgan pulled open the door and disappeared inside.

For a moment, I didn't move. This had to be some sort of joke; the hut couldn't be more than two feet square. I was going to waltz inside and Morgan was going to piss himself laughing that I'd been so gullible. When he didn't re-emerge after what seemed like a long minute, however, I stomped in after in. There'd probably be more cobwebs inside, I thought gloomily. And massive spiders.

I slipped in the door. The sight that greeted my eyes wasn't anything like I'd expected. I stared round, awestruck, then immediately turned on my heel and left the same way I'd entered. I looked at the exterior of the hut. Nope: it was definitely just a hut. Then I went back inside again. This really didn't make any sense.

'Get a move on, Maddy,' Morgan said, sounding amused. He was standing at least twenty feet away and leaning against a highly polished mahogany bar.

'Is this some weird faery place?' I asked, without moving an inch.

There was a loud snort from behind the bar then a young woman stood up and flicked a derisive look in my direction. She had spiky blonde hair that shot out in all directions and, if I wasn't mistaken, was tinged with blue at the tips. A pair of round glasses was perched on her nose, giving her green eyes an owlish aspect, while the stained denim dungarees she was wearing suggested she had a nursery of small children hiding at her feet.

'Weird faery place? Seriously?' She glanced at Morgan. 'Has

this idiot been asleep for the past ten years?' Then she stared back at me. 'Wait. I know who you are. You're ...'

'Madrona,' Morgan said. The woman flinched visibly, her skin paling. 'She's got amnesia,' he added as if to calm her.

'You brought *her* here?' The strange faery woman pushed her glasses up her nose. 'Do you have any idea how much trouble it is to relocate myself whenever one of them finds out where I am?'

'Arty, she doesn't remember Rubus. She doesn't remember working for him and she doesn't remember what she's done in the past.'

'Arty?' I interrupted. 'Is that name because you've been playing around with finger paints?' I pointed at the multi-coloured daubs all over her dungarees.

Arty's face twisted. 'It's Artemesia to you,' she said coldly. She turned back to Morgan and started berating him for daring to bring me here. What*ever*. I zoned her out and paid more attention to my surroundings. The room really was quite extraordinary.

For one thing, it was large. It might have looked like a tumbledown shed from the outside, inside of which you'd be lucky to swing your hair let alone a cat, but from this vantage point it was massive. It stretched back almost as far as my eyes could see and there was a long narrow room beyond the bar. Each wall was covered in shelves and each shelf was laden with bottles in myriad colours and shapes and sizes. It was as if I'd strolled into Aladdin's cave; the sight was genuinely dazzling.

The aroma was equally alluring; heady spices mingled with florals and earthy smells. The combination should have been sickly but it made me want to inhale as deeply as possible. It was exotic and delicious. I shook my head in amazement. This was what being a faery should all be about. Forget the grey streets of Manchester and trailing after Morgan or Rubus or whoever happened to be on the menu; I felt like I could settle in a corner and stay here forever.

To my left, there was a small wooden table with elaborately carved legs. A silver bowl lay on top of it containing a heap of small, jewel-like sweets. I reached for one.

In a flash, Artemesia was beside me and slapping away my hand. 'Those are for customers,' she snapped.

'I'm here, aren't I?' I said. 'That makes me a customer.'

'You couldn't afford my rates.' She tossed her head and glared.

I examined her. 'Is the look you're going for that of a clown? Because I'm not sure they're very popular these days. More people are afraid of clowns than amused by them. Not that you're very scary, but your hair and your clothes and your—'

'Enough, Madrona.' Morgan did not sound pleased.

There was a flicker of hurt vulnerability in Artemesia's eyes and an odd feeling rose inside me. Gasbudlikins. Was that guilt?

'Sorry,' I muttered. 'I'm under a lot of stress right now and my mouth has a mind of its own.'

Artemesia blinked at me. 'Good grief,' she said. 'You really do have amnesia.' She looked over her shoulder at Morgan. 'You know it doesn't mean that she's changed. She just can't remember. And when her memory returns, which it probably will, she'll go running back to Rubus.'

Actually, I didn't think I would. Whatever reasons I'd had before for being with him, there was no indication that he was the sort of person I wanted to spend any time with now. Whether I was truly evil or a secret hero, a girl had to have some standards.

'We need your help, Arty. You should listen to what she has to say about when she woke up. I think there might be something there.'

'Memory loss or not,' she told him, 'if I do this it's for you, not for her. You know having her here means I'll have to move again. Otherwise my uncle will find out where I am and I'll end up screwed.'

I looked at her. 'I don't understand,' I said.

'No,' she replied. 'I don't suppose you do.' She stepped back, as if the very air around me was tainted, and swept around her arm. 'This is my shop. I'm an apothecary. All my family are. My uncle and I were here collecting ingredients when the border closed and both of us were trapped. Once it became clear that it wasn't going to open again any time soon, we opened up a new outlet.' Her nose wrinkled. 'Under the auspices of Rubus. The things he asked us to do and the potions we were told to make were not ... pleasant.'

I had a sudden epiphany. 'Dust,' I breathed. 'You created pixie dust.'

'To help faeries like us, not to hurt them. To ease the homesickness and lessen the ache.'

I raised my hands irritably. 'Why doesn't anyone believe that I sold pixie dust for the very same reason?'

Her mouth turned down. 'Because my uncle took my recipe and adapted it. My intention was for it to be a good thing, not a concoction designed to hold faeries up and down the country in thrall to Rubus. Not to create addicts. You sell dust and you know full well what effect it has on us.' Her tone left little doubt as to what she thought of me.

'Actually,' I said, 'right now I don't know much of anything.'

Artemesia frowned at me. 'Well you're here now,' she said eventually. 'Let's hear the story.'

Morgan, who'd been watching our exchange carefully but without interfering, jerked his chin at me. 'Tell her what you told me, Maddy. About how you felt when you woke up with no memory.'

I sighed. 'Sore ribs. Pounding headache. Stiff limbs. Rotten taste in my mouth. I cut my finger on a rowan-poisoned sword and didn't receive treatment for it until it was almost too late.'

Artemesia bit her lip. 'I need more detail.'

I shrugged. 'It was long and pointy. I only gave myself a small cut but—'

She glowered. 'Not about that. You're not poisoned by rowan now,' she said, as if I possessed the intellect of a wet paper bag. 'The taste in your mouth. I need specifics. Tell me more.'

Slightly confused, I clicked my tongue. 'Do we really have time for this? Shouldn't we be doing something to help Julie instead of worrying about my taste buds?'

'Just answer Arty,' Morgan drawled.

I would have snapped at the command in his voice but something about the stiff, unyielding way he held himself gave me pause. He'd also focused on the foul taste I'd described on my tongue. I reminded myself that I was like a minnow floundering in a world full of knowledgeable sharks. What the hell did I know about anything anyway?

'Wet dog,' I muttered. 'I tasted wet dog.'

Artemesia immediately whirled around, speeding back to the bar and hopping over it. From underneath it, she pulled out a massive leather-bound book and began flicking through its pages. 'It's just as well that I managed to rescue this from my uncle,' she said, as much to herself as to Morgan and me. 'He has to rely on memory while I have the apothecary's bible.' She bared her teeth in some sort of a smile. 'His memory's not like it used to be.' She glanced at me. 'It's not as bad as yours, though.'

I snorted. Well, that was a given. I walked up to the bar and sat gingerly on a narrow barstool next to Morgan. 'Why doesn't the Metropolitan look like this?' I enquired, while Artemesia continued to flip through the yellowing pages.

'Some of us choose to maintain a façade for humans,' he

answered. 'While some of us provide services solely for faeries. The cash the bar makes provides help for many of us. The potions Arty makes do the same, albeit in a different way.'

I pursed my lips. I supposed it made a sort of sense. I knew without asking that Rubus didn't have the same sort of symbiotic relationships or faery services. There was no longer any lingering doubt in my mind that my old self had chosen the wrong side. I glanced at Morgan. I wanted to tell him that. It might not alter anything between us but I desperately needed him to know. Before I could even draw breath to speak, however, Artemesia spoke again.

'I've got it,' she said, jabbing at a page. Her eyes danced. 'Well, well, well.'

Morgan raised his eyebrows. 'Are you going to share?'

'From what she's said, her amnesia wasn't an accident. It was wholly deliberate.'

I inhaled sharply. 'Go on.'

'The taste in your mouth is what gives it away. It's an after-effect of the potion. Myosotis is commonly termed forget-me-not by humans, for obvious reasons. However when combined with Dragon's Blood, it has the reverse effect and causes memory loss. If you add a little faery magic into that mix, well...' She gave a low whistle. 'The effects can be life-altering.' She raised her eyes to me as if awe-struck. 'Cool.'

I wrinkled my nose. 'Not so much. Let's back up here a second. Dragon's Blood?'

'So,' Morgan mused, 'Maddy wasn't just poisoned with rowan, she was also poisoned with this amnesia-causing potion.'

Artemesia nodded, beaming at him. 'Yep!'

I held up my hand. 'Dragon's Blood?'

'It would explain a great deal,' Morgan said.

'Hello?' I waved my hand vigorously. 'I'm still here, you

know. Are you trying to tell me that as well as faeries there are dragons? Just strolling around without anyone noticing?'

'Don't be silly,' Artemesia told me. 'Why on earth would you think that? Dragon's Blood is a type of tree resin. Real dragon's blood doesn't do a damned thing.'

I rolled my eyes. How exactly was I supposed to have known that? 'But dragons exist?'

'Apparently,' she sniffed. 'Not that I've ever met one.'

Morgan seemed unconcerned. 'The only dragon I've heard of near here is Chen and he's an ornery bastard who hates the lot of us.'

'Does he breathe fire?'

'No. He looks just like a human. He can't fly or perform magic or eat unsuspecting villagers. Generally, all dragons do is collect gold and treasure and moan a lot.'

Boring.

'Dragons,' Artemesia scoffed. 'Honestly! Like things aren't bad enough with all the faeries and bogles and redcaps around here. At least werewolves and vampires aren't real.'

I stiffened, shooting her a quick glance; fortunately she was too absorbed with the book in front of her to notice. The same flare of pain I'd felt earlier, when I'd been thinking about mentioning Julie's ethnicity, snapped through me. I grimaced. That wasn't fair. I hadn't been going to say anything.

Morgan, annoying arsebadger that he was, didn't miss a trick. 'What is it, Maddy?'

'Nothing,' I answered quickly. 'Except that now I'm more disturbed than ever. You're saying that someone did this to me deliberately. They wanted me to forget everything I knew.'

'Not *someone*.' Artemesia sounded grimly satisfied. '*Rubus*. The only person on this demesne other than me with the skill to create this kind of potion is my uncle. And he works for Rubus.'

So Morgan's brother had tried to make me forget something, no doubt relating to something terrible that he'd done. He obviously hadn't been convinced that it had worked because he'd also sent those blasted Redcaps to kill me. I curled my fingers into the soft palms of my hands, digging in so deeply that I almost drew blood. 'I'm going to kill him,' I whispered.

'The truce—' Morgan began.

I screeched, 'Let me have my freaking metaphors! Obviously I won't really kill him.' Frankly, I doubted I could. I hissed out a curse and started stomping around the room. A good stomp seemed about all that was left to me.

Morgan watched me for a moment before returning his attention to Artemesia. 'Is her memory going to return? Or is there some sort of antidote she can take?'

Her eyebrows flew up. 'You want her to be the same bitch she was before? She's bad enough now as it is.'

I stopped my stomping. 'Hey!'

Both Artemesia and Morgan ignored me. 'Rubus did this for a reason,' he said. 'I need to know what he wants her to forget.'

This whole situation was as mad as a box of frogs. I bet even Julie's scriptwriters couldn't come up with anything as nutty as this. 'This is ridiculous,' I muttered. I put my hands on my hips and stared hard at Artemesia. 'Well?' I demanded. 'Is there a cure?'

'Not that I know of,' she answered, holding her nerve. 'I can look into it. But everything might not be lost.' Her smile took on a triumphant edge. 'This is why my uncle wishes he still had this book. The magic used to create the forgetting potion is unstable.'

I didn't know why she looked so bloody happy. 'Unstable? You mean I'm likely to explode?'

Artemesia laughed. 'If only. No, it means that reality is going to seek to re-assert itself. Due to the magic bound in the herbs, the potion that must have been thrown down your throat is wholly unnatural. And nature always, *always,* seeks to re-assert herself. It's why faeries were permitted to visit the demesne in the first place. We were needed to re-balance nature, for both our sakes and the humans.'

'Yeah?' I growled. 'And how exactly is that working out for us?'

She gave my words a dismissive wave. 'Something went wrong. But sooner or later the border will re-open and nature will take over once again. I have faith,' she added serenely. 'But that's not what is important in this current scenario.' She pointed again at the page in front of her. 'The unnatural essence of the amnesia potion means that your body – or your consciousness, if you will – is going to continually try to solve the problem. You'll be drawn towards situations and people where the truth will reveal itself. Without realising it, you'll be forced to find out what it is that you've forgotten.'

It took a moment for her words to unjumble themselves. When they did, troubled clarity struck me like a thunderbolt. 'Dave,' I breathed. 'I was supposed to meet him. My consciousness drove me towards him, which in turn drove me to you.' I nodded at Morgan.

'Sure,' Artemesia said easily. 'Whoever Dave is.'

I thought about it. The same could be true of Julie: a part of me could have known that she was a vampire, so I was drawn to her in much the same way.

I realised that both Artemesia and Morgan were staring at me and I hastily dissembled. 'I was drawn to you as well,' I pointed out to Morgan. 'And I've still not even seen Rubus.'

Artemesia shrugged. 'Probably because whatever counts as a soul inside you knew that Morganus would help you and Rubus wouldn't.'

Morgan flashed a quick smug grin then tapped his mouth. 'So, we just need to be patient and see where events take

Madrona. Natural order, as in her memory, will be forced to re-assert herself.'

'She might not remember consciously,' Artemesia explained. 'But she'll be led towards people and situations that will provide the missing information to solve her problems.'

Morgan looked at me. 'Where do you want to go right now?'

'I want,' I said through gritted teeth, 'to find Julie.'

'We don't know where she is.' His answer was annoyingly calm. 'Where do you *feel* like going?'

My stomach grumbled. I shrugged; if nature was the answer, then that was the call I would answer. 'Food,' I replied. 'Preferably greasy and with as many calories as possible.'

He waved towards the door. 'Lead the way.'

'I really don't see how this will work,' I said doubtfully.

Artemesia grinned. 'I reckon it will. I'll hunt around and see if I come up with some sort of antidote but I can't guarantee it will work. Even if I don't find anything, you shouldn't be concerned. Be patient and forces unseen will take you to where you need to be.'

Forces unseen. Yeah. Mad. As. A. Box. Of. Frogs.

CHAPTER TWENTY

I took a bite out of my kebab, chilli sauce dripping down my chin and onto my fingers. 'This is all very well,' I said with my mouth full, 'but Julie isn't here. Time is still ticking. If we don't find her, goodness knows what Rubus will do to her.'

Morgan, who was somehow managing to eat his food without looking like a messy toddler, looked at me assessingly. 'You really are different without your memory,' he said. 'This interest in another person's wellbeing is most unlike you.'

'I only have your word that I'm a bad person.'

'Has anyone you've met so far suggested anything to the contrary?'

The unfortunate answer to that was no. 'I've obviously not met the right people,' I said. I looked at him, the shadow of stubble round his jaw and the faint laughter lines at the corners of his emerald green eyes, and I knew I was lying to myself.

I scratched my neck awkwardly and put down the kebab. 'I'm sorry,' I said, my words barely audible even to my own ears. 'It's clear that I treated you badly before.' That was a bit of an understatement. 'Despicably,' I amended. 'I want to be better. Maybe,' my fingers twitched, plucking at the paper napkin, 'maybe I could spend more time with you and learn how to be better. I'm not angling for anything here, Morgan. I...' I swallowed. 'I like being around you. A lot. More than I probably should.'

I avoided looking at him. When I finally peeked, the blazing hope in his expression before he quickly shuttered his emotions filled me with optimism.

'That might not be so bad,' he said gruffly. 'I don't hate spending time with you either.'

I supposed that was about the best I could hope for right now.

'You know,' he continued, 'you're pretty cute when you look at me appealingly with your big eyes like that.'

'Cute?' I spluttered. 'I'm not a puppy!'

He let out a bark of laughter. 'Just checking,' he said. 'It's good to know that the real Madrona is still in there somewhere. I'd hate to think that I beat that sharp tongue out of you. It's actually rather refreshing to be with someone who says exactly what they think. Children are like that before they reach a certain age, when they're still innocent enough to tell people exactly what they think.'

'In that case,' I said, 'I think you're a sexy beast.'

Morgan laughed again, although this time it was tinged with surprise. 'For all your faults, Maddy, you're pretty damned sexy yourself.'

We grinned at each other – then something caught Morgan's eye and he glanced out of the steamed-up window, his whole body stiffening. 'Well, I'll be damned,' he said. 'It looks like Arty was right after all.'

I frowned and followed his gaze. When I saw what he was looking at, I also tensed. I slowly pushed the kebab away from me and wiped my mouth with the napkin. 'Unbelievable,' I murmured.

If I hadn't had the evidence right in front of my own eyes, I'd never have believed it. Out there in the street, scoping out an upper-floor flat, were two nastily familiar Redcaps, the same two who were part of the trio that had attacked me at the golf course. The same two who had circled round us out on the quiet country road and abducted Julie. Without thinking, I rose to my feet. I was going to smash their ugly faces into the ground.

Morgan placed a warning hand on my arm. 'Don't,' he said.

I gave a deep growl. 'You already said the truce doesn't apply to them. I can do what I want.'

'They're strong.'

I lifted up my chin. 'I'll be stronger.'

'They'll have learnt from their mistakes and coated their weapons with rowan. You survived before because your wound was just a tiny nick. If a bullet hit you, the rowan would flood your system.'

'Then I'll dodge their damned bullets.'

'They probably want to kill us more than you want to kill them. We killed their buddy.'

'Brother, I reckon,' I answered. 'They look alike. They have to share the same gene pool. They're probably freaking triplets.'

'That doesn't make this situation any better,' Morgan pointed out unnecessarily. 'Remember, they've slipped from our grasp before. They could do it again.'

I was growing irritated. 'This time I won't let them.'

Morgan's grip tightened. 'If you kill them, you might never find your boss again.'

'She's my friend,' I answered softly. 'I might not have known her for long but I know that she's a friend.'

His answer, when it came, was equally quiet. 'I would like to think that over the last hours we've become friends again too. And friends don't let friends make daft mistakes.'

'Is that what we are?' I probed, keeping my eyes trained on the Redcaps loitering outside. 'Friends?'

When he didn't answer immediately, I allowed myself a quick glance at him. His face was inscrutable. I sighed; it was pointless angling after something that Morgan was unwilling to give. Whether I could remember or not, I'd given up any opportunity to claim more of him when I'd abandoned him for Rubus's camp.

'Fine,' I sighed. 'What would you suggest? We can't just let them go.' I paused. 'My own consciousness and the latent magic from the amnesia potion led us here in the first place.' That, and an empty belly. 'We can't waste this opportunity.'

'We watch them,' Morgan answered without hesitation. 'We see what they're up to then we follow them back to Rubus's lair. We'll be able to scope out his place, find your friend and deal with whatever comes next. There are plenty of faeries on my side who'll help me against my brother if need be.'

For a heartbeat I didn't answer. When I did, my voice was distant. 'On *our* side, Morgan.'

He gave a tight nod. 'Our side. As you say.'

At least he didn't argue about it; I wasn't sure what I'd have done if he had. I nodded and dismissed the subject. I couldn't be pedantic about grammar now. 'We're sitting ducks here,' I said. 'Even with the windows steamed up, it'll take only one glance and they'll spot us.'

'Then,' Morgan agreed, 'we need to make sure they don't spot us.'

He released his grip on my arm, pushed his chair back and stood up. Together we marched over to the counter and the young, pimply human behind it, who looked as if he were asleep on his feet. 'Is there a back way out?' Morgan asked.

The assistant blinked and yawned, as if startled to be asked a question. 'Uh, yeah, but...'

'Great,' Morgan said, flipping up the counter so that we could pass through. 'It's this way?'

I could see the boy weighing up his options; no doubt there were rules that customers were not permitted to be in this area. The steely look in Morgan's eye, not to mention whether it was worth raising an argument when you're on minimum wage, made up his mind. 'To the right,' he muttered.

I beamed at him. 'Good lad.' We skirted past him and the small galley kitchen. I glanced at Morgan and lowered my voice. 'Apparently I'm not the only one who's prepared to engage in a little intimidation when the situation calls for it.'

'I didn't intimidate him. I merely asked a question and he answered.'

Yeah, yeah. At least if was good to know that none of us were perfect – even if I pretended otherwise.

While Morgan tussled with the dented steel door, I straightened my shoulders and cracked my knuckles. I was nervous that the Redcaps would already have vanished. When we finally made it out, I breathed a sigh of relief. Their shadows were still visible from the lamppost up ahead. Not only that, but the angle of the buildings and the narrow alley we'd emerged into hid us from their view. This was going to be a piece of cake.

'The Madhatter rides again,' I whispered.

Morgan shot me a look. 'Where did you hear that?'

I gazed at him blankly. 'Huh?'

'Madhatter. That nickname. Where did you hear it?' There was an odd light in his eyes.

'From those bastards up ahead. That's what they called me.'

Morgan was frowning slightly. 'That's interesting.'

'Why?'

Before he could answer me, there was the sudden sound of breaking glass. We both stopped moving and turned in the direction of the noise. 'They're breaking in somewhere,' he murmured.

I tightened my lips. 'Right across from an all-lights-blazing, twenty-four-hour restaurant. Sloppy.'

'I don't think the kid in there is going to do anything.'

I tutted and slid forward, keeping close to the wall to avoid the Redcaps noticing. When I reached the corner of the building, I craned my head round for a brief look then pulled back. 'They have a rope,' I said. 'They're climbing up to the first floor.'

Morgan's mouth twisted. 'We'll have no choice but to intervene if they're hurting someone.'

I grimaced. 'You were right before. If we confront them now, we could lose any chance of finding both Rubus or Julie.'

'Are you willing to risk someone's life for that?'

Gasbudlikins. No wonder I'd chosen to be evil; working out the most heroic path to take was much harder than simply going hell for leather and being bad. I shrugged. 'I don't know,' I whispered. I ground my teeth, searching for the right answer. For any answer. 'We divert them,' I said finally. 'We do something to make them abandon whatever it is they're up to.'

'We could call the police.'

I thought about it. 'This might be over by the time they get here.' I bit my lip. 'You stay here. I have a plan.'

Without waiting for Morgan's agreement, I darted into the road. The Redcaps were busy trying to hoist themselves upwards. As sneakily as possible, I tiptoed until I was almost directly underneath them. I could feel Morgan's eyes boring into my back. He didn't need to worry; I wasn't going to engage the Redcaps.

On the edge of the pavement lay a brick, no doubt the same brick that they'd used to break the window. I scooped it up, ran to the nearest lamppost and threw the brick upwards, smashing the light with my first attempt. Glass tinkled down and I froze, worried that the Redcaps might notice, but they were too focused on their nefarious deeds. They were heaving themselves through the window. Heart thudding, I jogged to the next lamppost and did the same thing. I was pretty impressed by my aim; maybe I should take up cricket.

At least a minute had gone by and there was no sign of the Redcaps now. I ran several feet away, made sure my back was turned, threw back my head and began to shriek for all I was worth. I almost shattered my own eardrums, let alone those of the poor innocent people who lived on the street.

It didn't take long before curtains began twitching in the houses and flats around me. Worried faces peered out and a few bedroom lights were switched on.

'Help meeeeeee!' I screeched, reaching true caterwaul point. No one would stay in the land of nod if I could help it.

Doors opened. I waited until three people, hugging dressing gowns round them, emerged. Then I made a run for it, pelting away from where the Redcaps were. I continued to raise hell as I went.

As soon as I came to a crossroads, I veered off and circled round, back to the spot where Morgan was waiting. I doubled over, breathing hard.

'Impressive,' he murmured.

'Has it worked though?' I said, in between gasps. 'Did I spook them enough?' From my position, I couldn't see a thing.

Morgan looked out of the alley. 'There are still people going back into their houses.' He frowned. 'None of them are checking down the street to see if you're okay.'

'I screamed like a madwoman and ran away,' I said drily. 'They're forgiven.'

He snorted then his body went still. 'Wait.'

I rolled my eyes. 'I *am* waiting.'

Morgan ignored my gibe. 'The humans have gone and the Redcaps are coming out.'

I held my breath. 'With anyone?'

'No. They're alone.'

Whew. 'Good.'

I must have looked relieved because Morgan squeezed my arm. 'That was impressive work.'

I offered him a mock curtsey but unfortunately he'd already turned back to focus on the Redcaps. I blew him a kiss as well, for good measure.

'What are you doing, Maddy?' he enquired.

Did the man have eyes in the back of his head? 'Nothing. What are the Redcaps doing?' I asked.

'Getting into a van. We'll have to retrieve the bike and follow them.'

'Can you keep out of sight?' I asked. It was an honest question. 'We can't afford for them to spot us.'

Morgan glanced back at me. '*Please*. They don't stand a chance.'

CHAPTER TWENTY-ONE

By the time we got Morgan's bike and set off in pursuit, the Redcaps had quite a lead. That was fine by me; as long as we didn't lose them altogether, it was imperative that we stayed well back. It was the middle of the night and there were virtually no other vehicles on the road, let alone motorbikes with engines louder than my own banshee-style screaming. Fortunately, Morgan's confidence wasn't misplaced and he was more than capable of keeping the arsebadgers in sight without them noticing us.

There was only one point, when they made a sharp right turn, that I felt concerned and even then the numerous traffic lights and the Redcaps' unwillingness to trigger any traffic cameras meant that we found them again quickly enough. It was almost disappointing; I'd been hoping for a high-speed chase through the deserted city streets. Next time, I comforted myself. Next time.

The building they pulled up in front of was depressingly similar to the warehouse where Dave had been camping out. Broken windows, graffiti-laden walls, air of desolate desperation; check, check and check.

I grimaced as Morgan and I remained at a safe distance and watched the Redcaps enter a side door.

'What's wrong?' he asked.

I flipped up the visor on the helmet and scowled at his back. 'How the hell do you know something's wrong? You're not even looking at me.'

'I know you, Maddy.'

That was hardly much of an explanation. I thumped him between his shoulder blades. 'Explain yourself,' I said sternly. 'Do faeries have special three-sixty vision?' I experimented with my own eyes, swivelling them first one way then the other.

'We do. It's a difficult technique to master, though. Get off the bike and I'll show you – it might come in handy.'

Cool. I slid off and ambled round till I was facing him.

'What you have to do is tilt your head back fifty-two degrees,' he said

'Fifty-two? How am I supposed to know how far that it is? It's not like I'm carrying a protractor.'

He laughed. 'Do your best.'

I did as he bade. It was awkward but not entirely uncomfortable.

'Now,' he said, 'lick your lips three times, spin around and do a star jump.'

To my shame, I started to. I licked my lips at least twice. Then I came to a halt and glared. 'You're taking the piss out of me, aren't you?'

Morgan's face split into a massive grin. 'I am indeed.' He unhooked his leg from the bike and shook out his hair as if he were in a shampoo advert. I wasn't complaining. 'We faeries are impressive but we're not so impressive that we can beat the basic laws of biology.'

I frowned. 'Then how do you always know what I'm doing?'

'As I said,' he told me, 'I know you. When you're so close,

I'm ... attuned to you. I could hear your breathing change. And your body was pressed up against mine. I felt it when you tensed.'

My mouth was suddenly inexplicably dry. He was paying that much attention to me? Slightly discombobulated, I shuffled my feet. 'Spiders,' I said, by way of explanation.

Morgan blinked at me. 'Pardon?'

'There were lots of cobwebs in the last place we went to. Rubus's old hide-out. Fortunately I couldn't see any spiders but the cobwebs were massive.' I shrugged awkwardly. 'I guess I have mild arachnophobia.'

'Don't be ridiculous.' His tone was so dismissive that I bristled.

'It's a phobia. It's not supposed to be logical. It just *is*. I can't help the way I feel.'

'The Madrona I knew wasn't afraid of spiders. She wasn't afraid of anything.'

I pulled back my shoulders. 'The Madrona you knew dumped you for your brother and was by all accounts an evil bitch. At least *I'm* trying.'

He stilled and his eyes met mine. For a long moment, we simply looked at each other, surrounded by night and silence and the whisper of old, broken promises that I couldn't remember.

Eventually I shook myself. 'We should get going,' I said. 'Julie is in that building and I'm going to rescue her. You can do whatever you want with Rubus. I just want to get out of there with my new boss still alive.' I sniffed. 'And I want to find out what happens with Stacey and her husband.'

'Who the hell is Stacey?'

I smiled. 'I'll tell you all about her once we're out of this place.' I raised my eyebrows. 'Coming?'

He growled in the affirmative.

With my shoulders hunched and my back slumped, as if poor posture could hide me from any prying eyes, I slipped across the street. Morgan followed. The last thing either of us needed was to end up trapped in Rubus's lair without knowing how to get out, so I went left while Morgan went right. We met up round the back of the derelict warehouse.

'No other doors round this side,' I whispered, 'apart from the one the arsebadgers entered, and the front door itself. There's a low window that is ajar though. It's on a latch that can't be reached from the outside, but it's an option for an escape route from inside if we need it.'

Morgan nodded. 'There's a door back that way,' he told me, pointing in the direction he'd just come from. 'It's padlocked and chained so it doesn't look like an option.'

'Then it looks like we enter the same way they did.' I glanced around. The streets were still quiet but there was a faint glow appearing on the horizon. 'Dawn isn't far off. If we're going to do this, we should do it now.'

I was prepared to argue with him; I couldn't face staking out this place until we were sure about who was inside. I didn't have the energy and I wasn't convinced Julie had the time. Fortunately, Morgan offered a low murmur of agreement, pivoted and led the way back to the first side door.

The door handle was a simple affair. Morgan twisted it and I gave a brief sigh of relief when the door swung open. Weak florescent light poured out. Morgan looked round the edge of the door and held up his arm to me with his fingers curled into a tight fist. It was obviously some kind of silent signal but, not being SWAT or even in possession of a memory that might tell me what he wanted me to do, I simply stared. Then I stepped past him and into the building.

Morgan grabbed my shoulder. 'What are you doing?' he hissed.

'Breaching the stronghold.'

'I told you to wait!'

I shook my head. 'No, you didn't.'

He made the gesture again. 'This means wait.'

I tilted my head. 'How am I supposed to know that?'

Morgan rolled his eyes in despair. He beckoned with one hand. 'This is come.' Then he circled one index finger in the air. 'This is return to the rally point. That's here.' He moved his hand up and down. 'This is crouch down.'

I flung my arms up in the air. 'This is Y,' I said.

'Why what?'

I ignored the question and moved my arms again, curving my fingers down to my head. 'This is M.' I switched. 'This is C. And this is...'

'Very funny.' For some reason, he wasn't smiling. 'How is it that you know the dance moves to a stupid song but you can't remember anything important?'

'I think you're underestimating the role of the Village People in human culture. And I don't know why I remember that. I don't know why I remember how to drive or how to speak English. Nothing about any of this makes any sense to me.'

'You don't make any sense to me,' he growled.

I flipped up my middle finger. 'I remember this signal too.'

Morgan clenched his teeth. 'Fine. Forget the signals. Just...' he sighed in irritation. 'Just let me go in front and follow my lead.'

I saluted. 'Aye, aye.'

He tutted and pushed past me.

The exchange had loosened the knot of tension inside my stomach and helped me to relax slightly. That was good; if I jumped at every shadow or tiptoed along on tenterhooks, I'd get both of us noticed. The banter seemed to have helped

Morgan, too, despite him appearing vexed. His shoulders were less rigid. I decided that could only be a good thing.

In any case, now that we were inside the time for fun and games was over. Rubus must be here – which meant the entire building was probably teeming with his minions. The fact that I was supposed to be one of those minions didn't exactly fill me with joy. Whatever he'd been to me in the past, if he'd harmed one hair on Julie's head just because she was a vampire, I'd burn this place to the ground and everyone in it.

I closed the door behind us, using a piece of cardboard to wedge it open so we could make a fast exit if we had to. Then I caught up to Morgan, my eyes swinging this way and that for any signs of life. So far there was nothing more than a long corridor with cracked bare walls and overhanging strip lights. Rubus's life certainly wasn't as glamorous or luxurious as I'd expected. What was the point in being evil if it didn't translate into gold-plated penthouse apartments?

We must have gone at least twenty feet down the dingy hallway before we came to a doorway. We came to a halt outside it, listening for any sounds. After a moment, Morgan turned to me and frowned. I shook my head. Nope. I couldn't hear a damned thing, either. I knew enough about my own abilities by now; if someone was beyond that door, even if they were only breathing, I'd have been able to hear them.

Morgan's expression was stony; he clearly wasn't happy with the lack of life we'd come across so far. He squared his shoulders and set off again. I stayed as close to his back as I could. There was no way I was going to be left behind.

The same thing happened three times. There were three more closed doors; each time, we stopped and waited, listening with all our faery might, but there was nothing. The warehouse appeared to be completely deserted.

There was a right turn at the end of the corridor. Morgan

started down it but I touched his shoulder in a bid to forestall him. 'Something about this isn't right,' I whispered.

'I know.'

'It's too quiet.'

'I know.'

'We're probably walking into a trap.'

His expression tightened. 'I know.' He looked back down the corridor. 'Maybe you should wait outside.'

I snorted. No chance. I wouldn't even deign to comment on such a ridiculous suggestion. 'Perhaps the actual lair isn't here at all. Perhaps this part is just for show and the main den is underground.'

We looked down on the off-chance that the floor would give us some clue. 'It's possible,' he conceded quietly. 'But we've still got a lot to explore on this level first.'

'Wouldn't we have heard something by now if anyone was up here?' I asked. At that very moment, my ears prickled at a distant sound.

I stopped moving. Morgan looked at me. 'What did you hear?'

'A clink.' It hadn't lasted long but it wasn't a natural sound.

He nodded. 'That's what I heard too.' He pointed round the corner. 'Let's go.'

We set off, our footsteps even lighter and quieter than they had been before. There were no more clinks but I felt more confident that we were heading in the right direction. I couldn't fail Julie again; it simply wasn't an option. Images of her corpse flashed through my mind with stomach-churning regularity. There was nothing to suggest she actually was dead; if Rubus had wanted that outcome, no doubt the Redcaps wouldn't have bothered kidnapping her in the first place. The alleyway attacker would have used a stake, not a Taser. All the same, my trepidation was growing and it wasn't a feeling I enjoyed.

We kept walking, turning right twice. The corridor remained depressingly similar. It wasn't until we reached the second-to-last doorway that my senses started to prickle again.

I stopped. Morgan, who'd continued on ahead, turned his head. He frowned at me, indicating silently that there was nothing to be heard beyond the doorway I was standing beside. I jerked my head at it. He was right that there were no sounds but there was something about the quality of the silence through the old oak veneer that was different. As Morgan moved back towards me, I reached for the handle and gently pushed it down, revealing a glimpse of the room beyond. When I saw what was covering the inside of the door and the walls, I knew we were finally getting somewhere.

Not daring to open the door more than an inch or two, I pointed. Even from his awkward angle, he could see the black soundproofing foam covering every inch of the space. His jaw tightened. I grinned; at least this wasn't going to be a wasted visit. Rubus was indeed a canny arsebadger.

I edged inside. The room was about eight metres square, with two more foam-covered doors at opposite ends. Nothing else was visible – but if this was merely the gateway to the lair beyond, that wasn't surprising. I strained my ears again but I couldn't hear anything other than Morgan's and my own breathing.

I stayed on the balls of my feet and headed for the door on the left-hand side, motioning to Morgan to take the one on the right. His mouth twisted briefly, as if he were unhappy at us splitting up. Although I was more than happy to keep him by my side, I was getting bored with skulking around.

'Three minutes,' I mouthed, indicating that we should meet back here after that time was up. He blinked at me in reluctant agreement and, with one final glance at each other, we went our separate ways. I opened my door and Morgan opened his then we vanished from each other's sight.

Unsurprisingly, the short corridor that greeted my eyes was covered in soundproofing foam, just like the previous room. There was one more door. Grimly, I stalked up to it, pressing my ear against the foam triangles in case there was anything to be heard. When not even a whisper reached my ears, I pulled back and braced myself. I was more than ready for what lay beyond.

With one swift movement, I yanked on the door handle and flung it open, leaping inside with a short-lived roar.

'Goodness,' Julie murmured from a red-velvet chaise longue. 'That's quite a dramatic entrance, Mads. Being around me has rubbed off on you already.' She took a sip of the gin and tonic in her hand and smiled. 'Chin-chin.'

CHAPTER TWENTY-TWO

My yell died on my lips and my mouth fell open. 'What the gasbudlikins...'

Julie tutted. 'Darling, you look terrible. Have you not been sleeping?'

I stared at her. To make doubly sure she wasn't a figment of my imagination, I shuffled forward and poked her. She was definitely real. Then it occurred to me that she might be a faery wearing a glamour. Could Redcaps glamour themselves? If I could do it surely they could. I crossed my arms. 'If you're really Julie,' I said, 'tell me what you were buying the first time we met.'

'Who else would I be if I wasn't Julie?'

'Answer the fucking question.' My voice was low. I didn't have the faintest idea what was going on here but I wasn't going to relax until I got some answers.

'Darling!' Her eyes opened wide in mock shock. 'Language! If you really need me to say it, I was buying some Valium. Or rather Mark was buying it for me.'

I stayed where I was. No glamour then; this really was the Julie I knew. That only meant I had more questions now. I stepped back, suddenly desperate to keep some distance between her and myself. 'You need to tell me what's going on here,' I said. 'And you need to tell me now.'

The door behind me thumped open. I sprang back, spotting Morgan facing off against both Redcap arsebadgers. My stomach dropped. I jabbed my thumb at Julie and growled, 'Stay here,' then I jumped into the fray to help him.

The Redcaps were gunning for Morgan, grim fury on their faces. I had to draw one of them away from him. I needn't have worried; it took both Redcaps less than a second to recognise me. As soon as they did, they abandoned their onslaught on Morgan and spun towards me.

The shorter of the two reached me first, slamming a punch into my stomach that I wasn't fast enough to avoid. I doubled over, winded and in agony. The second Recap thumped my spine and I crumpled, wheezing. All I could think about was the pain.

One of them gave a strangled cry. 'You killed him!'

I rolled onto my side, barely managing to draw my knees up into a foetal position so I could protect myself against more attacks. Some fabulous fighter I was, I thought dully. Morgan roared as he threw himself at the Redcaps, fury lacing every indistinct syllable. Through brimming eyes, I registered him grab the backs of their heads and shove them together so their foreheads bounced off each other. The shorter one took the worst of the impact; he fell backwards with a groan before tumbling down onto the floor next to me.

While I willed my body to recover, Morgan and the second Redcap went at it, fists and feet flying. Neither paused to speak; I wasn't sure they even paused to breathe.

Morgan grabbed hold of the Redcap's arm, twisting it hard behind him. The Redcap reacted by swinging his head backwards and connecting with Morgan's nose. Morgan fell back a few steps, his body landing against the foam-covered wall. He pushed himself off and jabbed a kick at the Redcap's chest. In response, the Redcap lashed out with his foot. Even I heard the crunch of Morgan's ribs.

The fallen arsebadger next to me moaned and twitched. He was already starting to move again; another moment or two and I knew he'd be back on his feet. I couldn't allow that to happen – Morgan had his hands full as it was.

Pain still throbbed through my body, although it was lessening by the second. I tensed my stomach and rolled, managing to get on top of the Redcap and pinning him in place to stop him re-joining the attack on Morgan. I wasn't sure it was going to do any good, however, because the other Redcap had pulled out a gun and pointed it at Morgan. What was it with these guys and their damned guns?

My stomach sank. This wasn't a country road with plenty of room to manoeuvre; in this small space, there was nowhere to go and no moves to make. Morgan froze, lowering his fists. I did the only thing left to us and straddled the Redcap underneath me, wrapping my hands round his throat and squeezing. He choked, his face turning a fascinating shade of purple. In my peripheral vision, I spotted his brother pressing his gun even harder against the underside of Morgan's chin. Stalemate.

All of a sudden there was a sound behind us. Before I could glance round, a cold liquid drenched me. I heard the Redcap holding Morgan swear loudly and I realised that exactly the same had happened to him.

We all stopped what we were doing and stared at Julie, who was holding an empty glass in one hand and a half-empty bottle in the other. 'Waste of good gin, if you ask me,' she said. 'This would be far easier if you all simply spoke to each other instead of attacking first.'

The Redcap underneath me spat out, 'She works for Rubus.'

His words were barely understandable given that I was still gripping his throat but it didn't stop me from snarling at him. 'I work for *her*!' I retorted angrily. 'Or at least I used to. I'm not sure what's going on now. The only ones around here who work for Rubus at this moment in time are you and your ugly buddy.'

'You're a fucking idiot.'

I tightened my grip. 'Say that again,' I said. 'Go on. I dare you.'

Julie sighed loudly. 'You're *all* idiots.' She walked over and kicked the Redcap.

'Good,' I said. 'He deserved that.' I'd barely finished speaking when she slapped me sharply on the cheek. 'Hey!'

'You deserved that too,' she answered serenely. 'Let's all go and sit down in the next room and talk about this like adults.'

'I'm not going anywhere.'

'Madrona,' Morgan said in a strained voice. 'Do you have any idea what is going on here?'

'Not a gasbudlikin clue.'

The Redcap holding the gun snarled at Morgan. 'Why are you with her?' he asked. 'You're supposed to hate your brother. Are you back with him now? Is that what this is all about?'

Julie flung back her head and let out a high-pitched scream. Yet again we all looked at her. She stopped the ear-piercing noise and smiled benignly. 'That's better. Honestly, I thought actors were hard to deal with but they've got nothing on you lot.'

'We're not sitting down on the sofa and having a little chat, Julie!' I said. I didn't trust her, not with the way she was acting and the fact that she didn't appear to be a prisoner.

'That's fine then,' she answered. 'Stay here. Then once everyone has said their piece, you can kill each other and I can go on my merry way. But let's talk first.' There was something about her tone that brooked no argument. 'You start, Mads.'

I was about to refuse but something in Morgan's eyes stopped me. 'Alright.' I glared at both her and the Redcaps. 'I'm a faery.'

'They said that too,' Julie murmured. 'We'll have to compare supernatural notes later.'

If there was going to be a later; right now, I wasn't so sure. 'Yeah,' I said unconvincingly. 'Anyway, I woke up on a golf course last Saturday night. I don't remember anything before then, not my name, not my ethnicity, not anything. There was a dead body next to me and, before I could call the police and ask for help, those arsebadgers attacked me and tried to kill me.' I narrowed my gaze at the Redcap underneath me.

'You're still alive, aren't you?' he said, his expression twisting. 'The same can't be said for Winn. You killed him.' He flicked a disparaging look at Morgan. 'So did you. You did it together. We were going to approach you for help. Just as well we chose not to.'

'Winn? He's the Redcap who came at us on the country road?' I asked.

He sniffed. 'Yeah. He was our brother. He was a good guy and you broke his neck without a second thought.'

'That was not our intention. We weren't trying to kill him,' Morgan said. 'His death was entirely an accident. We were only trying to stop him from killing us.'

'And abducting you,' I added to Julie. 'Although I'm beginning to think all that stuff about getting stalked and kidnapped was a lie.'

'I wasn't lying,' she said very quietly. 'Not about any of it.'

The Redcaps exchanged glances. 'We were trying to kidnap her,' admitted the one next to Morgan. 'But we have our reasons.'

'Go on then,' I hissed. 'Spit them out.'

'There's actually only one.' He hesitated, uncoiled tension

lingering in his large body. He looked at Morgan and then at Julie, who nodded encouragingly. He sighed and rubbed his forehead with his free hand. 'Rubus. We're trying to stop him.'

My brow furrowed. 'But you work for Rubus.'

He shook his head. 'We pretend to work for him. As Redcaps, we're beneath his notice. He'll use us for dirty jobs when he needs to but most of the time he ignores us. That suits us because we're smarter than he thinks and we know exactly what he's up to. Our plan is to stop him. There's no other choice.'

'How are we supposed to believe that?' I asked.

'How are we supposed to believe you have amnesia?' he countered.

I shrugged. 'It is what it is. You *did* kidnap Julie.'

His answer was calm and pragmatic. 'She's special. We can use her. She'll help us bring the fight to Rubus and she can help us win. At least,' he added with a sneer, 'we've not hurt her. The only killers around here are you faeries.'

'Not through lack of trying on your part!' I responded.

The Redcap I was sitting on stiffened, his anger flaring up again to match mine. 'We were only trying to wound you, not kill you. Our bullets would only have slowed you down. Even if we'd hit you, the fact that you're a faery means you'd have survived. Besides,' he sniffed, 'if we'd succeeded in ending your life, Winn would probably still be alive.'

I tightened my grip on his neck and snarled. I wasn't going to take the blame for this mess. I wasn't convinced I could have done any differently, given the information I'd had at the time. Besides, I knew that murder had been on their mind that night up at the golf course, no matter what they said.

This time, both Morgan and Julie stepped in to soothe the waters. Morgan offered me a reassuring smile, his posture relaxed despite the gun still pressing into his flesh, while Julie knelt down and smiled at the Redcap I was holding. His chest rose and fell with fast, furious breaths; he still looked as if he'd happily slit my throat given half the chance. I imagined that the expression on my face was the same.

'I apologise for what happened to Winn,' Morgan said. 'We were only trying to wound him and protect ourselves. I vow to you that killing him was not our intention.'

Morgan's Redcap, who was maintaining more stoicism than his brother, jumped in. 'We can point fingers and lay blame later. Let's stick to information sharing for now, shall we? We got the idea to use others from Rubus. He's been using humans to do his work for him. He tried to get a dragon to work for him too but that didn't pan out. Luckily for us, he doesn't know that any other supernatural species exist. In our demesnes, they're common knowledge. If vampires and werewolves are there, it stood to reason they were here too. We just had to find them.' He raised his shoulders in a massive shrug. 'We researched. We found her.'

Julie smiled prettily in response and stood up again. 'Lucky old me.'

'There are werewolves?' I asked.

Morgan coughed. 'She's a vampire?'

We looked at each other. 'Well,' I said to him, '*we're* faeries.'

Both Redcaps snorted in unison. 'All you high-faluting species are the same. You have so much power, you think you're the best, that there's no one else like you. There are faeries and there are vampires and there are werewolves and there are dragons. Just because you don't see them, or haven't met them, doesn't mean they don't exist. You're so up yourselves, you never to stop to consider whether there are other magical beings like yourselves.'

I had to concede that he might have a point. 'Ethnicity and egos aside,' I said, 'what is Rubus doing that's so bad you have to infiltrate his organisation and spy on him? I mean, I understand he's evil.' I shot a quick look at Morgan, whose expression was suddenly inscrutable. 'I don't remember who Rubus is or what he looks like, but I've learnt enough to believe that he's not a good faery. But why do you care if he sells drugs to other faeries and gets some humans to help him? What's the big deal?'

The Redcap beneath me laughed humourlessly. 'You really don't remember anything, do you? Pixie dust is just a sideline. Rubus,' he all but spat the name, 'has far more grandiose plans. He thinks he'll find a way back home. He couldn't be more wrong.'

I frowned. 'What do you mean? What way back home?' I noticed that Morgan had gone pale, as if he already had a dreadful inkling about what the Redcap was referring to.

'Rubus thinks all he has to do to re-open the borders and get everyone back to where they belong is to destroy this demesne.'

'The entire planet?'

'In a sense.'

That was stupid. 'What's he going to do?' I enquired. 'Set off a nuclear weapon? Or several?'

The Redcap shook his head. 'He's going to flood this demesne with magic.'

I still wasn't getting it. 'How is that a bad thing?'

'This world is run on technology,' Morgan said quietly. 'Magic has no place here. This demesne can withstand small amounts but a surge of magic could destroy everything. That's why altering time is forbidden. It's too much magic to use in one go.'

'You mean every time I did that, I almost brought down the apocalypse on all our heads?' I shrieked. 'Why didn't you say so?'

'I did.'

'No, you bloody didn't! All you said was that it was forbidden!'

'Well, there you go. I told you more than enough.'

'You're very lucky we're friends now,' I told him.

'Actually,' the tall Redcap said, 'altering time, as long as it's just a temporary, short-lived measure, isn't going to cause that much harm.'

'There are still risks,' Morgan said, ignoring my look. 'Even if they are minor.'

'Anyway,' the Redcap said, 'we've heard enough whispers and seen enough evidence that Rubus has worked out how to bring magic here. Chen, the ancient Chinese dragon I mentioned earlier, was working on a device that would suck magic from other demesnes and bring it here. He thought it would help him in his bid to garner more treasure from other worlds. He only realised after its inception what damage it might cause. He had no trouble keeping it away from Rubus.' His mouth flattened. 'Dragons are good at keeping their possessions to themselves. But he died last week and now all bets are off. From what we've gathered, the device is still here in Manchester. We don't know exactly where it is or what it looks like, but we know that Rubus doesn't yet have it.' He pointed at me. 'She was hunting for it. So were others. That's why we were on her trail. We thought she'd found it and we were prepared to do anything to stop her.'

I stiffened. 'The bogle. On the golf course. The dead bogle whose head…' My voice trailed away. I looked first at one Redcap then the other. 'Did you do that? Did you kill him?'

Both of them looked confused. 'We're pretty sure that was you.'

'Me?' My voice almost reached a screech. Without thinking, I released my hold on the Redcap and stood up. Julie and Morgan were watching me with concerned expressions, although there was a far steelier watchfulness behind Morgan's eyes.

'The sword was yours. We saw you with it earlier in the day.'

'No.' I shook my head vehemently. 'It was coated with rowan. That's poisonous to faeries, not to bogles.' I checked with Morgan. 'Right?'

He nodded. 'That's correct.'

The Redcap stood up and dusted himself down. He glanced meaningfully at his brother and, in response, his brother lowered the gun from Morgan's throat. Relieved, I ran a hand through my hair. When I realised that hand was shaking, I dropped it hastily. Alas, from the others' expressions, I wasn't fooling anyone.

'DTs,' I said quickly. 'I think I might be an alcoholic.' I licked a few drops of gin from my bare arm. 'Mmm. That's better.'

The Redcap next to Morgan scratched his head. 'I always wondered why you were called the Madhatter,' he said. 'Now I know.'

Morgan snapped his fingers. 'I should have realised.' He looked at me. 'I gave you that nickname for no other reason than that Rubus hated it. He forbade anyone from using it. Anyone loyal to Rubus would have done whatever he asked, but you said they called you Madhatter at the golf course.' He raised his eyes to the Redcaps. 'You really aren't loyal to him.'

They bowed together. The slightly taller one nudged his companion. 'It's details like that which can get us killed.'

I hissed. 'Can we get back to the part about me on the golf course carrying a big, old, poisonous sword? Because that can't be true. I don't believe I killed anyone.'

'All I'm telling you is what we saw,' said the Redcap 'We didn't know what was going on when we found them so we disposed of both the body and the sword. We drove them to the coast and tossed them off the nearest cliff.'

'Maybe, Mads,' Julie interjected, with an inappropriately bright tone, 'you wanted everyone to think that this bogle attacked you, instead of the other way around. Coating the weapon with something that's poisonous only to you would make everyone believe your story.'

I tried to ignore the oily upsurge of nausea. 'You're saying that I followed that bogle up there with the intention of killing him and then covering it up. You're saying I'm a murderer. You're saying I committed premeditated murder.'

'It's only a theory.'

'Do you know anything about the bogle?' I demanded. 'Who was he? Why would I have killed him? If...' I swallowed. 'If I killed him.'

'His name was Charrie. He showed up from time to time. As far as we can tell, he was tasked the same sort of jobs as we were. We know he visited Rubus three days before he died, but we don't know any more than that. You should know more than us – you're the one who's closest to Rubus out of all us.'

'I don't know anything about Rubus!' I realised I was shouting so I tried to lower my voice. 'I don't remember anything about him,' I said, my shoulders slumping in defeat. 'I don't even know if I *want* to remember anything any more.'

Morgan moved over to me. The Redcaps tensed but all he did was put his arm round my shoulders and squeeze them gently. I leaned into his embrace for the briefest moment then something vital occurred to me and I pulled away. 'Wait,' I said. 'The bogle guy had a sheath.' At their expressions of confusion, I explained further. 'At his back – he had an empty sword sheath. So either you're mistaken or,' I added grimly, 'simply lying through your crooked, yellow teeth. The poisoned sword had to be his.'

'We're not lying. We were not present when the murder took place but you were definitely the one who brought that weapon to the golf course. For one thing, the reek of rowan is how we managed to tail you.'

'You had money,' I said, reaching for any detail I could use to protest my innocence. 'You all had exactly the same amount of brand new bank notes in your pockets. You were paid to come after me.' I glanced at Morgan. 'Probably by Rubus.'

'You need to stop jumping to conclusions. Yes, we had money. We were planning to get hold of you and take you to Morganus. We realised we were out of our depth and we needed help to stop Rubus. We each had the same amount of money because we emptied our bank accounts and split the cash between us so if we were separated...'

'Or killed,' interrupted the other Redcap.

His brother nodded. 'Or killed, we'd each have our own bargaining power. We'd have a chance of escaping.'

Morgan's eyes were dark. 'You thought you could pay me off? Throw me a bit of money and I'd do whatever you asked?'

'Not really. But we thought we could shoot her,' he pointed to me, 'and bring her to you as both proof of Rubus's deeds and as collateral. Then you might listen to us and consider helping.'

Morgan rubbed his chin thoughtfully while I just glared. 'Shoot Madrona?' he murmured. 'And bring her injured, bleeding body to me?' He nodded. 'Yeah. Good plan.'

My jaw dropped. Arsebadger. He flashed me an amused smile. I rolled my eyes.

'Julie,' I said suddenly. 'She had threats. Nasty letters and icky animal parts shoved through her letterbox. You can't tell me you're pretending to be the heroes of this piece when you did things like that to her.'

'That wasn't us.'

'But we found the guys who were doing it,' his brother said.

He bared his teeth. 'They won't try anything like that again.' His eyes took on an odd sheen of glee that was somehow the most terrifying thing about all of this.

Julie grinned. 'Once you've sorted out this Rubus fellow, you should think about becoming bodyguards. Is it a profession either of you have considered?'

'Hey!' I protested. 'What about me?'

'Darling,' she said, 'I was abducted from right under your nose. I'm no longer convinced this is your best career path.'

She had a point but that didn't mean I had to be happy about it. I'd never even got chance to wear a real earpiece or had time to learn kung-fu.

'What are your names?' Morgan asked, addressing the Redcaps.

They exchanged looks. 'Why do you want to know?'

'Yeah, Morgan,' I drawled. 'Their names don't matter.' I paused. 'Unless you need them for their gravestones.'

Morgan grimaced, exasperated. 'You are not helping, Maddy. We need to know their names because it'll be easier when we start working together.'

Julie clapped her hands in delight and the taller Redcap pursed his lips. The other Redcap and I exploded. 'We're not working together!' we spat in unison. Then we turned and glared at each other.

'You killed our brother,' the Redcap yelled at me.

'It was an accident! And you tried to kill me!'

'We weren't trying to kill you! We just wanted to make you bleed a bit and kidnap you!'

'Well, that makes everything better then, doesn't it?' I said sarcastically.

Morgan sighed. 'We keep going round in circles. Whatever has happened before, and however we feel about each other, it appears we have a common goal.'

The tall Redcap nodded. 'Stopping Rubus once and for all.' He looked at Morgan. 'I'm Jinn.'

'Don't tell them our names!' his brother howled.

I smirked. 'He's Jinn. Your brother was Winn. Let me guess ... you're Rubbish Binn?'

'He's Finn.'

Finn huffed and stamped his feet. Jinn raised his bushy eyebrows at him. 'The enemy of my enemy is my friend.'

'That bitch is not my friend!'

'You got that right,' I added.

Julie tutted. 'You're frenemies. I have loads of them and they really can be tremendous fun. Let's go back into the other room. There are more glasses and there's definitely more gin.' She smiled at me. 'As hideouts go, this really isn't so bad.'

I sniffed. 'The décor leaves something to be desired.'

Jinn shrugged. 'We had to do something to hide her from the super hearing of faeries like you.'

I nudged Finn. 'Super hearing. That's because we're super-heroes. Unlike you.'

'Enough, Maddy!' Morgan roared.

'Is Jinn as annoying as Morgan is?' I asked him.

Surprisingly, Finn's mouth twitched in amusement. 'You have no idea,' he muttered.

Morgan and Jinn simultaneously folded their arms in irritation. This shaky partnership could actually be quite a lot of fun, I decided.

'I vote,' I said aloud, 'that we go back to the golf course. There will be some sort of clue there that I didn't kill that bogle.'

'It doesn't matter whether you killed the bogle or not,' Jinn said. Except it mattered to me. 'What matters is finding out what Rubus is up to and stopping him before he destroys this entire demesne and all the humans in it.'

Morgan frowned. 'The bogle, Charrie, went to the golf

course, presumably on Rubus's orders. So did you Madrona. There must be something there that will provide a clue about Rubus's plans.'

'We scoured the area. There's nothing,' Finn grumbled. 'There's no need to go back. We even used a reveal spell after we recovered from the Madhatter's attack.'

I coughed loudly. '*You* attacked me. Not the other way around.'

He waved dismissive. 'Anyway, we used the spell in case there was any magical residue, or anything you or the bogle had inadvertently left behind. There was nothing.'

'You used a what spell?' Julie asked.

Morgan smiled at her. 'When there are some faery-related objects or spells, or—'

'Not just faery,' Finn interrupted.

Morgan inclined his head, acknowledging the point. 'I apologise. When there are some alternate demesne-related objects or spells or whatever, they are often hidden from sight. If any humans noticed them, they either wouldn't understand what they saw or they would put themselves in grave danger by attempting to make use of them.'

Julie was fascinated. Frankly, so was I. 'Like what?' she asked.

He scratched his cheek. 'Um...'

'Wishing wells,' Jinn interjected.

'But I've seen wishing wells,' Julie said. 'They exist.'

'You've only seen the fake ones. The real wishing wells are dangerous things. Even for us. In fact, especially for us. If every wish you made at a wishing well came true, imagine what would happen.'

I screwed up my face. 'I'd wish for Rubus to be stopped. Job done.'

'Sure,' Jinn said. 'Then you might wish for all Redcaps to be dead. Morganus might annoy you one day and you'll wish for him to be dead. And so on and so forth.'

'I'm really not that petty,' I snapped. 'For you I can be persuaded though.'

'You get my point,' Jinn said, smiling slightly. For a large, bullish guy, he was very earnest. I sighed and nodded reluctantly. 'So,' he continued, 'Mother Nature conspires to keep the real wishing wells hidden. We don't believe there are many of them. You would have to know the exact location, and be in that exact spot, to use a reveal spell that allowed the well to be displayed. Not even Fey idiots like Rubus are crazy enough to go looking for one. But sometimes there are other things that are more useful to locate. Hence, reveal spells.'

Julie shook her head in amazement. 'I'm 173 years old and I never had an idea about any of this. Or about any of you.'

Jinn shrugged. 'Why would you? We keep ourselves hidden from each other all the time. We're so determined to keep up the façade that we're something else or someone else that we don't notice what's going on right in front of our own eyes.'

Her eyes shone. 'All this is simply fabulous.' She licked her lips. 'So do you have magic wands? Do you wave them in the air and say the magic word?'

Morgan and Jinn laughed. 'No, it's not like that. Usually spells are bound up in objects of their own,' Morgan said. 'Virtually all magic needs something physical to cling onto. Any such objects are difficult to create and enormously valuable. I've only seen a few myself.'

Jinn agreed. 'Rubus has been collecting these objects for years. We've even hunted down a few of them for him. But there was no sign of any magical object or spell on or around the bogle's body. Word is that the dragon's magic-sucking device is very small. Of course, that makes it even harder to find. We've been trying to locate the dragon to see if he can help us trace it. That's what we were doing now. We had a lead on a nearby flat which we attempted to search but,' he frowned at both Morgan and me, 'we were interrupted.'

'Magically-bound objects,' Julie breathed. 'How wonderful.'

I bit my lip. 'Um...'

'They are quite few and far between,' Morgan cautioned. 'It's not easy to create such objects in the first place, let alone use them.'

I put my hand tentatively up in the air. 'Hello?'

'But anything could be a bound object?' she enquired.

I waved my hand around a little. 'Just a little thing I should mention,' I said.

'What is it, Maddy?'

'You're saying that you searched around the golf course for a magically bound object because retrieving it might have been why the bogle was at the golf course?'

Finn shrugged. 'Yeah. But it's probably irrelevant to all this. We've not found a thing. There definitely wasn't anything like that at the golf course, so there's no point worrying your pretty little head about it.'

I scowled at him. 'Enough with the patronising,' I said. 'Because I'm going to save all our skins. You lot,' I pointed at each one of them in turn, 'are going to bow down to me and be pathetically grateful.' They looked at me. 'I have amnesia. If I'm not given relevant information, I can't possibly help out. Now you've given me the relevant information, I can save the day. It's quite simple really.' I beamed.

'Go on,' Morgan growled.

'Charrie the bogle did have something strange with him on the golf course. I know because I took it out of his pocket and kept it. I didn't know what it was – in fact I still don't. It's a smooth metal sphere, not much larger than a marble, which is attached to some sort of hook. It's so odd looking that I'd happily believe it's one of these bound objects, maybe even the world-destroying one that we're looking for. The bogle took it from the golf course and I took it from him.' I spread my arms. 'Ta da!'

Jinn stared at me. 'You have a magically-bound object from the bogle? But we searched your hotel room in case you'd taken something. And even when we were right behind you, there was no sign of a magical trail clinging to your body.'

My grin stretched from ear to ear. 'I can't promise it's magical or it's the dragon's magic-sucker – and I really think we ought to come up with a better name than magic-sucker – but I can assure you that I've had something of the bogle's all this time.'

'You didn't think to mention this before?'

'To be honest, I'd completely forgotten about it. Between dead bodies, saving soap stars, amnesia and running for my life, a little chunk of shiny metal didn't seem all that important.'

'Well, get it out.' Julie gave an excited little skip. 'Let's take a look at it, darling!'

Ah. 'I don't have it *here*.'

Morgan frowned. 'Where is it?'

'It's, uh, in my coat pocket.'

'Where's your coat? At Julie's house?'

I winced. 'No. It's, um, underneath a car. Near Mike Timmons – Begonius's –Travotel.'

Now everyone looked confused. 'Mads, darling,' Julie said. 'Why would you put a coat under a car?'

I raised my shoulders helplessly. What could I say other than the truth? 'I didn't want to give away my secret superhero identity if I could help it.'

Finn stared at me. 'That doesn't make any sense.' He flicked a look at his brother. 'No wonder we didn't notice anything magical. We didn't realise how crazy she was and we didn't think to look under the chassis of every vehicle we passed.'

'If you possessed a super brain like mine, you'd understand why I did what I did,' I said airily. 'Or if you possessed any brain at all.'

He started towards me but Jinn put a heavy hand on his shoulder, holding him back.

Morgan passed a hand over his eyes. 'Why are we all still here? Let's get to that hotel and get hold of that coat.' He was obviously still unhappy with me. 'It would have helped if you'd mentioned this before, Madrona.'

Yeah, yeah. I pointed at his wrist. 'Are you wearing Jinn's Rolex?' I asked. 'The one you took from me, which I took from him?'

Jinn, Finn and Morgan bristled. Julie looked entertained; I knew I could count on her. 'It's back at the Metropolitan Bar,' Morgan said, glaring at me. 'I'll return it to Jinn as soon as I can.'

I thumped him on the shoulder and smiled broadly. 'Good for you!' I tripped over to the door. 'Now that it's agreed that I'm not the only one around here who's made catastrophic errors of judgment, let's vamoose.' I spun round like every good superhero should and headed out. The others would follow.

CHAPTER TWENTY-THREE

Despite my blithe superhero styling and sauntering, I couldn't prevent the constant niggles gnawing away at me, like those spa fish that nibble away dead skin from your feet. Except these metaphorical fish weren't just nibbling; they were chomping at both my inner calm and my soul.

Despite everything, I found it hard to believe that I could have killed anyone but there wasn't anyone else who could have lopped off the bogle's head. For all their faults, I didn't believe that Finn or Winn were lying about their story. Neither, it appeared, did Morgan. So, either my former self had been working behind the scenes, just like the Redcaps, and doing everything she could to undermine Rubus and save the day – or she'd been working for Rubus all along and was as nasty and evil as he was. I tried to imagine myself being responsible for the end of the whole world. I'd go down in history. Except history would no longer exist. Gasbudlikins.

When we reached a set of traffic lights and Morgan was forced to bring his motorbike to a stop behind the Redcaps' van as we waited for the green, he turned his head towards me. 'Stop it,' he murmured. 'You're thinking too hard.'

I grimaced. 'I can't help it.'

'We're on the right track, Maddy. We know exactly what Rubus is up to, so now we can work with the Redcaps to stop him.'

'The Redcaps whose brother we killed, you mean.'

'That was an accident,' he pointed out, although his eyes looked pained.

'Sure,' I said, '*that* was an accident. But it's the second death I'm responsible for.' I turned baleful. 'What if I did kill Charrie the bogle? What if my former self was fully aware that Rubus is looking to destroy this demesne and I was helping him?' I swallowed, making a weak attempt at keeping the atmosphere light. 'If he achieves his goal then there will be no more *St Thomas Close*. No more gin. No more Pot Noodles!' A car pulled up behind us. I glanced at the sleepy-looking people inside and my stomach dropped. 'No more families on the school run,' I added in a strained whisper. 'What if that's the world I'm seeking to create, Morgan?'

'Maybe it *was* what you were seeking.' A muscle throbbed in his cheek. 'Hell, Maddy, I'd have had no trouble believing it of you a week ago. But even if that was the case, I don't believe it is now. You're not the same person you were then.'

I dropped my eyes. 'You don't know that for sure.'

'Yes, I do.' His voice was quiet but his expression didn't flicker. He held my gaze steadily.

The car behind us beeped its horn loudly and Morgan and I both jumped. The traffic lights had turned green and the Redcaps, with Julie beside them, had already accelerated away. Rather than rushing, however, Morgan leaned his head towards mine and with a feather-light touch brushed his lips against my cheek. Only then did he turn back around and rev the engine to move on.

For convenience's sake, both Morgan and the Redcaps parked in the Travotel car park. The beige blinds on the window of Timmons' office twitched. For old times' sake, I gave him a little wave. He didn't wave back.

Julie got out of the van and frowned at the hotel. 'I don't understand, darlings,' she murmured. 'Why would a faery be a manager of a hotel? And a hotel like this, to boot? Surely you're all more fabulous than this?' She waved a hand and I had to admit she had a point. Everything around us was dull and nondescript.

'We try to keep a low profile,' Morgan told her. 'We don't want humans learning of our existence.'

She sniffed. 'Darling, I'm a vampire with a high profile but you still didn't know about *my* existence. Secrecy is no excuse for drabness.'

I tried to muffle a giggle and glanced at the Redcap brothers. 'I understand that you both want as many supernatural creatures on your side as possible but, vampire or not, Julie doesn't have that many special abilities. How is she going to help bring Rubus down?'

Jinn shrugged. 'It's less what she can offer and more *who* she can offer. She can bring other vampires to us. We obviously can't involve humans. We don't know which faeries to trust and there aren't many of us Redcaps. But there are quite a few vampires around. If we can take care of idiots like the vampire hunters in exchange for their help in taking care of Rubus, we all win.'

Julie coughed delicately. 'I did try to tell them that there aren't many of us. And that it's been quite a while since I've been in contact with the others.'

'Let's not forget your age,' Finn said, failing to notice Julie's grimace. 'That gives you a great deal of knowledge, wisdom and experience that we can put to good use.'

Jinn nodded enthusiastically. 'Once we get the werewolves on our side, we'll have all the fighting power we need.'

'What about the dragons?' I asked, utterly fascinated.

'They're terrible fighters,' he said. 'But as well as the ability to create world-ending magical objects, they also have lots and lots and lots of gold. Rubus is minted – we'll need considerable funds of our own if we're going to match him.'

'Obviously there will be plenty of faeries involved too,' Morgan said. 'Together we'll easily overpower Rubus.'

Jinn's eyelid twitched. 'That's very good of you,' he said. 'But we have to point out the obvious.'

Morgan frowned. 'Which is?'

'Rubus is your brother.'

He stiffened. 'In blood only. We have not been brothers in any other sense of the word for a long time.'

'That may be but the Fey truce means you can't attack him directly. And the family ties mean that you might not want to.' He jabbed a squat, hairy finger in my direction. 'And none of us know about *her*. None of us know whether she'll run back to Rubus as soon as her memory returns. She could betray us all. Even *she* doesn't know what she'll do when she remembers.'

'*If* she remembers,' I butted in. 'And I won't betray you.' I met his eyes. 'I give you my word.'

He didn't blink. 'I'll believe that when I see it.' He lifted up his chin. 'Now where is this car? We need to retrieve the dragon's magic-sucker.'

I sighed. I'd have argued about my integrity but I wasn't sure I believed in myself any more than anyone else did. And the magic-sucker was indeed what was important. I pointed down the street. 'It's that way.'

We set off with me in the lead. I could only begin to imagine what an incongruous group we made: two hulking Redcaps, with overhanging foreheads and bulging ears; two green-eyed faeries – one of whom at least was eminently desirable – and a bottle-blonde soap star who was actually a vampire in hiding. You couldn't make this shit up.

I stopped thinking about it when Morgan's fingers repeatedly brushed against mine as we marched. Every time we touched, a delicious tingle ran across my skin. He didn't look at me and I didn't look at him but I was almost certain that he was thinking the same. After all, there was a hotel right behind us with plenty of beds. Once the object was safely back in my possession – presuming it was actually more than just an oddly shaped key chain – I'd direct us gently in that direction.

I breathed out when we turned the corner, relieved that the dilapidated old car was still in the same spot. I grinned at the others and darted forward to it, crouching down to try and grab the bundled-up coat. When I couldn't quite reach it, I got down even lower, my belly on the pavement, then I shuffled underneath the car. I'd done an even better job of hiding the coat than I'd realised.

I'd only just snagged my fingers on the material, grimacing when I spotted the considerable amount of oil that had dripped onto it, when a new set of feet appeared from nowhere and a gruff, male voice spoke. 'Hand her over.'

My eyes widened and I froze, one hand still clutching the dirty raincoat. Another set of feet appeared, then another – and those were only the ones I could see. Morgan wouldn't give me up – of that I was almost sure – but I reckoned Jinn, and certainly Finn, wouldn't hesitate. Gasbudlikins.

'We're not going to do that.'

If I'd not already been lying down, I would have fallen down. That was Finn's voice. My winning personality must have brought him round to my side despite what happened to his brother. I relaxed slightly and grinned. Go me.

'You don't know who she really is,' the disembodied voice continued. 'Or what she's capable of. She's an evil creature of hell.'

That was a bit melodramatic; even Morgan thought I'd changed. Not to mention that I was a faery, not a hellish demon.

'We know exactly what she is,' Jinn said. 'She's under our protection. You're not having her.'

I felt touched that he was standing up for me. Shaking myself out of my fugue, I scrabbled in the pocket of the raincoat, my fingers immediately finding the smooth metallic sphere. I drew it out and clutched it tightly in the palm of my hand. The Redcaps wouldn't give me up and I wouldn't give up the dragon's magic-sucker. If that's what it was.

'We'll kill you if we have to. She is unnatural. She doesn't deserve to live.'

Steady on.

'Is that what you're planning to do?' enquired Morgan's cool voice. 'Kill her?'

'What we are planning to do is keep the rest of the world safe from her kind.'

'You mean lock her up.'

'Perhaps.'

'Torture her?'

The response was mild. 'Only if it means we can uncover more of her kind and learn more about her capabilities.'

Hang on a minute. There was something about this...

'You're no better than I am!' There was considerable venom in Julie's voice. 'I'm not a bad person. And I won't give up anyone else, no matter what you do to me.'

Ah. So this wasn't actually about me. Maybe the world didn't revolve around Madrona the Madhatter after all. The

Redcaps had been convinced they'd taken care of the vampire hunters. Apparently they were wrong. Oh well. I shrugged; what was a girl to do? I started to roll in the opposite direction so that I'd emerge on the road away from the vampire hunters rather than next to them.

The voices continued. 'We're not prepared to fail again. One way or another, that creature is coming with us.' Apparently the hunters had run out of patience. No doubt that accounted for their bid to send everyone they had to pick up Julie, even though it was now broad daylight. 'We can do this the easy way or the hard way.'

I rolled my eyes. Us villains had to do better with our patter than tired old clichés. Honestly. These guys could learn from me; it was a shame they would never get the chance.

Freed from the car, I sprang upwards. The hunters obviously hadn't realised I was there because all three of them turned to me in astonishment. Fortunately, Morgan, Jinn and Finn wasted no time in taking advantage of the situation.

Jinn drew his gun, grabbing hold of the nearest man and putting him in a chokehold with the gun pressed against his neck. Morgan threw a punch towards the second one, while Finn faced off against the third.

'I thought you took care of the vampire hunters!' I yelled at him, running to his side to help.

'I thought we did too,' he hissed.

The vampire hunter in front of us laughed. 'You can't scare us off. We do the work of the righteous. We stop evil. If you are protecting that vampire bitch, that makes you as evil as her.'

Julie's face contorted. She darted forward, smacking the man on the side of his head. He snapped his arms and two black canisters emerged from his sleeves. He sprayed one in my direction and one in Finn's, and clouds of pepper spray hit us both at the same time.

I shielded the worst of the damage by raising my arm in the nick of time but it wasn't good enough. I yelled as burning pain flashed through my eyes and face. Finn made a similar, inarticulate screech. Unable to see clearly, I fumbled forward, trying to grab hold of the hunter before he grabbed hold of Julie.

'I've got her!' I heard him yell over the sounds of fighting.

I kicked out in the direction of his voice and Julie screamed in agony in response. 'Mads! You're supposed to be on my side!'

Gasbudlikins.

Something struck me from behind and I fell forward onto my hands and knees, eyes still streaming with agonising tears. There was a faint buzz in the air and then a gentle hand reached for me. I blinked and blinked. Morgan.

'You've messed with time,' I gasped. 'I thought that was forbidden.'

'It is,' he growled. He used his sleeve to wipe my face. The pain was still extraordinary and my vision was still blurred but it was better. I glanced around. One of the hunters, no doubt the one who'd struck me, lay on the ground behind me. Finn was doubled over while Jinn and the other hunter had their hands wrapped round each other's throats, struggling together in slow motion.

'I can't hold it for long,' Morgan grunted.

Seeing the strain on his face, I nodded quickly. I darted for Julie and wrested her away from the hunter, then I did for Finn what Morgan had done for me and wiped away the worst of the pepper spray residue. I hoped I was doing more good than harm.

There was a rushing sound and time returned to normal.

'Wh – what?' Julie blinked, obviously confused at her changed position. I didn't waste time explaining it to her and thrust her towards Finn. 'Take her!' I yelled. 'Take her to the hotel! Mike Timmons will help you!' I hoped he would, anyway.

Still barely able to see, Finn nodded. He and Julie half ran, half stumbled in the direction of the Travotel. It was still some distance away. We still weren't safe.

The hunter who'd grabbed Julie shook off his confusion, recovering from the time lapse with scary swiftness. He glanced from Morgan to me and back again, obviously judging that Morgan was the more dangerous opponent. 'You lot are vampires too, aren't you?' he snarled.

'Guess again,' Morgan said.

The hunter laughed. 'It doesn't matter what you are. You're unnatural and you don't belong here. We won't kill you here. But we will stop you then we'll take you in and treat you just as we'd treat her.' He spat this last word, making it clear what his opinion of Julie was.

'What's your beef?' I asked, keeping Jinn and his own fight with the other hunter in my peripheral vision. He was holding his own – for now. 'She's not doing anyone any harm. She's not hurting anyone. She's a damned soap star! Why don't you just leave her alone?'

'Her kind shouldn't be allowed to exist,' the hunter grunted, with the sort of racist fear-borne mentality that fuelled wars in every corner of the globe. 'And apparently neither should yours, whatever it may be. Don't worry though,' he said with a spiteful smile, 'we learn from our mistakes.' As that hissed promise left his lips, he drew out a gun and sprang towards Morgan.

I should have known better. His action was no more than a feint; the hunters were better equipped, better prepared and better manned than any of us had realised. Just as Morgan kicked, forcing the hunter to drop his weapon, I caught a flash of light from one of the nearby rooftops. There was a crack and Morgan fell to the ground. A split second later, so did Jinn.

Yet again, I reached for my faery magic but it wasn't time I messed with. From somewhere – I didn't know where – vicious anger uncoiled within me. There was an odd vibration from the sphere that I was still clutching in my right hand. With grim intent, I thrust out my left hand and sent a spark of fire in the direction of the hidden sniper. I knew I'd caught him – I heard his scream – but it was still too late. I was thrown backwards by the force of a bullet smacking into my side. The sphere fell from my grip and rolled away towards Morgan's fallen body.

The two remaining hunters turned, taking off in the direction of the hotel – and Jinn and Julie. I could already feel my body using its inherent Fey magic to knit itself back together again and seal the wound caused by the sniper's bullet. I wasn't convinced it would heal quickly enough for me to do anything to stop the arsebadgers from reaching my friends. In the end, neither Jinn nor Morgan nor I had been any real match for the hunters, and now we had Julie and Finn's wellbeing to worry about as well.

I stretched out my hand, my fingertips just able to brush against the cold steel of the fallen gun. It was no good; I couldn't grab it properly. I lifted my head, groaning with the effort. Morgan and Jinn were out for the count and I prayed they were still alive. There was no way the hunters knew about the poisonous effects of rowan and had coated their bullets, so Morgan would probably survive. With any luck, the bullet that had hit Jinn hadn't done any real damage. But neither of them was moving – so I had to. I had to get up. No one else could do this; it had to be me.

I forced myself upwards, rolling to my side and managing to raise myself onto my knees. The sun was in my eyes, though, and tears still streamed down my face from the effects of the pepper spray. I could just make out the silhouettes of the two hunters who were near the corner; they were almost out of sight. Then, to my left, a hand appeared. It reached for me and, without thinking, I grasped it, allowing myself to be hauled to my feet.

I blinked, pain juddering through me and reverberating through my bones. It felt as if the marrow itself was disintegrating. 'Stop,' I gasped, 'them.'

The good Samaritan tilted his head as if confused. 'Why? Who are they?'

His face swam in front of my eyes and I forced myself to focus on his features. When green eyes and a face even more ruggedly handsome than Morgan's, but with the same swarthiness and a similar jawline, blurred into view, I knew immediately who I was looking at. I didn't even have the energy to be scared.

'Rubus,' I whispered.

He didn't react; he simply watched me with a studied lack of expression. 'If you really want those two men stopped, Madrona, you simply have to say the word.'

If there had been any alternative, I'd have taken it but I was out of options – we all were. 'Please,' I said, my voice barely a croak. 'Stop them.'

'Your wish is my command,' Rubus answered. He gestured to the group of faeries and humans standing at his back, whose presence was only just registering in my painful brain. Five of them immediately peeled off.

Rubus didn't watch them go; his gaze remained trained on me. 'Lunaria told me you had amnesia. Begonius said the same. Is it true? Can you really not remember?'

'Yes,' I said, wetting my lips. I didn't know which way to turn. Fear for Julie, Finn, Jinn and Morgan clawed at me from all directions. 'I really can't remember.'

'And yet,' Rubus murmured, his voice silky smooth, 'you are with my brother. You found him. You remember him.'

I shook my head. 'No. It's not like that.'

Rubus leaned forward until his lips were at my ear. 'What oily lies has he been pouring into you?' he asked. 'You can't trust him, you know.'

I didn't know the right answer. I had to keep Morgan safe from Rubus but I didn't know how. My thoughts were too sluggish and I simply couldn't think straight. Still, if I'd learnt one thing about myself it was that I didn't take anything lying down.

Rubus terrified me but I was tired of being a meek little ex-minion and I could tell he was already growing irritated with my mild-mannered responses. If I acted like the bitch I was supposed to be – the bitch I *was* – maybe he'd relax. And that scenario would be to my benefit – and to the others'.

'Well,' I drawled, 'I'll try to see things from your point of view but I'm not sure I'll be able to get my head that far up my arse.' For a moment the silence was deafening. Not one of his minions so much as dared to breathe.

Rubus didn't move for at least ten seconds then he threw back his head and gave a loud laugh. 'Amnesia or not, you've certainly not forgotten how to charm, Madrona.'

I exhaled. The line of his body was less tense than before. That was something. Even so, as if afraid to give me the freedom to speak again and show him up, Rubus snapped his fingers. The tall Amazonian Fey, who I took to be Lunaria, sent me a quick, apologetic glance. Then she handed Rubus a small box.

'Do you know what this is, Madrona? Do you remember?' Rubus asked.

Confused, I shook my head. What was he doing? There wasn't time for any of this shit, not with those hunters still on the loose. A ghost of a smile crossed Rubus's lips. He flipped open the lid and, despite myself, I peered inside. When I saw what it was, I hissed and drew back. Spider. Giant spider.

'Amellus worked to create this.' He held the box up to his eyes as if in admiration. 'An entire species designed to do just one thing.' He looked at me, gauging my reaction. When I just stared at him, he shrugged. 'It's a Truth Spider. It senses changes in a person's physiology and reacts to them appropriately. More specifically, if you lie to me, it can tell. It will bite in return and flood your system with venom. One bite won't kill you – it takes at least three or four to achieve that sort of release.' He bared his teeth in what I supposed was a smile. 'I'm told the pain is quite extraordinary. Making use of this beautiful little creature doesn't affect the truce because the choice about whether to lie or tell the truth is entirely yours. You don't have to be hurt. It's exactly the same as a Truth Draw, except this is about a hundred times more powerful.'

I took a step backwards but suddenly there were Fey at my back, holding of my upper arms and forcing me to stay where I was.

'This hurts me more than it hurts you, Madrona,' Rubus murmured. 'Believe me.' He tipped the box towards me so that the spider fell onto the bare skin of my arm. I flinched and let out a tiny squeak of fear. Rubus didn't give me any respite. 'Do you have amnesia?' he asked.

I couldn't answer. My tongue cleaved to the roof of my mouth and I could feel my heart rate rising.

'Let's try that again. You have to answer, Madrona. I won't accept silence.' He leaned forward. 'Do you have amnesia?'

Thankfully, my voice returned. Barely. 'Yes. I don't remember from before the weekend. Not who I am, not who you are. Not anything.'

The spider scuttled a few inches up my arm.

'What is the first thing you remember?'

'Waking up on a golf course,' I whispered.

Rubus raised an eyebrow. 'Golf? Is that a new hobby?' he

enquired. Then he waved his hand. 'Don't answer that one. Do you know what caused the amnesia?'

I shook my head.

'You have to say the word, Madrona,' he pressed.

'No,' I managed. 'I don't know what caused it.'

Rubus's mouth split into a huge smile but it didn't, alas, detract from the hard edge to his eyes. 'Good. That's good.' His eyes dropped to Morgan's unconscious form. He was still breathing, I noted with relief. Morgan wasn't dead yet. Neither was I. 'Did he tell you we're brothers?'

'Yes.'

'How do you feel about him, given that you don't remember anything about him?'

My eyes widened fractionally and I tensed. I stared at the spider. It had stopped moving and seemed to be waiting for my answer as much as Rubus was. 'I ... uh ... I...'

Sudden anger flashed across Rubus's face. 'Never mind,' he said curtly. 'Don't answer that either.' He passed the box to Lunaria and folded his arms. 'We have a standing arrangement,' he told me. 'You stay away from Morganus and I allow him to continue living.' I stopped breathing. 'As you do indeed have amnesia, I shall let you off on this occasion.' His voice deepened. 'Do not disobey me again, however, Madrona.' He aimed a sharp kick in Morgan's direction, although I was grateful that his foot didn't connect. That truce crap actually had its uses. 'I don't want to see you anywhere near Morgan ever again.'

'It seems too much of a coincidence that Charrie disappeared at the same time as Madrona did,' Lunaria said, before Rubus could try another shot at his unconscious brother.

Rubus nodded. 'Indeed. Do you remember speaking to Charrie?' he asked me. 'About six foot tall? Slightly greenish skin, blond hair and a squeaky voice?'

I counted my lucky stars that I could answer truthfully. 'No,' I said. 'I don't.'

Rubus pursed his lips. 'Hmmm. Then the bogle is still on the loose and still has my fucking dragon sphere.' His skin was turning a mottled red colour. 'I can't break the fucking border without my fucking dragon sphere!'

My eyes dropped. Morgan didn't move an inch but I knew that the slight lump next to his right sleeve was the sphere in question. I swallowed hard and quickly looked away. Rubus pointed at the spider and Lunaria darted forward, scooping it back up and putting it into the box again. Thank goodness.

'That Redcap,' Rubus said. 'Did you put him down or was it those humans?'

I glanced at Jinn. His chest was rising and falling slowly. He was still alive too. Just. 'The humans,' I said, hoping that the truth would encourage leniency on Rubus's part.

Rubus jerked his head. Suddenly, I wasn't sure he cared either way. 'Lunaria said you'd told her that the Redcaps were trying to kill you.' He tutted. 'We can't have that. They're supposed to work for me. They're supposed to do what *I* say.'

Too late, I realised the danger. 'I was m–mistaken,' I stammered. 'The Redcaps were just trying to help me. They wanted me to go with them so that they could take me to you. They were helping not...'

Rubus raised a hand in my direction. All of a sudden, my lips sealed together, glued with some bizarre magic. I struggled forward, moaning insistently.

'Cease,' he ordered. 'I don't need a Truth Spider to know that you're lying now. You always did have too soft a heart, Madrona.' He sighed. 'All that work I've put into training you and now it seems I'll have to start all over again.'

Footsteps sounded. Everyone turned in their direction and

watched as the group who'd gone after the vampire hunters returned, looking considerably worse for wear.

'Must have been military,' one of the Fey muttered. 'They put up a hell of a fight. We put them down though. They won't be a problem again.'

He was lucky we'd softened them up for him first, or it would probably have been a different story. I tried to growl at him to indicate this but all that escaped me was another moan. At least he hadn't mentioned Julie or Finn; I prayed that the pair of them had managed to get away. Maybe Timmons was hiding them. Please, a voice whispered inside of me, please let that be the case.

Rubus grunted, disinterested. 'Give me a knife,' he instructed.

The Fey didn't hesitate. He reached for a sheath hanging at his belt, drew out a long, sharp blade and handed it to Rubus. With sudden horror, I knew exactly what he was going to do.

I didn't think. I lunged forward, hands flailing, but I was too late. The hands holding my arms pulled me back while Rubus spun round and slammed the knife directly into Jinn's throat. 'There's a lot of things a Redcap will recover from,' he murmured. 'But that certainly isn't one of them.' He wiped the blade on his trousers, staining them with dark blood, before handing it back.

My knees gave way. Rubus glanced over at me and frowned. 'Yeah,' he sniffed, 'like I said. A lot of re-training is required.' He motioned to the Fey at my back. 'Let's take her home. Be careful, though. I don't want her hurt any more than she is already.'

The arms tugged gently, leading me towards a car nearby. All I could see as I was bundled inside was Jinn's blood leaking onto the road and Morgan's unmoving body. Then the door closed and darkness descended.

ABOUT THE AUTHOR

After teaching English literature in the UK, Japan and Malaysia, Helen Harper left behind the world of education following the worldwide success of her Blood Destiny series of books. She is a professional member of the Alliance of Independent Authors and writes full time, thanking her lucky stars every day that's she lucky enough to do so!

Helen has always been a book lover, devouring science fiction and fantasy tales when she was a child growing up in Scotland.

She currently lives in Edinburgh in the UK with far too many cats – not to mention the dragons, fairies, demons, wizards and vampires that seem to keep appearing from nowhere.

OTHER TITLES

The complete *FireBrand* series

A werewolf killer. A paranormal murder. How many times can Emma Bellamy cheat death?

I'm one placement away from becoming a fully fledged London detective. It's bad enough that my last assignment before I qualify is with Supernatural Squad. But that's nothing compared to what happens next.

Brutally murdered by an unknown assailant, I wake up twelve hours later in the morgue – and I'm very much alive. I don't know how or why it happened. I don't know who killed me. All I know is that they might try again.

Werewolves are disappearing right, left and centre.

A mysterious vampire seems intent on following me everywhere I go.

And I have to solve my own vicious killing. Preferably before death comes for me again.

Book One – Brimstone Bound

Book Two – Infernal Enchantment

Book Three – Midnight Smoke

Book Four – Scorched Heart

Book Five – Dark Whispers

Book Six – A Killer's Kiss

Book Seven – Fortune's Ashes

A Charade of Magic complete series

The best way to live in the Mage ruled city of Glasgow is to keep your head down and your mouth closed.

That's not usually a problem for Mairi Wallace. By day she works at a small shop selling tartan and by night she studies to become an apothecary. She knows her place and her limitations. All that changes, however, when her old childhood friend sends her a desperate message seeking her help - and the Mages themselves cross Mairi's path. Suddenly, remaining unnoticed is no longer an option.

There's more to Mairi than she realises but, if she wants to fulfil her full potential, she's going to have to fight to stay alive - and only time will tell if she can beat the Mages at their own game.

From twisted wynds and tartan shops to a dangerous daemon and the magic infused City Chambers, the future of a nation might lie with one solitary woman.

Book One – Hummingbird

Book Two – Nightingale

Book Three – Red Hawk

The complete *Blood Destiny* series

"A spectacular and addictive series."

Mackenzie Smith has always known that she was different. Growing up as the only human in a pack of rural shapeshifters will do that to you, but then couple it with some mean fighting skills and a fiery temper and you end up with a woman that few will dare to cross. However, when the only father figure in her life is brutally murdered, and the dangerous Brethren with their predatory Lord Alpha come to investigate, Mack has to not only ensure the physical safety of her adopted family by hiding her apparent humanity, she also has to seek the blood-soaked vengeance that she craves.

Book One - Bloodfire

Book Two - Bloodmagic

Book Three - Bloodrage

Book Four - Blood Politics

Book Five - Bloodlust

Also

Corrigan Fire

Corrigan Magic

Corrigan Rage

Corrigan Politics

Corrigan Lust

The complete *Bo Blackman* series

A half-dead daemon, a massacre at her London based PI firm and evidence that suggests she's the main suspect for both ... Bo Blackman is having a very bad week.

She might be naive and inexperienced but she's determined to get to the bottom of the crimes, even if it means involving herself with one of London's most powerful vampire Families and their enigmatic leader.

It's pretty much going to be impossible for Bo to ever escape unscathed.

Book One - Dire Straits

Book Two - New Order

Book Three - High Stakes

Book Four - Red Angel

Book Five - Vigilante Vampire

Book Six - Dark Tomorrow

The complete *Highland Magic* series

Integrity Taylor walked away from the Sidhe when she was a child. Orphaned and bullied, she simply had no reason to stay, especially not when the sins of her father were going to remain on her shoulders. She found a new family - a group of thieves who proved that blood was less important than loyalty and love.

But the Sidhe aren't going to let Integrity stay away forever. They need her more than anyone realises - besides, there are prophecies to be fulfilled, people to be saved and hearts to be won over. If anyone can do it, Integrity can.

Book One - Gifted Thief

Book Two - Honour Bound

Book Three - Veiled Threat

Book Four - Last Wish

~

The complete *Dreamweaver* series

"I have special coping mechanisms for the times I need to open the front door. They're even often successful..."

Zoe Lydon knows there's often nothing logical or rational about fear. It doesn't change the fact that she's too terrified to step outside her own house, however.

What Zoe doesn't realise is that she's also a dreamweaver - able to access other people's subconscious minds. When she finds herself in the Dreamlands and up against its sinister Mayor, she'll need to use all of her wits - and overcome all of her fears - if she's ever going to come out alive.

Book One - Night Shade

Book Two - Night Terrors

Book Three - Night Lights

~

Stand alone novels

Eros

William Shakespeare once wrote that, "Cupid is a knavish lad, thus to make poor females mad." The trouble is that Cupid himself would probably agree...

As probably the last person in the world who'd appreciate hearts, flowers and romance, Coop is convinced that true love doesn't exist –

which is rather unfortunate considering he's also known as Cupid, the God of Love. He'd rather spend his days drinking, womanising and generally having as much fun as he possible can. As far as he's concerned, shooting people with bolts of pure love is a waste of his time...but then his path crosses with that of shy and retiring Skye Sawyer and nothing will ever be quite the same again.

Wraith

Magic. Shadows. Adventure. Romance.

Saiya Buchanan is a wraith, able to detach her shadow from her body and send it off to do her bidding. But, unlike most of her kin, Saiya doesn't deal in death. Instead, she trades secrets - and in the goblin besieged city of Stirling in Scotland, they're a highly prized commodity. It might just be, however, that the goblins have been hiding the greatest secret of them all. When Gabriel de Florinville, a Dark Elf, is sent as royal envoy into Stirling and takes her prisoner, Saiya is not only going to uncover the sinister truth. She's also going to realise that sometimes the deepest secrets are the ones locked within your own heart.

~

The complete *Lazy Girl's Guide To Magic* series

Hard Work Will Pay Off Later. Laziness Pays Off Now.

Let's get one thing straight - Ivy Wilde is not a heroine. In fact, she's probably the last witch in the world who you'd call if you needed a magical helping hand. If it were down to Ivy, she'd spend all day every day on her sofa where she could watch TV, munch junk food and talk to her feline familiar to her heart's content.

However, when a bureaucratic disaster ends up with Ivy as the victim of a case of mistaken identity, she's yanked very unwillingly into Arcane Branch, the investigative department of the Hallowed Order of Magical Enlightenment. Her problems are quadrupled when a valuable object is stolen right from under the Order's noses.

It doesn't exactly help that she's been magically bound to Adeptus Exemptus Raphael Winter. He might have piercing sapphire eyes and a body which a cover model would be proud of but, as far as Ivy's concerned, he's a walking advertisement for the joyless perils of too much witch-work.

And if he makes her go to the gym again, she's definitely going to turn him into a frog.

Book One - Slouch Witch

Book Two - Star Witch

Book Three - Spirit Witch

Sparkle Witch (Christmas novella)

The complete *Fractured Faery* series

One corpse. Several bizarre looking attackers. Some very strange magical powers. And a severe bout of amnesia.

It's one thing to wake up outside in the middle of the night with a decapitated man for company. It's another to have no memory of how you got there - or who you are.

She might not know her own name but she knows that several people are out to get her. It could be because she has strange magical powers seemingly at her fingertips and is some kind of fabulous hero. But then why does she appear to inspire fear in so many? And who on earth is the sexy, green-eyed barman who apparently despises her? So many questions ... and so few answers.

At least one thing is for sure - the streets of Manchester have never met someone quite as mad as Madrona...

Book One - Box of Frogs

SHORTLISTED FOR THE KINDLE STORYTELLER AWARD 2018

Book Two - Quiver of Cobras

Book Three - Skulk of Foxes

The complete *City Of Magic* series

Charley is a cleaner by day and a professional gambler by night. She might be haunted by her tragic past but she's never thought of herself as anything or anyone special. Until, that is, things start to go terribly wrong all across the city of Manchester. Between plagues of rats, firestorms and the gleaming blue eyes of a sexy Scottish werewolf, she might just have landed herself in the middle of a magical apocalypse. She might also be the only person who has the ability to bring order to an utterly chaotic new world.

Book One - Shrill Dusk

Book Two - Brittle Midnight

Book Three - Furtive Dawn